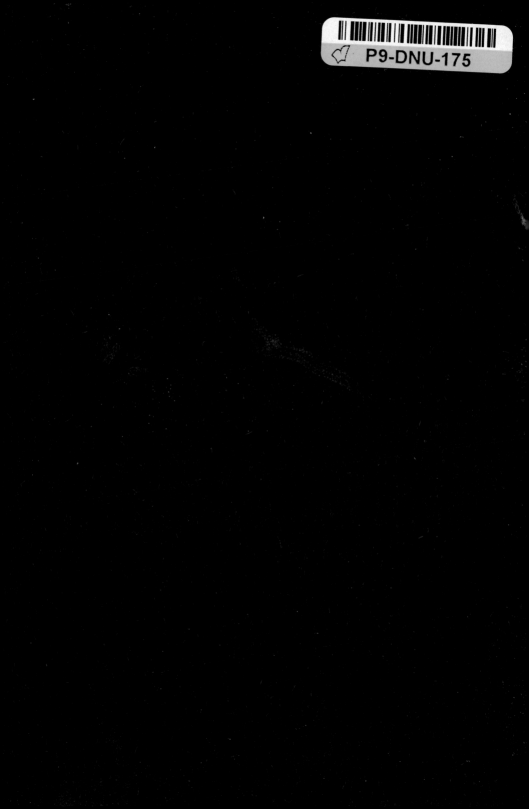

THE SLIDE THAT BURIED RIGHTFUL

RICH SHAPERO

THE SLIDE THAT BURIED RIGHTFUL

A NOVEL

HALF MOON BAY, CALIFORNIA

TooFar Media
500 Stone Pine Road, Box 3169
Half Moon Bay, CA 94019

Library of Congress Cataloging-in-Publication Data is available.

ISBN: 978-1-7335259-6-1

Cover artwork by Paul Rumsey
Cover design by Adde Russell and Michael Baron Shaw
Artwork copyright © 2005 Rich Shapero
Additional graphics: Sky Shapero

Printed and Bound by CPI Group (UK) Ltd, Croydon, CR0 4YY

25 24 23 22   2 3 4 5

1

A peak with a nodded crown rose into the arctic sky, lit by a crescent moon and the rippling drape of a lime aurora. Below its icy front, jetties of rock extended on either side, forming a horseshoe around a small village. Cabins were huddled, half-buried in snow, and paths winding between the doorways formed a web, with a larger building at the center. Its roof and tar-papered walls were plastered with rime. A hand-painted sign, fringed with icicles, hung over the door: *Eisenhart's Mercantile.* Between piles of lumber and rusted equipment, three sleds were parked, and the dogs that had pulled them were curled in the powder. For the lower windows, portholes had been cut in the drifts. All the store's windows were lit.

Inside, four dozen people were seated on benches, watching, silent. Some were white, from the States. Most were

I

Eskimo. The white women wore dresses, and their men wore jackets and ties. The Eskimo women were in bright-colored drill. Many had facial tattoos, and all had their hair parted in the middle and braided on either side. The Eskimo men wore parkas. Counters and provisions had been pushed against the walls.

Beside a wood stove, a bride and groom stood facing the pastor, Lars Koopman, a man in his late twenties, slight with stooped shoulders, fresh-faced and earnest. His hair was simply groomed, short with a small wave in front. He bowed as he prompted the bride, raising and lowering the black book in his hand as if weighing it.

"I, Sara Eisenhart," she said, "take you, Hiram Somebody—"

She stopped, turning red as a laugh went around. The groom laughed too.

The pastor nodded acquittingly.

"—take you, Hiram Sumderby," she corrected herself, "to be my wedded husband—"

She was blond with big brown eyes. A giggle emerged from her painted lips as she glanced at the groom. Her gown had lace sleeves, and it was long in the waist and loose at the bodice. Sumderby gave her a victory grin. He was six-two and chinless, the part in his hair was crooked and his cheeks were pimpled. He stood stiffly in a tux and white tie, eyes on Sara as she completed her vows.

"—to love and to cherish, till death do us part."

Pastor Koopman handed the ring to Sumderby. The bride held out her hand.

Sumderby's lips parted. As the pastor gave him the binding words, the young man's brow kinked, as if he feared he might say the wrong thing and the spell would be broken.

"With this ring, I thee wed," he said, and his unsteady hand slid the ring onto Sara's finger. It didn't fit, as hard as he pushed.

She shifted the ring to her third finger. Sumderby noticed the amusement on the guests' faces and joined in, grinning, happy to be the center of attention.

Ruth Eisenhart, Sara's mother, stood a few feet away, watching the ring slide onto the proper finger. Her jaw was quivering, and she seemed to be twisting inside her green gown. Her husband, Jonas, tall and thin, had one shoulder stooped, and his head was cocked. He looked puzzled, waiting to be let in on a secret. Jonas grasped Ruth's wrist and squeezed it. She sighed, raised her free hand and touched the tortoiseshell comb in her hair. Then she turned and forced a smile for him.

"God, creator and preserver," the pastor said, "author of the everlasting, send your blessing upon this man and this woman." He joined their hands together. "I pronounce you man and wife."

As Sumderby kissed the bride, her father nodded to show his approval. The kiss cheered the observers, except for two Eskimo boys wrestling on the floor and a white woman in a homely dress at the rear. She was weeping, softly but audibly. Her sorrow wasn't sentimental. Something was crushing her. Small, her silvery hair bound at her nape, she put her hand over her spectacles, then removed it, facing the pastor with a pleading look, like a battered child.

Koopman turned away.

Amid the congratulations, Sara approached another young woman seated in front. Yvetta was her name, thin and wispy, with striking blue eyes. Her blond hair was braided on either side, the Eskimo way. Sara flashed her ring, and the two women embraced. On Yvetta's neck was a black tattoo, a paw with four toes, like a print in snow that a fox would leave. Seated beside her was John Jimmy, a young Eskimo man with a bronzed, diamond-shaped face and a set jaw. His eyes were solemn, distant as a sage's.

Two Eskimo men stood by a window at the rear of the gathering. One wrinkled his nose as if he was smelling something. The other stepped quickly forward, and when he reached John, he whispered in his ear. John turned to face the other, pointed, and the man circled the crowd, heading for the door. Yvetta faced John and put her hand on his thigh, calling him back. John met her gaze and relented.

The father of the bride pinched a gold chain at Sumderby's waist, pulled a pocket watch out, checked the time and returned it. Then Jonas raised both arms and asked the guests to help move the benches aside. He faced the sideboard and grabbed a small box. To the left was a white cake with orange blossoms; to the right was an Edison phonograph, its large black tulip horn aimed at the center of the room. Jonas opened the box, removed a blue cylinder and slid it onto the Edison's armature.

An Eskimo man stood a few feet away, watching with one open eye. The other was sealed with a shoelace scar. Jonas noticed him, pulled him closer, then took his hand and set it on the phonograph's silver crank. The one eye flared, wondering. With Jonas' hand on his, together they turned the crank, winding the mainspring.

"Give them some space," Jonas called over his shoulder. "Somebody—" Jonas motioned to the groom.

As the floor cleared, a small man in his fifties, Clayburn Pike, unlinked arms with a younger woman, freckled with ginger hair. She raised her brows and pinched her ring finger. Pike laughed and continued forward. He was thin and lithe, with an aquiline nose, eagle eyes and a billow of white hair.

"Take off your slipper, my dear," Pike told Sara.

She blushed and did as he asked.

Pike's hand dipped into the pocket of his dinner jacket and emerged with a large gold coin. He smiled and showed the coin around. When Sara held her slipper toward him, he dropped the coin into it.

As she put the slipper back on, Jonas set the stylus on the blue cylinder and flipped the Edison's latch. The cylinder began to turn and music blared from the horn. A string band was playing a waltz, and a tenor sang:

> *Somebody's tall and handsome,*
> *Somebody's fair to see . . .*

Sumderby grinned, embraced Sara and swept her around the floor. Twisted crepe streamers were tacked to the ceiling above the couple. The Eskimos stood watching—all but the One-Eyed Man, who faced the Edison open-mouthed. Pastor Koopman put his Bible on a barrel and strode past the natives toward the woman with her hair bound at her nape.

"Mattie—"

She shook her head as if she was fighting a cloud of mosquitoes.

"We did the right thing," Koopman said.

His words seem to pierce her. Mattie stifled a cry, then clenched her eyes. "I know," she whimpered.

Her submission enfeebled him. As she wiped her tears, he felt his own starting. Was he going to break down in front of them all? Koopman turned and strode toward the door, choking on remorse as he crossed the threshold. He continued into the cold, crunching divots, shivering and hugging himself. The reflected glow caught his eye, and he looked up, seeing the curtain of rippling light crossing the heavens.

"Lars," Mattie cried.

He turned and saw her silhouette in the doorway, with the lanterns flickering behind her. Koopman was about to reply when a loud thump shook the snow beneath him, followed by a huffing and grinding. He gazed at the frozen surface around him, and then up at Butcher Peak. Smoke was coiling from its flanks. Cracks appeared in the slopes as he watched, the white field shattered, puzzling and crazing, breaking into cakes.

A terrible hiss rose in the valley. Then it drummed, turning throaty.

"Mattie," he shouted. She was still in the doorway.

Spans of rock were breaking away, the white cakes descending, buckling, turning to powder. A freezing wind struck Koopman down, and the sounds united in a deafening roar. Through slitted lids, he saw the churning mass, praying it would spend itself. But it wasn't slowing or thinning. Its billows were consuming the sky, while its thundering front descended on the valley.

Its leading edge bucked and curled, crashing onto a shelf and boiling over, mowing down thickets. The surge vanished in a hollow, then erupted from it, rising over the Mercantile in a white wave.

The flimsy walls shuddered, then the wave fell on its roof, and the store exploded as if a bomb had gone off. The building collapsed, and a sound like a fist closing on crackers filled Koopman's ears, planks and beams flying, lanterns popping like heated corn. The wreckage churned and moved downslope, then the slide's margin reached him and turned him end over end.

Partway up Butcher Peak, beneath a giant blade of rock, a musher stood on his sled runners while rivers of snow roared past on either side. His nose and lips were spiculed with ice. Beneath the arc of his parka ruff, his eyes struggled to see through the roiling clouds. The crunch of the store echoed in his head, along with the fear of what that meant.

The tumbling ice grated and groaned. The hiss and rumble faded. Then it stopped altogether.

Garris shouted to his dogs, and the sled broke free of its ruts, descending.

The clouds were thick, whirling on either side. The way down was blind, but he trusted his team and his able lead. Rips in the drifting sheets, glimpses through on the right. A jumbled morass, boulders of ice and rock piled in hillocks, riddled with pits and ravines. And the store—

The sled bucked and heeled. They were charging beside the fan, following its broken edge, blocks purple and blue, mortared with crush. And the way ahead— The ice dust was filtering down, but there was no store to see. Zoya, his lead dog, hugged the slide's border. But the store—

Wind cleared the drifting dust, and the curtain was drawn.

Where was it, where? Then a moment of horror: nothing remained. The store had been leveled. And his daughter, Yvetta—

She was mixed with the ice or buried beneath.

The crescent moon was over his shoulder. Above, the folds in the aurora plunged like pink and gold swords.

Was she thrown free? Was she on the surface?

Garris scanned the slide in the spectral light, looking for movement.

He could see the extent of the avalanche now. It had knocked down Mattie's cabin. All that remained was a wall and a window. The remains of Pike's was visible, mixed with the churn—snapped logs, splintered planks and a piece of

8

roof. The flow reached the boulder bed and lapped over it, petering on the banks of the Rightful River.

Garris braked his team, and as the sled fishtailed to a halt, he saw Koopman rising from the snow. The pastor faced the slide, batting the powder from his suit. Garris shouted, and Lars turned.

Stillness reigned now. There was only the sighing of the wind.

"My god," Koopman said, waving his arm.

Garris called to Zoya and the sled moved toward the pastor, skirting the fan's border. The air thickened again, hazed with drifting powder. When Lars reappeared, he was limping closer, squinting, trying to see.

The runners whisked, dogs panting, then Garris dropped his anchor and jumped off his sled, padding forward. The two men embraced. Garris was strong as an ox and built like one, thick-chested with broad shoulders, large legs and giant hands.

"I thought you were inside," Lars said.

Garris unclasped the smaller man, loosened his hood and brushed it back. He had a squarish head and a determined jaw, but his brutish face was foiled by eyes fearful and soft. He faced the slide. "Yvetta," he bellowed.

Lars turned too. "Mattie," he yelled, gazing numbly around. "Yvetta! Can anyone hear?"

Garris threw back the sled cover, grabbed a pair of snowshoes and strapped them on. Then he drew a shovel and ax from the basket, passing the ax to Lars. "You'll freeze," he said, retrieving a pair of blankets and wrapping them around the

9

shivering pastor. Garris hurried forward, shoeing over the ice. Lars limped after him, punching holes in the snow.

Of the store, there was only debris—splintered timbers, jags of glass, a broken chair, a length of stovepipe.

"Yvetta," Garris shouted.

The people— Where were they? Not a one was visible. Was Yvetta with them? Was she still alive?

"Yvetta!"

"Mattie, Mattie!" the pastor joined in.

If the snows hadn't crushed her, Garris thought, how long would she have? How long before her air ran out or the cold froze her?

He skirted a pit and passed between boulders twenty feet high, calling, listening and looking. The fan looked like badly cooked oatmeal. Remains of the store were everywhere—canned goods, splintered posts, bolts of fabric, scraps of tar paper.

"Answer me," Garris demanded. "Yvetta—"

"Please," Lars cried.

Plats of ice were compacted, firm as concrete. Garris strode past them, fearful, imagining. He paused at a looser area, digging his shovel in. "Yvetta—" There are people beneath me, he thought. Crushed, suffocating in darkness, feeling the unbearable cold.

Lars groaned. Garris turned to see him in powder to his knees. The pastor began to sob. Garris dug his shovel in. Was she protected? Was she free and struggling, or cemented in place, choking at that very moment? Something shadowed the surface between his snowshoes. He spaded away the loose beads, uncovering a slab of bacon.

"*Ickeang naktook*," a man yelled.

Garris turned. On the far side of a blue boulder, an Eskimo man named Toluk was down on his knees, holding another. Garris hurried toward them. The motionless man was tangled with crepe streamers. Toluk stripped them away. Garris recognized him. The man's eyes were open, but his face was still. Toluk removed his mitt and felt the man's neck. Then he shook his head. "Help, help—"

"I can't leave," Garris said.

"Dogs." Toluk stood, pointing.

Garris nodded. "Take them." Pleasant, a nearby village, was an hour away.

As Toluk hurried toward the sled, Garris scanned the slide. "Yvetta," he cried.

The silence was absolute, unearthly.

Conscripted for slaughter, he thought. Mirabel dead. And now this, cruelest of all— Yvetta. He blurted a wordless protest, and his tears welled up. Why, he thought. Why had he ever brought her here?

ONE YEAR EARLIER. APRIL 11, 1921, 4 P.M.

The first green sprigs had pierced the snow, but the land was still in the grip of winter. The river was frozen, its icy banks lined with wind-carved ledges. Higher up, the slopes looked bony and smooth, polished with age. A petrified world, white and silent, with no sign of man.

They'd left Nome at dawn and it was late afternoon. Garris walked beside Yvetta on a trail that followed the frozen river. He carried a packboard on his back, and his daughter bore one too, almost equal in size. Behind them, Sumderby pulled a sled loaded with their belongings. A battered cello case wobbled between a leather trunk and a plaid valise. Two canvas duffels were lashed to the sled rails, along with a wooden stool. Sumderby wore a dark coat, patched work pants and a rain hat with spittoon brim. His shirt cuffs were frayed, and his cheeks were dotted with pimples. He'd been sent to Nome to escort them.

"I don't mind telling you," Sumderby said, "I've got a girl."

Garris shared a weary look with Yvetta. Shy and reserved at first, the young man had grown increasingly talkative. Yvetta smiled, amused but tolerant. They'd learned about Sumderby's boyhood, his job, how he'd fixed up his cabin, and how he'd fathomed the mysteries of ledger accounting. The man who employed him, Garris thought, was kindhearted to a fault, or a fool himself.

"How much farther?" he asked.

"We're almost there," Sumderby said. "She's a beauty. She could have any man in the world, but it's me she wants."

The river turned north, and the trail turned with it.

"I shouldn't be talking," the young man admonished

himself, "but I'm wild about her. There's no hiding it, when you're in love."

A raven winged past, and its grating call was like the rattle of gravel in a hungry craw. Garris followed its flight, and a mountain range swung into view.

"We're not headed up there."

"Gosh no," Sumderby laughed. "No one lives in the Teeth."

The ridgelines were jagged. Amber spires rose through the snows.

The trail continued to turn, and a peak with a nodded crown appeared directly before them, its snowy front studded with rock, rusty and iron-black.

"This is our valley," Sumderby announced. "Rightful."

Garris looked at Yvetta, and they slowed together. He raised his arm, removed his black beret and drew the crisp air into his chest. When he exhaled, he imagined the poisons had left with his breath. The insanity was behind them.

"That's Butcher Peak," Sumderby said. "Can you see him?"

"I can," Yvetta replied, pointing at the mountain's top. "There's his head. He's sitting, and his legs are spread to either side."

She had grown so quickly, Garris thought. A few inches more and she'd rival him. Her reedy body had hints of her mother's curves, though modest still and hidden by her tired brown coat. She wore a ribbon of silk in her hair that he'd given her on her tenth birthday. Sky blue, it matched her eyes.

"Do you see?" she asked.

Yvetta had his gravity, but her zeal was her own, bold and incautious—a bright flower on a flexible stem.

"Father?"

Garris scanned the peak, and the butcher resolved. His head was bowed, lopsided and shaggy. His shoulders were slumped, elbows drawn to his sides.

"That's the Cleaver," Sumderby pointed.

The butcher was holding a giant blade, a vertical slab streaked with iron stains. The sharp edge gleamed as if about to come down.

"Pike named him."

"Where's the village?" Yvetta said.

Sumderby motioned, and the three continued along the trail.

Rightful appeared in a fold beneath Butcher Peak. They saw the store first, and then the cabins scattered around it. Some were made of driftwood, others of planking and canvas. A few looked well kept, but most were in disrepair. One was roofless, another had a wall stove-in.

"We're here because of Pike," Sumderby said. "He found gold floaters upriver and tracked them to a deposit below those boulders."

"When was that?" Garris asked.

"In '01, during the rush."

The place looked abandoned. It had been a long time since gold had been found in Nome or anywhere near. "He left," Garris guessed.

"Oh no," Sumderby laughed. "That's his cabin there."

"Is it warm in the summer?" Yvetta asked.

"Heaven," Sumderby said. "Grow whatever you like."

The Mercantile was on the far side of a winding creek. As they crossed a plank bridge, the door opened and a tall man in overalls stepped onto the porch. He was in his forties, tall and thin, bushy-headed and cheerful. He greeted them, thanking Garris for coming. Then he hurried to help with their baggage.

"I'm Jonas Eisenhart." He gripped Garris' shoulder, shaking it as you would someone's hand.

Over the shopkeeper's shoulder, Garris surveyed the store. Its doors and windows were out of square and the eaves were sagging. The unstable ground beneath played havoc with its timbers.

A woman appeared on the porch in a long black skirt and a white blouse. She was statuesque and big-breasted, with her hair piled high.

"Ruth," she introduced herself, "and this is our Sara."

A young woman stepped forward, blond with daring brown eyes and full lips. She wore overalls like her father and had a pencil behind her ear. At the sight of her, Sumderby removed his hat.

"The mice were chewing last night." Ruth tapped her cheek, eyeing the pimples on the young man's face.

He blushed and covered his sores with his hand.

"I wouldn't wrap fish in those trousers," Ruth said. "You wash them or I'll strip them off and do it myself."

Sara giggled.

"Soon as I get their things upstairs," Sumderby nodded.

Ruth turned to Yvetta. "Just set your pack down. Somebody will manage it."

Sumderby grinned and began to unload the sled. "I'm 'Somebody,'" he said.

"How was your journey?" Ruth motioned Yvetta onto the porch.

"I like the mountains," Yvetta replied, ascending the steps.

"You'll get your fill of them here," Ruth replied.

Somebody lifted the cello case over his shoulders for Sara's benefit.

"Careful with that," Garris said.

"I've made biscuits," Ruth told Yvetta. "Will you have something to eat?" She took Yvetta's arm and led her inside.

Garris followed, with Jonas behind. As they entered, the mingled odors of store and kitchen greeted them. A large table appeared on the right, with places set. Ruth moved a bowl of biscuits and a kettle of tea from the stove's top. Garris shrugged off his pack.

"Set it by the bench," Ruth directed, raising her arm to check the pins in her coif. "We don't often see people wearing hats like that."

"It was my uncle's." Garris removed his beret. "He and my father were from New Brunswick."

"You'll love Ruth's cooking," Jonas said as they sat down.

"We would take our meals with you?"

"You may count on breakfast and dinner," Ruth said. "Lunch is unpredictable."

"I'll be dusty," Garris warned.

"I know dust," she smiled. "I'm married to it."

Somebody appeared, lugging the duffels. Sara traipsed in front of him, as if daring him to force his way past. Ruth shot Jonas a look of alarm.

"Sara," Jonas barked.

She rolled her brown eyes and took a place at the table as Somebody started up the stair.

"How old are you, dear?" Ruth tidied her blouse.

"Sixteen," Yvetta said.

"Three years behind Sara. Did you like Nome?"

Yvetta nodded. "I love seeing new places. We walked on the beach before the snows came."

"And before that?" Ruth asked.

"Juneau. And San Francisco. That's where we're from."

Garris heard her voice falter. She glanced at him.

"California has painful memories for us," Yvetta said.

"I *love* San Francisco." Sara's eyes glinted.

"She's never been," Ruth muttered.

"Somebody knows all about it," Sara snapped.

Garris looked from mother to daughter. They seemed to have little in common. Ruth carried herself with an erectness that accentuated her classical profile—her high forehead, her straight nose, the finely tapered chin. An attractive woman. Sara was slighter and shorter. Her face was boyish, round and indelicate, and her hair hung thin and loose, like an unwatered plant. She was chattering at Yvetta, but her gaze shifted as Somebody reappeared with more baggage.

17

Sara dropped her biscuit. She bent to retrieve it, dipping her head beneath the table. Somebody turned with a sly grin. Ruth grabbed Sara's shoulder and jerked her upright.

A bell rang. Jonas shouted, "We're here," and the door opened.

Voices sounded, then two Eskimo women and a child crossed the threshold. The women were short with broad faces, plump cheeks and flat noses. One was middle-aged and carried a load of pelts in her arms—seal skins, spotted and silver-gray. The other was elderly. She had a chin tattoo and held a little girl by the hand.

Ruth rose and approached them, calling them by name.

"Very nice," Ruth said, taking the pelts. "What do you need?"

The younger woman rattled off a list of foods and supplies.

The little girl had fixed on Garris. She let go of her granny and ventured forward, small features ripening, wide-eyed, smiling. She was dressed like an Eskimo hunter, in a fur parka with a sunbeam ruff, mukluks and hide leggings.

"Help them, will you?" Ruth told Sara. And to the girl, "Who wants a biscuit?"

The child beamed. Ruth wet a cloth, cleaned the girl's hands and face and handed her the treat.

"Would you like to come?" Sara asked Yvetta.

She glanced at Garris, and he nodded. Sara escorted the three Eskimos and Yvetta away.

Garris turned to Jonas. "They're local."

"Yes. There's a camp up the river."

"May I see the sleeping quarters?"

"Of course."

Jonas led the way upstairs.

"How long has Somebody been in your employ?"

"A year and a half," Jonas replied.

"Hard to get help in a place like this," Garris guessed. It wasn't a question, and Jonas didn't reply.

The lodgers' room had two double bunks and a washbasin on a small stand beneath the window. A couple of pictures taken from magazines hung in handmade frames. "You're not far from the stove." Jonas pointed at the floorboards.

Garris nodded.

"We're in the room across the hall."

Jonas suggested they look at the work to be done, and they returned downstairs.

"We came to Alaska with the rush," he said. "My family had a store in Milwaukee. I started buying and selling in Nome. Pike was one of my customers. When he struck it, I came along. Set up a tent, built a one-room shack. By then Ruth was pregnant."

"Twenty years ago," Garris said.

Jonas regarded him.

"There were a lot of people here," Garris said.

The shopkeeper nodded. "Till the gold ran out."

Outside, Jonas led him around the building. The siding was a patchwork of rotting planks, and the duckboards needed replacing. Two windows were broken. "You have the glass?" Garris asked. Jonas said he did, then showed him the remains

19

of a collapsed dog shed. "I want a larger one. We're thinking about the future." The roof had some leaks, he added, and a tarp covered each.

He faced Garris. "Where did you learn your trade?"

"In Maine, from my uncle."

"You've been making cabinets in Nome."

"I've done it all," Garris said, "framing, roofing, furniture. I built barracks for soldiers in the Great War. In Russia, on frozen ground."

"Russia?"

"That's where they sent me."

Garris kept his words spare and direct, the way he struck nails with his hammer.

"You have a lovely daughter," the shopkeeper said. "Can I ask—"

"A cancer took her," Garris answered. "That's not your affair."

"No, it's not. I didn't mean to—"

"I have some questions for you," Garris stopped him. "There's not much to your village. You have the money to pay me?"

"I wouldn't have asked you here—"

"Snug me up with tea and biscuits, then chisel me down when the job's done."

"Look—"

"I've been cheated by grocers and robbed by doctors. I was pushed in front of mortars by Professor Wilson. I know what to expect. You want me to fix up your place, you'll pay in front."

Jonas was speechless. He had expected neither scorn nor literacy, Garris thought, from an itinerant carpenter. The hint of a smile formed on the shopkeeper's lips. Did he mean to placate him?

"I said in my letter," Jonas laughed, "I'd give you an advance. But now that we've met— I'm not sure I can stand having you around."

Garris laughed in return. When Jonas extended his hand, he shook it.

"Shall we see what the women are up to?" Jonas motioned.

As he followed the storekeeper through the rear door and down a hallway, Garris unbuttoned his coat, feeling foolish. Beside one suspender, the white of his shirt showed a half-dollar spot where varnish had dropped. It was like a knot in a slab of wood. He was no more sensitive than the lumber he handled, as flat and hard as if he'd just arrived from the mill. He'd been clumsy with others all his life. The years had only made things worse.

"The Mercantile serves four other villages," Jonas explained, "along with the natives who come to trade. We get lodgers, mostly in winter."

The store was unevenly stocked. The shelves were half empty. Goods were stacked at odd intervals, in baskets and barrels, piled against the walls. Sugar and tea, canned fruit, blankets and sacks of grain, shot and kerosene, salmon planks and dusty medicinals. Sara was showing the Eskimo women bolts of cloth. Ruth made marks on a clipboard ledger. Yvetta sat in the corner singing to the little girl.

The Eskimo women turned and approached the girl. The granny came up behind her and felt for her shoulder, the old fingers brown and banded. As Garris stepped closer, the granny turned, the lines in her face trenching deeply. Her gray hair was thin and stringy and lay broomed across her crown. There was an ancient kindness in her eyes. Garris felt it pass through hardship and pain to reach him.

"What's your name?" the little girl asked in perfect English.

"They go to a mission school," Ruth explained.

"Garris," he answered, kneeling.

She grinned, eyes wide. "What's your name?" she asked again.

"Garris." He mimicked her elfish smile.

"What's your name?" she asked still again.

"Garris," he laughed, shaking his head.

The little girl shook hers too, mimicking him.

"Play for her," Yvetta said.

Garris looked at Ruth. "Would you mind?"

"We'd be delighted," Ruth said, nodding at Jonas and Sara.

Garris returned to the front room and mounted the stairs to the lodgers' quarters. He lifted the cello case onto the bed and opened it. A battered guitar lay inside, surrounded by clothing.

He returned to the store, self-conscious, head bowed. Yvetta was seated on the floor. Garris sat beside her. The little girl stepped closer, reaching to touch the instrument's face. Garris plucked a few strings, turned a few pegs, then

22

he rocked back and forth to set the tempo and began to play. Yvetta joined with her voice.

It was a witless ditty with too many rhymes, a favorite of Yvetta's.

The little girl bobbed, eyeing Yvetta with reverence. Four or five, Garris guessed. Wonderful years. While he played, Ruth watched his stubby fingers dance over the fretboard. When the guitar's final notes rang, a clapping sounded at the rear of the store. Garris raised his head to see a slight man with stooped shoulders stepping forward.

"My father wrote that," Yvetta told the little girl.

The slight man smiled at Garris. "There's something of heaven in music," he said. "We have a mission here."

"I've heard," Garris said.

"The Society of Friends," Ruth explained. "Lars is our pastor."

"You're the carpenter," Koopman guessed.

"That's right."

"I want you to see what we're doing."

The weather was clear, so Garris began with the roof repairs. He set up his shop on the first floor, curtaining himself off from the household with tent canvas. As always, the shop was a home for him. Yvetta brought meals in, and he would eat at the table where he sawed and planed. At night, by lantern light, he fashioned posts and boards for the dog shed.

Indoors or out, his saws spoke as they worked, and so did his chisels and drills, and the nails as they sank. They had a lot to say, and he gave them thoughtful replies, lips moving till weariness overcame him.

Yvetta schooled herself from the books they'd packed with them and helped in the store. Sara taught her to weigh out goods and barter with the natives, and when their hours were free, they walked in the valley together. Garris learned from his daughter about Sara's affection for Somebody. The attachment was deeper than her parents knew.

Often he rose before Yvetta. If he tired during the day, he'd stretch out and nap in the sawdust. No one complained about his odd hours and habits. He enjoyed working long into the night.

Pastor Koopman visited in the second week to make good on his invitation. "I want you to meet the People," he said. He spoke of his mission with pride, as if he imagined Garris would be stirred by it. Politely, Garris said no. He had little interest in the Friends or the natives. A few days later, the pastor interrupted their dinner to ask him again.

"Can we please?" Yvetta begged.

"Of course," Garris said. Her eagerness gladdened him. He'd had worries about bringing her north. Would the harsh conditions or the rough-hewn residents trouble her? The friendship with Sara was a great relief. Yvetta's happiness was the most important thing in his life.

Koopman and his fellow missionary, a woman named Mattie, met them on the Mercantile porch, and the four followed the trail to the Eskimo camp.

Mattie was small and sturdy-looking, and a decade older than Koopman. With spectacles and a bun at her nape, she looked stern and pious, but there was a delicacy in her gestures and expressions that drew Garris. Did she sense he was an unbeliever? She did nothing to test him, and her words were thoughtful, unassuming and warm.

Thirty-eight Eskimos lived in the camp, she explained. Their ancestral home was to the west, on the coast. They had numbered over three hundred, then gold was discovered and the new arrivals brought the "Great Death"—measles, diphtheria, syphilis, TB and the influenza. Those who survived sought help from the whites. Children without families were sent to orphanages. Others sheltered in Nome or with missions like theirs.

"I want them to learn modern carpentry," Koopman said. "They're in desperate need of skills like yours."

Garris didn't reply.

The river narrowed and turned. Butcher Peak vanished and the Teeth grew numerous. Bristling and spiny, ridge beyond ridge, the crests were lined with cusps. A rocky wall rose on the right, bounding the river, and the Eskimo camp appeared. It was a rugged place and an intimate one, filled with the rumble and hiss of wind and current.

"In Rightful, we're one community," Koopman said.

Garris regarded him. "With one faith."

"That's their choice. We're not here to convert them. That's not the Friends' way. Those who have found our Lord have found Him through guidance and prayer." The pastor met his gaze. "Is He in your thoughts?"

Garris shook his head.

"You seem like a good man," Koopman said.

"Don't let your faith divide us."

"I promise," Koopman nodded, "it won't."

As they drew closer to the camp, dogs chained in a pen began to bark. A dozen people were about.

The shelters were mound shaped, mortared with mud and roofed by sod. A few were shingled with scrap metal or flattened cans. From the outside they looked like snow-covered hillocks, with threads of smoke rising from their tops. Garris wondered how they were lit and where the entrances were. Between the dwellings, the ground was littered with crates, washtubs, cans and jars. Seal skin pelts were hanging on racks and lines like laundry.

As they stepped through the yard, Garris saw faces turn, following him and Yvetta. Mattie hailed a woman bent over a large bird, pulling feathers from its breast. When the woman looked up, Garris saw she was white. She had a heavy jaw and intense eyes, dark as an Asian's. Her hair was long and black, and twin-braided.

"This is Garris," Mattie said, "and Yvetta."

The woman stood, faced his daughter, then turned to him. "The carpenter." Her voice was cordial, but her eyes were somber. It was as if they had met before and she recognized him. "Kiachuk," she said.

"Garris." He nodded.

"I can't shake your hand," she said, glancing at her bloody fingers.

She stooped and took a pinch of down from the swan's breast. Then she rose and set it on his shoulder.

Was she making fun of him? Testing, curious— Troubled by something? Her expression was unaccountably grave. He couldn't look away.

Yvetta shifted beside him. Garris saw his daughter watching, smiling to herself.

"I want him to meet Ned," Koopman told Kiachuk.

Before she could answer, a native boy interrupted, circling them, waving the swan's severed wings and crying, "Flying Man, I'm the Flying Man."

Mattie and Koopman stared at Kiachuk, looking agitated.

Kiachuk knelt, spoke gently and extended her arm. The boy put the swan's wings in her hand. Then she rose and passed them to Mattie, with an expression apologetic but unperturbed, as if the boy's misbehavior was something she was inured to. "He doesn't know any better."

"We'll be in the nursery," Mattie said. She smiled at Yvetta, and the two started down to the river.

Kiachuk turned toward a gathering across the yard. "They're getting ready to leave," she said.

Koopman motioned to Garris, and they stepped forward, following Kiachuk.

"Smelt have reached the Channel," the pastor explained. "They're first, then candlefish and herring. The water will be black with them. The Eskimos net them, as they did in centu-

27

ries past. They fish and hunt, but they've learned some agriculture too. You'll be surprised.

"They call themselves 'Inupiaq,'" he said. "'The People.' Ned Jimmy is their leader, the elder. Kiachuk's his daughter."

Garris was confused by that. The woman was as white as he was.

Two men were folding nets. Others coiled ropes and lines, and loaded supplies into open packs. Cured skins, bleached by the sun, had been spread on the ground, and a man was rolling them up.

"Walrus hide," Koopman said, "to patch their skin boat."

Garris spotted an older native, short and gray at the temples but muscular despite his years. His brows were thick, his cheeks grizzled. He was dressing the head of a spear while he spoke to a man with a long face and one eye, who sharpened hooks with a flint.

Kiachuk came to a halt before her father. "This is Ned," she said, and she spoke to the grizzled man in his native tongue.

Ned inspected the spear as if he hadn't heard her, as if they weren't there.

Garris stood motionless, silent. The One-Eyed Man stared at him.

Finally Ned straightened himself, squinted at Garris and spoke.

"It's a pleasure," Kiachuk translated.

Garris didn't reply. Ned's meaning seemed closer to, "What're you doing here?"

Koopman tried to smooth things over with a kindly smile. "Ned's children," he said, "are the most literate natives in the Arctic."

Kiachuk translated the pastor's words for Ned. He grunted and spoke.

"My father questions the value of my learning," Kiachuk said. "He thinks white schools teach us the wrong things," she explained. "'A man needs to know how to kill a walrus. Christ makes our sons soft,' he says."

Her speech was measured, but her eyes were hard. She was used to this kind of treatment, Garris thought. However Ned's contempt might have pained her, she seemed to accept it.

"Tell him he's going to miss my lesson," Koopman said.

When Kiachuk translated, Ned grinned, seeing the humor. He spoke to Kiachuk, and when he finished she turned to Garris.

"'Good luck with your repairs,' my father says. 'I built a home your way. Cut logs with a saw and nailed them together. It blew down in a storm.'"

Garris laughed. Koopman shook his head. Kiachuk smiled, but the darkness in her eyes remained.

"How are they made?" Garris asked Ned, looking at a nearby hut.

Kiachuk posed the question to her father and translated his answer. "The framework is driftwood," she said. "Woven branches. We cover the branches with mud, then grasses and moss grow over it."

29

"Are the branches fixed together?" Garris asked.

Kiachuk translated the question, and Ned's eyes flashed as he answered.

"We lash them with hide," Kiachuk said.

For frozen ground and fierce winds, Garris thought, it was a smart solution. The frame was free to shift and stretch. For those inside, the hut was like a thick sweater.

"Tell him I understand," Garris said. "I admire your resourcefulness."

He watched as she translated. An intelligent woman, literate and intuitive. Her dark mood would be unattractive to some, but not to him. Ned was watching him watch his daughter, mouth skewed, as if he was chewing on one side.

"Good netting," Koopman wished Ned. He turned away from the Eskimo elder, leaning closer to Kiachuk.

"Our goods have arrived," Koopman told her.

"We'll get them hauled," she said, "when the men leave."

Fresh supplies from the spring freighters had reached the store the previous week. The Friends, it seemed, were provisioning the People.

Koopman motioned to Garris, and they started back across the yard.

"Here comes Yvetta and the children," the pastor said.

Garris saw his daughter with the little Eskimo girl, holding her hand. Mattie and a crowd of other youngsters hurried beside. Yvetta looked buoyant, sunny and bright. There was a time when he'd felt that kind of joy in life. He still knew wonder and satisfaction, but his pleasure now came from working wood. And the finer his craft, the more solitary and involuted the pleasure had become. Shadowy thoughts. Had the Eskimo woman triggered them?

"Kiachuk was adopted," Garris guessed.

"No," Koopman said, "she's Ned's by birth. Before the rush, the government had a station at Teller. Ned endeared himself to one of the white women there. When Kiachuk was born, Ned took her."

"And the mother?"

"She returned to Auckland with her husband," the pastor said.

A half-dozen women and children had collected in a clearing. Mattie, Yvetta and the little Eskimo girl approached. The little girl beamed, let go of Yvetta's hand and ran toward him, circling his knee and tugging his pant leg. "What's your name?" she asked.

"I adore them," Yvetta said.

Garris put his hand on the little girl's head.

More natives joined the assembly, reaching the clearing from the huts and the yard, and the nursery downriver. Koopman left Garris' side.

As the pastor mounted a rise, his flock found their places. Some sat on a log, a bucket or a handmade bench, while others settled on the ground.

Koopman gazed at the river, then turned his back to it. A young Eskimo man stepped toward him, halting a few feet away. He was average height, broad shouldered and long in the waist. His bronzed face was diamond shaped, with a sharp chin and black hair parted on either side of his brow.

"John Jimmy," Mattie said, "Ned's son."

Koopman took a Bible from him and began paging through it, reading passages while John trialed Eskimo translations aloud.

Koopman's voice reached them. "Do we have it?"

John Jimmy replied, "We have 'righteous' and 'wicked.' 'Kingdom' is always hard, but I'll get the idea across." His English was as flawless as Kiachuk's.

Koopman put his hand on John's shoulder. They might have been father and son.

"What is the subject?" Garris asked.

"The Kingdom to Come," Mattie replied.

The natives were seated and ready. They were all in warm clothing. The sun was higher, but the air was cold.

The pastor planted himself and raised his head. John took his position six feet to one side and two feet forward.

"God's judgment will be visited on the earth," Koopman began, "and in that long-awaited hour the righteous will be separated from the wicked. Those who cling to evil will be doomed, and those who have Jesus in their hearts will enter His kingdom."

John faced the Eskimos, translating the words for them.

"We think we know life. But there is more to know. We think we see how life begins and ends. But there is more to see. When the breath stops, and the body is bound in cloth, is that the end?"

Koopman spoke earnestly, pausing after every statement. John rendered the thoughts with a spirited delivery. Phrase by phrase, the message reached the natives through the mind and lips of the youth.

An Eskimo woman sat on an overturned crate, sewing and pursing her lips. Another wove blades of grass into a basket. A mother and daughter were skinning a seal, sectioning blubber, putting pieces in a bucket. The woman stopped and peered at John with a fistful of fat in her hand.

"Though the body is still and lifeless, there's a deeper life within that continues to think and see. The dead wait for their day, and on that day, they awaken. Do they wake in this world? Do they put on their parkas and mukluks and trudge down to the Kuzitrin to haul out their fish? No. The world they wake into is a world of the spirit, where they know themselves and each other in the deepest and most personal way.

"On this day, those of pure heart, those who have God's spirit within them, will find their eternal reward in heaven. And those who are corrupt, who cast God out of their hearts in life, will find their reward in hell."

Koopman was trying to make divine justice comprehensible, and he seemed to be succeeding. There was thoughtfulness in an old woman's face, and emotion in a younger's eyes. The baby she'd been nursing had fallen asleep.

"Will the time of judgment be tonight, after dinner? Or

while we're asleep, lost in dreams? None of us know the hour or day. But God has it in mind." The pastor touched his finger to his head. "The moment when he will bring an end to this world—every man and woman in it—and measure who we are.

"My friend— Picture the expression on Jesus' face when your spirit rises before him. You'll want to be counted among His righteous. Won't you?"

Koopman scanned the faces.

"Last week, on Wednesday, Edna left her hut to wash clothing in the river. Her necklace disappeared—the one with the blue beads that her grandmother gave her. I don't know who took it and neither does Edna. We may never see it again, in this life. But when the thief stands before Jesus in the hour of judgment, our Lord will raise his hand and that necklace will be in it."

Garris laughed to himself. Edna's necklace.

"Our world doesn't reward us as we wish it would," the pastor said. "When we do what is fair and just, we aren't recognized. Our bad deeds aren't seen for what they are and punished by man or God. Not in this world. That is our sadness, our grief, our curse. That is the trial to which God puts us.

"To look beyond today and see the life of the spirit and the reward it will have. To see beyond the hardships of this dark, frozen world and embrace the kingdom of warmth and light. That is the message that Jesus brings."

The pastor's tone was solemn, but John Jimmy's was anything but. His gaze was fearless, and his voice rang out, loud and confident. It had an emotional depth and a fervor the

34

pastor lacked, and his physical presence cast a shadow over the milder man. John's nose was bold, the bridge sharp and bowed. He had his father's thick brows and bold almond eyes. The power in his voice boomed in his chest, and the hands he clasped behind him suggested there was more in reserve.

Mattie was nodding, and so were a dozen natives. Garris wondered how much of the lesson's impact was the translator's doing.

"Let the wicked and righteous grow together until the harvest," Koopman said. "On that day, I will send out my angels. I will cast the wicked into the furnace of fire, and the righteous will shine forth like the sun in my kingdom."

The translation was given.

"John," Koopman said, "will you sing for us?"

The young man took a step forward, collected himself and began to sing:

Why do we mourn departing friends
Or shake at death's alarms?

It was a hymn expressing indifference to death and affirming a heavenly reward. Music often reached Garris, and the hymn's melody swept him up. Its words reached him too. They expressed a yearning that seemed authentic. What did it matter that the subject was redemption? People had needs, dire needs that went unanswered. The hymn understood that.

Garris heard the baby crying. Its mother opened her tunic and gave it her breast.

Yvetta was rapt, fixed on John. Spine straight, his shoulders drawn back— His eyes were shut, but a great dignity shone in his face. His hands were still clasped behind him, but instead of holding his strength in reserve, it seemed now that he meant to bare it.

There was beauty in the hymn, and in the young man too.

Garris didn't often find beauty in people, but when he did, they seemed like wood. His uncle had been as clear as sanded birch. His father was the arm of an oak, twisted by life, hard to plane and patterned with scars. Mirabel was ebony, impossibly dense, with a grain hard to discern. John Jimmy had the fire of apricot wood. And Yvetta—she was glowing beside him like osage orange.

The look in her eyes—

It was as if John's voice was lifting her, carrying her away.

Garris felt the chill of separation, and the shudder of a parting without appeal. She was at the age. It was going to happen—

But not with him standing beside her. The attraction, no doubt, was weaker than he imagined. Still, he couldn't help himself. He wanted to protect her, and himself.

Garris remembered Mirabel and the day they met. For those who knew love, he thought, life made no exceptions; there was no allowance, no special treatment. The world was deaf to that music. If Yvetta loved deeply, she would feel pain. And what could he do? She would learn, as he had, how cruel life was.

The last verse celebrated a "great rising day," but to Garris it was less a cry to be joined with God than a cry to be reunited with humanity—a cry that faded quickly as the words were borne away by the wind.

Koopman stepped forward. The lesson was over.

John faced the river, hearing the birds perhaps, and the sound of wind and water, feeling the sun on his face with his eyes closed.

The Eskimos rose and returned to their chores.

"What do you think?" the pastor smiled.

"That's some hymn," Garris said.

"I learned it when I was a boy in Pennsylvania. God speaks through music."

"Music is a refuge," Garris said. "From God and everything else."

Koopman looked at Yvetta. "He's a hard nut."

She ignored the jibe. "Your message reached them."

"That's what matters," the pastor replied.

"Is there any way I can help?" Yvetta said.

"Schooling the children's a big job," Koopman answered. "Mattie's on her own."

"She has no religious training," Garris said.

"She doesn't need any."

Garris saw the excitement in Yvetta's eyes.

"In our work," Koopman added, "the teacher learns as much as the student."

"John has a wonderful voice," she said.

"You should hear his sister," the pastor told them. "She's the nightingale in the family. They were both schooled at the

Methodist mission. You'd think they went to an eastern prep school. A real credit to the work we're doing."

Every other day, Yvetta followed the trail upriver and spent the afternoon with the Eskimo children. In the first week, she returned with the story of how Edna's necklace had reappeared in the place where she'd kept it. Garris didn't believe his daughter was drawn solely by the mission and her affection for the children. The work she was doing put her in frequent contact with John.

May arrived, and the days were longer and warmer. He completed the roof repairs and the dog shed. The sawdust in the shop softened his steps, and the curls loosed by his planes grew like a garden. The air was a medley of scents—the honey of hemlock, the spice of birch, the tang of spruce; day and night he breathed the perfumes rising from the wood's pores. When Yvetta returned from her visit upriver, she would share her thoughts. "They're a special people, Mattie says. They have a natural sweetness which our race lacks. This is a good place for us."

Garris didn't ask about John. He tried not to dwell on what might be happening.

One evening after they'd eaten, they retired to the lodgers' room, and Yvetta opened her heart, hesitantly. She lay on the bunk with her head on his knee. She was fond of John, she said. They were the same age, born in the same month. Wasn't that strange?

Garris stroked her temple. They were spending more time together, Yvetta said. Garris didn't reply. He was her father. There were things she wanted to tell him, he thought. Things he didn't want to hear.

Had John kissed her? Had they—

It was foolish, he knew, but he felt the violation himself. His instinct to protect her made no sense at all. Her judgment was keen. If she trusted John, he should as well. It was his wish, his duty, to stand for love.

Yvetta was speaking of John's ideas.

"He hasn't just learned the lessons by rote. He's searching."

Sexual feelings could give rise to wild romanticism in a teenage boy, Garris thought. Yvetta knew nothing of that. John had no trade. He'd grown up in a hut, in a frozen land. Yvetta wasn't a child, but he couldn't help think of her as one. A special child—the only ray of sunshine in a dark world.

"John's uncle—" She looked up at him. "They called him 'the Flying Man.' He died from the influenza.

"John was close to him, like you were with Uncle Luc. The Flying Man saw things most people can't see. The Eskimos have the Christian faith, but a few still—" Yvetta stopped herself.

"Still what?"

"Sometimes," she spoke softly now, "when you're falling asleep— You see things and hear things. Others are with you. People, and creatures."

He removed his hand from Yvetta's brow. There was silence in the room.

39

"It's like looking at water," she said. "You can see your reflection and the reflection of others behind and around you. Blurred, rippling, in soft colors. Not the colors of life, bright and vivid; but pale and runny."

Garris sighed. "Between the Flying Man, his mission schooling, and Koopman's lessons, John's been fed a lot of hocus-pocus."

Yvetta was still for a long moment, then she rose and faced him.

"Do you really know better? If someone sees something you can't see, why must you ridicule them? You have no right to do that."

Garris was stunned. He thought to protest, to defend himself. But when he looked in her eyes, he dared not.

She turned, strode through the doorway and descended the stair.

A moment later, he heard the front door close, and when he looked out the window, he saw Yvetta in her parka, headed down the trail toward the river.

If she had hurt herself or suffered some setback, he would have known what to do. But the outburst rendered him helpless. He had understood his young daughter. But the woman inside her—mysterious, struggling to define herself—was a total stranger.

Garris watched Yvetta shrink to a dim silhouette and vanish.

2

*T*he aurora filled the sky, a great arc of green, bridging the darkness from the moon's silver crescent in the east to the ranks of glimmering Teeth that stood between Rightful and the Bering Sea.

Garris shuddered, gripped his spade and drove it into the crush. Had an hour passed? Every fresh pit he dug with reviving hope. "Yvetta," he called, praying she'd hear. "Yvetta, Yvetta—" Time, more time. Another minute for her. A minute of strangled breath, of freezing cold. He had to find her.

Lars was shouting his name.

Garris looked up. "Where are you?"

"Here, I'm here."

Garris scanned the jumbled ice. He didn't see him, and then he did.

Lars was clambering onto a boulder. He struggled for balance, tipping and waving his arm to be seen. "Hurry," he yelled. "I've found her."

Garris started toward him.

The lime aurora glowed brightest on the pulverized ice. Blocks were set in it, faceted and cracked like barbaric jewels, green-gold on reflecting faces, midnight blue in their depths. Timbers were everywhere, a dented fuel tank, a wad of linen, a casserole dish and a carton of soap. Garris saw Ruth's silver, scattered as if a thief had entered her kitchen and been caught in the act. "Hurry," Koopman cried.

As Garris wound through the blocks and hillocks, a dog barked and came bounding toward him, waving its tail. One of the native dogs that brought guests to the wedding. "Garris—"

Koopman was kneeling in a hollow, the ax beside him. As Garris drew closer, he saw a hand protruding from the snow a few feet from Koopman's face.

"It's Mattie," Lars said, shivering.

The hand was waxen, the fingers curled. There were grooves and pits in the snow around it. Garris handed the shovel over and grabbed the ax.

Koopman used the shovel blade to continue his chipping. "You're sure?"

"I know her hands," Lars replied.

Garris removed his mitt and felt Mattie's wrist. "There's a pulse."

The third finger moved. Koopman gasped, wild-eyed.

42

Garris rose, hefting the ax, bringing it down. "Jesus. It's like cement."

"Careful," Lars bleated, using the spade's point to scrape around her wrist.

Garris continued swinging. The ax blows left shallow dints.

"Be careful," Lars insisted. "She heard my voice. Her fingers," he opened his hand, "reached out."

The auroral rays were plunging from heaven to earth, as if they had some kind of score to settle. "We're here," Lars spoke to the buried woman. "We're here."

Garris struck with the ax, again and again. Koopman wheedled and chipped.

The rays of light were glowing silver. Mattie's elbow appeared. Then the tips of the rays turned red. Time was passing, but how much— The hand looked ghostly now, a visitation from some other realm.

Garris dropped the ax and sank to his knees.

"What are you doing?" Lars demanded.

Garris felt Mattie's wrist and sighed, thinking of Yvetta.

"Her heart's stopped," he said.

"No it hasn't. You're wrong."

"Look at her hand," Garris murmured. "It's turning gray." He imagined his daughter, pressed to death, freezing, unable to breathe.

"Please—" Lars broke down, sobbing, eyeing the curled fingers, a closed fist now. He seemed afraid to touch it.

The sight was too much for Garris. The unlucky pastor,

he thought. The gentle woman, so innocent, so well-meaning. They wanted a better world. How much they sacrificed, and how little it mattered.

Was Yvetta already lost? Broken, frozen. Smothered or crushed like Mattie. What could he do on his own or with Lars? And even if she was still alive, even if help arrived— Would there be enough time to save her?

Above, the luminous curtain was turning in on itself; and as it coiled, its color shaded from green to blue. While Lars sobbed, the glowing spiral expanded to fill the night. Garris felt like he did when Yvetta sang with all her heart, and the tears were flowing down both their cheeks.

They were all just helpless children. They longed for a life more kindly, more just than the one they'd been given. Like an imagined future, the great blue screw-thread trembled with tension and turned in the heavens.

Was the wind sighing, or was it the whisk of sled runners?

Garris stood. Dog teams were ascending the Rightful Valley in line on the trail. Help, from Pleasant. The light from above haloed them all, the dogs' icy fur refracting the glow, as if they'd been dispatched from some fabled realm. The man driving the first team came into view, mounting the slope. Garris raised his arms and shouted.

The man saw him. He drove to the edge of the fan and braked his sled. Garris hurried to meet him as the following teams pulled up on either side. Many in Pleasant were known to Garris, but the man stepping toward him was faceless. His head was hooded with a dark balaclava.

TEN MONTHS EARLIER. JUNE 9, 1921.

The repairs to the Mercantile were completed on schedule and to Eisenhart's satisfaction. By then, Yvetta had grown close to the Eskimo children. Her affection for John, and his attachment to her, had become a local story. The prospect of their departure lay heavy on Yvetta, but what could be done? They had to go where the work was.

Garris stepped along the path to Pike's cabin. Jonas had invited him there "to express our thanks." Summer had come. Most of the snow had melted off Butcher Peak. All that remained were fringes beneath the brute's spread legs, and a white sheet below his tarnished blade. Garris felt the sun on his brow, and the lightness that came with a project's completion. He felt, as well, the excitement of leaving, of setting out for some place new.

He knew the Arctic better now. Work on the roof and siding had given him a view of the country as the season changed. The Teeth in the distance grew longer. Their gums receded and the enamel dissolved, revealing fangs, pointed and cracked. The first rains came in early May, then two weeks of fog filled the Rightful Valley; and when the fog dissolved, sun beat on the melting ground. Summer was the time for building repairs, and the northland was sprinkled with villages.

Large gray rocks lined the pathway to Pike's door. On

the left, ptarmigan had been strung up to dry on a driftwood rack. On the right was a woodpile Somebody kept fresh. A mastodon tusk leaned against the cabin wall. The logs themselves were of uniform dimension, peeled and saddle-notched at the corners, and the window beside the door was the largest in Rightful, sporting eight panes.

When he knocked, Jonas opened the door and motioned him in. Garris hung his knapsack on a peg, and Jonas handed him a stein. Pike stood on his bear rug, and as Garris turned, he raised his tankard. The hawkish nose, red cheeks and billowing hair lifted as well. "To a job well done," Pike said.

"Well done," Jonas echoed, lifting his mug.

The three men drank.

Pike's amour, Blinne, sat at a plank table covered with rags and brushes, cleaning his shotgun. She was an Irish girl, short and trim, with ginger hair, thin brows and a delicate mouth. She looked fragile for the Arctic, but Garris had been there long enough to know better.

"You've added your piece to Rightful," Pike said, "and life tips out its reward." He nodded to Jonas.

The shopkeeper pulled a roll of greenbacks from his pocket and handed it to Garris. The repair work was paid in full, so this was a surprise.

"That's how the scales work." Pike motioned to a shelf above the stove.

A pair of brass scales stood there, circular trays hanging from triple chains. They were out of balance, with a small weight on one side and a fist-sized rock on the other.

46

"My first big haul," Pike remembered. "I brought a sample to the office in Nome, and after the assayer weighed out my worth, I asked him how much those scales were."

"Not the scales," Blinne said, without raising her eyes.

He ignored her, pointing at a framed photograph on the shelf. An elated Pike with dark hair stood between piles of gold bricks. "After it was smelted, I had 'em stack my gold, with a space for me to stand.

"Eighteen months before, I was sifting dirt back of Council. They kept talking about the gold on Nome's beach, so I went to have a look. Ten thousand men! And every one of 'em a fool— the sea floor was covered with gold, they said. It was coming in with the tide!" He laughed. "'Easy money' men. They packed the saloons and dance halls. A year later, they were all bums without a nickel. The government hired a ship to haul 'em back to the States."

Pike looked out the window. "Back then no one cared about these mountains. I thought, 'Might be something there.' Ten thousand loafers playing 'Kitty Climb the Pole,' and I'm tramping the Teeth, eating the cuffs off my shirt—"

"Piker—" Blinne rose.

He waved her down. "A man has to follow his star, Garris. Have the nerve and the daring, and he has to work—"

"You haven't done any work in twenty years," Blinne said.

Pike bristled. "What would you know about work, Cherry?"

"Smoking and reading newspapers?" she laughed. "Tramping to the bank in Nome?"

"The jades are like fleas—that's work. As soon as I hit town, they jump on."

She threw her rag down. "Clean your own damn guns."

"Happy to," he snapped. "They'll be cleaned right for once."

She started across the cabin. One of her legs was misshapen, and her foot dragged. The thigh was fine, but below the knee the leg was bent at an odd angle. Her limping left an uncomfortable silence in its wake.

Blinne slammed the door behind her. "You're sleeping alone tonight," she yelled.

Pike sighed. "My stocks are in those papers. I'm looking after my investments," he explained to Garris. "I smoke 'cause I'm in tobacco."

"Tobacco companies?"

"Yup. Autos gonna ruin the trains, electricity gonna ruin kerosene. But a man will always want a good smoke." He forced a laugh. "Watching investments is work. The only time I waste is with Cherry."

"Careful, Clayburn," Jonas said.

"Ah—" Pike waved his concern away.

"She's talked to Ruth about leaving."

"You think I care?" Pike was incredulous. He pinched the gold ring on his pinky, rotating it with authority. "A fellow like me deserves better. She was another man's wife. Bill overlooked her defects, and so have I. But there's a limit. Which brings me back to my point." He looked at Garris. "Life has rules. It doles out rewards based on the effort a man makes. I named this place Rightful because the riches were earned.

"Now," he spread his arms, "I live beside the Rightful River. I look out my window at the Rightful Valley. I sleep on a wool mattress, under a squirrel quilt. I have a copper teapot and a mercury thermometer. I stroll to the store and buy canned peaches on tick." He gave Garris a concluding smile.

Garris glanced at Jonas. The storekeeper was mum.

"Luck had something to do with it," Garris said.

"Oh sure, but it was daring and spine that gave luck its chance. You're an educated man. You understand what a symbol is." Pike held his palms out to either side and tipped them. "The scales weigh out to each his due."

He's sawing dovetails, Garris thought. Pike's focus was on the cut, and there was rhythm and determination in his strokes. He has some purpose, Garris thought.

"My story is what Lars would call a lesson," Pike said. He looked at Jonas. "We're going to pay him a visit, aren't we?"

Jonas turned to Garris. "Why don't you come along."

Garris nodded. "I was going to return some things."

Pike stepped over to his bed, took a small box from beneath his pillow and slid it into his pocket. The three men put on their rubber boots, and Garris pulled his knapsack from the peg.

As they exited, Pike spoke. "Give me a minute to make it up to her."

They started along the trail, and when they reached Blinne's cabin, Pike stopped and knocked on the door.

She swung it all the way back and stood glowering, hands on her hips.

49

"I treated you poorly," Pike hung his head. "I'm a rat and a goon." He removed the little box from his pocket. "I have something for you."

Blinne stared at the box. Then she laughed and took it. When she opened the lid, she laughed again. Then she sighed, "Oh my."

"Put it on," Pike insisted.

Garris saw her pin something to her shirt, below the collar.

"Specially made, for a special woman." Pike's voice dropped as the words left his lips, "My Cherry."

Blinne brushed a tear from her eye, embraced him and kissed his lips.

"Come with us," Pike said, taking her hand.

She stepped forward and Garris saw the brooch on her shirt—a silver cherry with a curled stem.

The trail to Koopman's was muddy. There were pools on either side, and meltwater trickled beneath the rocks, on its way to the river. Windflowers pushed through the heather and lichen, and the blueberry was ankle high. It was midday, but the sun shone from the south, and the clouds looked pearly.

"Perfect, isn't it," Pike said. His billow of white hair was iridescent.

They passed the water hole. Ten feet deep, blasted out of the rock, it collected runoff in spring and summer.

"I was out last night," Pike said. "Guess who was here, fishing."

"Don't tell me," Jonas said.

Pike laughed. "It was past midnight."

They were talking about Somebody.

"Is there anything to catch?" Garris wondered.

"Just fry." Pike held up his thumb and finger with two inches between. "They find their way from the river."

Beyond the water hole, cabins built by prospectors appeared. They passed one with broken windows. Its door was open, and the roofline had drooped. The boulder bed between the village and the river swung into view, fissures clogged with snow. The trail switched through a bog, and they followed the duckboards single file.

Pike hollered, "Lars, Lars," and Blinne joined in.

The missionary's cabin appeared. The pastor opened his door and welcomed them in. Mattie was seated at a table, mending one of his shirts. She lived there with him, a fact that was avoided in conversation. Garris strode to the bookcase behind Lars' desk, opened his knapsack and returned the books he'd borrowed.

"How was Emerson?" Koopman asked.

"Optimistic, as always," Garris replied. "Thanks for the use of your library." He faced the group. "You've been friends to us. It's hard saying adieu."

"Maybe we shouldn't." Pike nodded to Koopman.

An effort's been made to orchestrate this, Garris thought.

"We have a dream," Lars said, approaching, "something we've prayed for—and the dream is about to come true." He circled the desk and opened a box of letters. "The funds have been approved. The Society of Friends, together with the Bureau and Pike, are providing us the money to build a Meeting House."

He unscrolled a draftsman's drawing. "It will look like this."

Garris studied the drawing. "A church?"

"We're the church. This is a place for us to talk, to eat, to learn, to sing, in good weather and bad."

"It will have a steeple and clock," Mattie said.

Garris nodded. "Congratulations."

"We want you to build it," Pike said.

"You'd do a fine job," Jonas affirmed.

Garris was silent.

"It means staying here with us," Lars said. "Helping make Rightful a better place."

"It's just a sprout now," Jonas said.

"Imagine—" Pike spoke as if sharing a secret. "Streets with electric trolleys. Homes, nice ones, on either side of the river. Markets and shops." He cocked his head. "It's not so crazy. Towers with views of the Teeth," he predicted. "A suspension bridge across the Sinuk. And in the center of things, a park with statues of the Rightful founders—men who had a vision of the future.

"And women," he added. "Mine will be here this winter, won't you Cherry?"

"Oh sure. Who needs London or Paris."

"It would be an honor to have a man of your character with us," Mattie said.

An improbable vision, Garris thought. It was the last thing he expected.

"I'm sorry," he said. "I have other plans."

"Chances like this don't come along often," Pike insisted.

"You can't start now," Garris said. "You'll have to wait for the snows to haul lumber."

"Rezkov has a cache," Pike explained. "You've met him?"

Garris shook his head.

"A drift cruiser," Pike said. "He picks logs off the beaches, brings firewood in the winter. When it's warm, there's a trail he runs a wagon over."

Garris regarded Lars. "What's wrong with the mission as it is?"

"The Meeting House will give the People a sense of permanence. They need that badly. The camp is fifteen years old. Those huts are temporary lodging to them. During the Great Death their ancestral home was a charnel. They'll never go back."

Mattie was nodding.

"We will all better ourselves here," Lars touched the drawing. "It's not only faith and worship. Mattie will teach history, hygiene and medicine— She's much more than a schoolmarm and nurse. There are modern skills the People can learn. Cultivation, farming and breeding—a hundred things."

"A Meeting House," Jonas said, "will draw people from Nome and Council. They'll visit, stay a few days or a week."

"And shop at the Mercantile," Garris ventured.

"It's not just commerce," Pike said. "It's not just travelers we're thinking about."

"People need more than goods," Jonas agreed. "Among those who visit, there will be folks who might like to call this home. They'll attend Lars' meetings, they'll admire our industry. They'll see what we have here and want to be part of it."

"And they'll think about having a place of their own," Pike winked. "A summer cabin, or a house for all seasons."

"This could be the spark," Jonas said, "that ignites a fire."

Blinne raised her brows. "They're putting the hug on you."

Garris laughed, and then, with all eyes on him, he shook his head.

"It means a lot to me that you respect my skill," he said. "But—"

"You have a better offer?" Pike asked.

"I'm not going to settle here, or anywhere else."

Silence filled the cabin.

"Like the willows," Koopman said, "we need roots. And so do the People."

"I'm not going to lie," Garris said. "I don't think you're improving them."

Conversation stopped. Garris saw Mattie eyeing him over Lars' shoulder.

"They can't survive on their own," Jonas said.

"Before the missions showed up," Pike said, "they were drowning their daughters."

Jonas put his hand on Pike's shoulder.

"They never had enough to eat," Pike went on. "Too busy trading wives and conniving with their witch doctors."

"That's enough," Blinne warned him.

"I was here. I saw it. 'For godsake,'" Pike said, as if upbraiding the natives, "'get to work. Stop wasting your time with the Flying Man.'"

"Will you shut up?" Blinne snapped.

Garris laughed.

"To each his due," Pike declared. "The universal principle. Put them on the building crew—that's my idea. And a clock, up high where they can see it."

"Are you done?" Blinne said.

"There's no future for Rightful with a tribe of loafers in our backyard." Pike looked at Garris. "They've been the fleas on the dog for too long."

Lars sighed. "I wish all that's happened to them—the disease and starvation, their ruined families—was due to sloth. But it's not. Their misfortunes don't have anything to do with your 'universal principle.' They need more than jobs. They need to believe there's a cure for injustice, a divine reward."

Pike lifted his chin. "You don't buy that nonsense," he said to Garris.

Garris looked at Mattie. There was calm in her eyes, and patience. She was a forgiving woman, with a subtle strength. Her hair was down, and it was luxuriant. Did the pastor realize how fortunate he was?

"My wife was a Christian," Garris said gently. "But she couldn't persuade me." He looked at Lars. "I don't believe things are settled up when we die." He looked at Pike. "And I don't believe in your scales. I don't see right being rewarded in this world, and I don't see wrong being punished."

Mattie motioned to Blinne, and they stepped toward the rear. Two small beds were against the wall, a couple of feet from each other. An ivory curtain hung from a rod, separating the sleeping area from the rest of the cabin. They passed through, and Mattie closed the curtain.

"This is it." Garris opened his hands. "A man enjoys what he has, whether its earned or stolen. And then he's gone."

"If that were so," Jonas said, "we'd all be thieves."

"Maybe we would be," Garris replied, "if we knew we could get away with it. We're cruel creatures, and we're shameless."

"You don't believe that," Jonas said. "I know you don't. You don't believe it about Yvetta or the native children. You see too much to love in them."

"To love," Garris nodded, "and to pity." He looked from Jonas to Pike, thinking he should hold his tongue. "We're born with a desire to do good. But the world's a bad place. It breeds bad things in the purest hearts." He faced Koopman. "That's the real 'fall from grace.' The difference between what we imagine the world to be, and what it really is. Uncaring. Unjust. Godless. We learn and we're corrupted."

He met Pike's gaze, then Koopman's.

"I'm not building your Meeting House," Garris said.

/\/\/\

After he'd packed his tools, Garris headed for the Eskimo camp to fetch Yvetta. As he entered the yard, he spotted her at the river's edge, seated with John. Her head was on his shoulder. His arm circled her waist.

"It's a shame," a voice said.

He turned to see Kiachuk closing the distance. Garris halted. The white Eskimo woman's smile was wistful.

"We'll be leaving tomorrow morning," he said.

"They couldn't persuade you."

Children with baskets appeared on the upriver trail, approaching the camp.

"We gather eggs this time of year," she said. "Goose, snipe, seagull. Eider duck eggs are best. They have creamy yolks." She looked over his shoulder, toward the building site. "I'm no Christian. But a Meeting House would be good for the People. I was hoping—" Her dark eyes searched his. "To know you better."

"I've had thoughts like that myself."

Kiachuk gazed down the slope, at Yvetta and John. "She wants to stay."

Garris nodded.

"You're afraid of what might happen to her. And what might happen to you."

"What do you mean?"

"Injuries," she said. "Mistrust. I can feel it. You're afraid of being close."

The darkness in Kiachuk was a living thing, with senses and emotion.

"What happened to you?" she said.

57

Garris didn't reply.

"Please," she drew closer. "You weren't always this way."

"No. I wasn't."

"What happened?"

He looked in her eyes. She'd lived with despair. No doubt of that.

"There was a war," he said, "a 'Great' one, according to the papers."

"Yes, I know."

"I was drafted. We thought we were going to the Western Front, but they sent us to Russia to fight the Reds. Peasants. We slaughtered them. We burned their homes. They hated us. When they captured an American, they would cut off his arms and legs; put out his eyes; castrate him."

"You took others' lives," she said.

Garris shook his head. "I built barracks and bunks for the wounded." He turned his head. "When I came back to San Francisco, my wife—" His voice faltered.

Kiachuk reached out and took his hand.

In the silence, he shared his grief. Being gone for so long on a brutal, pointless political errand. Returning to find the woman he loved was slipping away.

Kiachuk's palm was warm. Her darkness was with him.

"My childhood friends," she said. "Aunts and uncles, the families we knew— Our elders are dead, our villages are gone. The strength and wisdom that bound us together— The Great Death destroyed it all."

Kiachuk faced him. "We might have borne our fate differently, if we'd had men like you."

Her words confused him.

"Devotion keeps you whole," she said. "You are homeless now, but still— Close to the earth and the beauty in life. Wood makes you strong. Your craft connects you. Your craft and your love for Yvetta."

She turned and gazed at the couple sitting by the river.

Garris did too, trying to imagine how the teenagers felt.

"She really cares for him," Kiachuk said. "She's happy here."

And that, too, was true.

They chose the best of the vacant cabins. It had a good roof and floor, and it was on the main path. A window at the rear, Yvetta pointed out, would give them a view of the river. The repairs were simple, and two weeks of balmy weather made them simpler. Garris fashioned a table and two chairs, and put them a few feet from a sheet metal stove, along with a dresser that held pots and utensils. A workbench ran along the side wall, and on the shelves above were his drills and planes, frame saws and hand saws, hammers and bags of nails. The cello case was in the corner, the guitar tipped against it.

While he worked on the cabin, Garris studied the Meeting House plans. They'd been drafted in Oregon under the eye of the Friends, and the design was simple and sturdy. He was pleased when he saw Lars' budget. There was money enough to do things right.

He and Yvetta moved their things from the lodgers' room, and Ruth hosted a housewarming party in their new abode. The next day, they attended a gathering in the Eskimo camp where Lars announced the project. All the whites in Rightful were present. The natives listened to John's translation, and the response exceeded Lars' expectations. After the announcement there were discussions and questions. Everyone including the children wanted to help. Kiachuk caught Garris' eye and left her father's side, patting her thighs as she came.

He stood at the rear of the gathering, and when she reached him, they spoke in muted voices. "Things have worked out," she said.

That night, Yvetta was unusually quiet. When they had finished eating, she said she wanted to share something important. Something "that must be kept private." About John.

Of course, he said. She could trust him. He would honor the secrecy of whatever she told him.

"You don't know scripture," she said.

"I remember passages your mother read me."

Yvetta nodded to herself. "John has had what the Bible calls a revelation."

He accepted her words soberly. "What has he seen?"

"We live among spirits," she said. "The world is full of them."

Her expression was anxious. Was she breaking some vow?

"Spirits," he said without derision.

"John is thankful to Lars and Mattie, and he loves the Bible. But his truest teacher was the Flying Man. John's been searching."

Garris put his hand on hers and stood. Yvetta stood too.

"He's been searching for his own belief," she said, peering at him. "And he's found it. He says it's because of me."

Garris saw uncertainty in her eyes. The child inside her was frightened.

"You're very close," he said.

"Very."

Yvetta reached out and embraced him. Garris put his palms on her back. His daughter was trembling. She put her brow on his shoulder and began to cry.

When her crying had stopped, he asked a few questions, but the sharing was over. She had no more to say. The next morning, when he rose, she was already gone.

Koopman had decided months before that the ideal spot for the Meeting House was midway between Rightful and the Eskimo camp, on a flat stretch of ground by the mouth of Bone Bag Creek. He and Garris walked the plot, and then Garris inspected it closely, looking for rock, digging pits to check soil depth and permanent ice. Three days later, he showed Lars where he thought the structure should stand, and the day after, he was laying out the site.

It was nearly noon. Garris was down on his knees, pounding a stake into the ground with a mallet. Yvetta was visible with Mattie and Lars, down by the river with a gang of Eskimo children. At the camp's center, women sat together, scraping seal pelts with their knives. The snow on the huts was spotty now, and the sod beneath was turning green. With the coming of spring, men were pulling fish out of the rivers, and grayling and trout hung from the drying rails.

Garris heard a clanging and jingling. He straightened, scanning the bench behind him. A string of epithets in the Eskimo tongue joined the jingling. Then Ned Jimmy appeared, tramping through the alders with a packboard loaded with dead animals. Weasel, mink and a large red fox— The animals were tangled in a mass of chains, foot traps and snare wires. He gave Garris an ugly look and spat as he passed.

Garris set down his mallet and rose. Ned was headed toward the camp. Garris followed him.

Work in the camp stopped. Ned was cursing loudly now for all to hear. The women stood, Kiachuk among them. Men approached from up the slope. A granny emerged from inside her hut. Ned was haranguing them all, waving his arms and shouting. When he reached the camp's center, he shrugged off the packboard and hurled it down, animals, traps and all. He continued to curse, his rage focused on the pile at his feet. The natives gathered around. They were quiet, respecting Ned's anger. A few men spoke, scowling, agreeing.

Garris halted twenty feet away. Ned noticed him and whirled around.

"Mink!" Ned snarled. "What he got going? Fox, mink—What he got going?"

Mattie was still by the water with Yvetta and the children, but Lars was hurrying toward the crowd. Kiachuk stepped forward and spoke to her father. He shouted her down, including her in his reproach. Lars strode up to them, breathless, and Kiachuk turned to explain.

"He found these on Bone Bag Creek. A trapper. White, he says. He thinks he knows who it is."

"Tom Astley," Lars said.

Kiachuk nodded.

"'It's our land, our creek,'" Kiachuk translated Ned's rage. "'These are our animals.'"

Lars gazed at the furry bodies and metal contrivances. "Let's separate the skins from the traps. He'll want those back."

"He can't trap here," Kiachuk said.

"No, of course not."

Ned gave Koopman a look of disgust and strode toward his hut. Kiachuk directed the women, and they stooped to the task while the men watched.

Lars signaled to Garris and stepped toward him.

"We'll put his gadgets back on the creek," Lars said.

"You'll talk to the man?"

"We can ask him if he'll work somewhere else." Lars sighed. "The law doesn't give them any claim to the animals."

"There are lots of other places to set his traps."

63

"Astley's new here," Lars replied. "They say he's a strange character."

An hour later, Ned and the men left for the coast to fish.

Kiachuk doled out the trapped animals, and the women skinned them and hung them to dry.

Lars, with Garris' help, gathered up the traps and returned them to the mouth of Bone Bag Creek, along with a note.

"Can he read?" Garris wondered.

Lars shook his head. "Who knows."

/\/\/\

By the end of the next day, the foundation was staked and the locations for post holes were marked with stones. Garris returned to the camp for Yvetta and, with Mattie and Lars, they started back to Rightful. The trail veered away from the river and passed a bluff. The Eskimos had a communal dog team, and the dogs were penned there. As they approached, they heard one yowl. Then another and another.

Lars halted. Mattie and Yvetta did too. Garris continued forward.

As the pen came into view, he saw a dark figure hunched over a dog lying on its side. The figure bent and rose, bent and rose. It was flogging the dog with a chain. Through the yelps, a croaking was audible. Ravens were perched on an outcrop of rock behind the pen, and a pair were circling above. The dog taking the beating jerked its legs and lay still. The man stopped and straightened.

He was short and lanky, and he wore a hide shirt and pants with rusty stains. He twitched like an insect and the hanging chain rattled, and when his head turned, Garris saw straight black hair and an oversized brow, too wide and too tall, with a skeletal nose.

The dog whimpered and moved. The chain rose, and the man resumed, hair slashing as he struck, hiding and revealing his face. Garris checked behind. Natives had heard the dogs' screams and were hurrying along the path. But as he watched, they halted. They could see what the man was doing. Why had they stopped?

Lars and Mattie were twenty yards back, but Yvetta was striding toward him.

"Don't look," Garris whispered, grabbing her, holding her close.

"What can we do?"

Garris shooshed her, but the trapper heard.

His arm froze in midair. He turned. Then he was staring straight at them.

The breeze raised hackles on his parka. His arm fell, the chain swinging beside his leg. His eye orbits were deep, and points of light glittered within.

"Let's go," Garris muttered.

He clasped his daughter's hand and continued along the trail.

The man's eyes followed him. Then they shifted to Yvetta.

Seconds passed. A grunt emerged from the man's throat. He turned, his frame spasmed and the chain rose and descended, laying on another dog. The dog screamed, and the man raged back, peering at Yvetta between the blows.

Garris closed his mind, hurrying, burning inside. When he looked back, the pen was hidden by willows. Lars and Mattie were close behind, fear in their faces. The corners of Lars' mouth sagged. Avoidance was the Friends' answer to violence. And it was his answer too, Garris thought. Keep Yvetta out of harm's way—that, above all. In a world of wrong, it was the best he could do.

Lars and Mattie caught up.

"Astley," Lars said.

Mattie shuddered. "He's starting something."

/\/\/\

It was 2 a.m., but it was near the solstice, so there was light in the sky. Rightful was asleep.

The cabin was divided by a blanket nailed to a beam. Yvetta lay behind it, on a cot by the stove. In front of the drape, Garris slept on a pallet near the door. On returning, he and Lars had agreed to talk with Jonas and Pike first thing in the morning. But the meeting came sooner.

A knocking woke him. Ruth was at the door in her robe.

Jonas was rousing Pike, she said. Ned and Kiachuk had come.

Garris could hear Ned making a commotion on the Mercantile porch.

He accompanied Ruth up the trail, and the group gathered in the kitchen, around the table. Everyone was seated but Ned. He was apoplectic.

As Garris sat down, Ned let loose an Eskimo torrent.

"One dog is dead," Kiachuk translated. "The others are bloody, with many wounds."

She spoke slowly, and her eyes met his. Garris saw trouble in them. Trouble and dread. Ned didn't wait for her to finish. He jabbed Pike in the chest and sneered while he spoke.

"The lead will never run again," Kiachuk rendered his words. "We will cut her throat and feed her to the others."

Ned was shouting, gesturing with both hands.

"She has no courage now," Kiachuk translated. "The white devil has taken it. He's letting off steam," she remarked.

Garris could feel her forbearance.

"What are you going to do about this?" she translated. "He wants to know. What are you going to do?"

Jonas looked at Pike.

Mattie tried to put her hand on Ned's wrist, but he slapped it away and began to rail again. He wasn't waiting for an answer.

"You steal our land," Kiachuk translated.

Ned glared at Pike, rage mounting.

"You kill our animals," Kiachuk rendered his words.

Ned turned his accusations on Ruth.

"You give us your disease and destroy our people." Kiachuk's voice sank.

Ned pointed at Mattie, then he jabbered at Koopman.

"The whites are a curse, a curse to the world and everything in it," Kiachuk translated. She closed her eyes, as if the words pained her greatly.

Then Ned turned to Garris, his eyes brimming with contempt. He spoke, and the delivery was low and malevolent. But the translation didn't follow. When Garris looked at Kiachuk, her lips were pursed.

"Go on," he said.

"Koopman poisons John with Jesus. And you poison him with Yvetta."

"You're an arrogant fool," Garris shot back. "Tell him that."

Jonas raised his hand, shaking his head.

"Tell him," Garris demanded.

Kiachuk translated. Her father just laughed.

Garris showed Ned his scorn. "You had to tear up his traplines."

When Kiachuk conveyed the reproof, Ned responded in kind.

"Bone Bag Creek belongs to us," Kiachuk translated. "What will you do?"

Ned scanned the group.

"We'll send word to the Deputy," Jonas said.

Garris looked at Ruth.

"He has an office in Nome," she explained.

Lars frowned at Pike. "Can we talk to Astley?"

"I ran into him once in Nome," Pike said. "Tearing up the saloon at 1st and D. Crazy man."

"He's been to the store," Jonas said. "He wasn't short on cash."

Pike lifted his chin. "Gets a good price for his furs, I'll bet."

Garris turned to Kiachuk. "Do the People trap on Bone Bag Creek?"

She shook her head.

"So it's not about the animals."

The room was silent. Ned stared at Kiachuk, wanting to know what had been said.

She took a breath. "My father—"

Ned burst out, red-faced, yammering in his native tongue. His mouth was skewed. Life had fed him something so tough, Garris thought, it could never be swallowed or digested. All he could do was to keep on chewing.

"He says he's going to find Astley," Kiachuk told them, "and do to him what he did to our dogs." She uttered the threats as if she'd heard them before.

"He's not serious," Lars said.

"Ned knows better than that," Jonas agreed.

Ned straightened, raising his hand as he spoke, as if he was making a vow.

"He says," Kiachuk looked at Garris, "if Astley isn't punished, we're done with the Meeting House. Build it on your own. It will be a place of shame for the People. None of us will ever enter that cursed place."

The room was silent. Lars' lips parted, but no words emerged.

Then Ned spoke again, gravely, circling the table.

"This is a matter of honor," Kiachuk rendered his words. "A man hopes for it. Hunts for it. He plans for the time, and when the moment arrives, he drives his harpoon into its chest and eats its liver."

With that, the camp's leader turned, and Kiachuk escorted him away from the table and out of the store. Garris watched her go, wondering what it would be like to be a mouthpiece for a man like that. Father and daughter couldn't have been less alike.

"'Our land?'" Pike laughed. "The government owns it. The mineral rights are mine, and the animals belong to whoever lays hands on them."

No one disagreed. Garris looked at Jonas.

"The law doesn't recognize Ned's claim," Jonas said, "and neither does history. Their ancestral home is on the coast. They moved here because they needed help from people like Lars and Mattie."

Koopman was pale and silent.

"Was he serious," Garris said, "about going after Astley?"

"Attacking a white man," Jonas said, "is a capital crime, no matter the cause."

"He'd hang, and he knows it," Pike said.

Ruth closed the lapels of her robe. "I've never seen him so angry."

Lars looked around the table. "Ned doesn't understand how badly they need the Meeting House."

"He doesn't have the power to stop construction," Jonas assured him.

"He's threatened us before," Mattie reminded Lars. "The People know us. They count on us, not just for food and medicine and schooling, but for faith and hope. They won't turn their backs on us because Ned's upset."

Ruth was silent, but Garris could see she wasn't convinced Ned's threats were toothless. "What about Astley?" he said. "Is there more to come?"

"He's got animals to skin," Pike replied. "Let him tend to his traps."

"I'll write a note to the Deputy," Jonas said.

Pike waved his hand. "Leave it be. Things will settle down."

No one challenged him.

3

*N*ew arrivals from Pleasant were crowding around him. The man with the dark balaclava held a lantern. Others had poles, blankets, picks and shovels.

"Who are you?" a woman asked.

He brushed the snow from his face and batted his parka hood back.

"Garris," one said. "The carpenter."

A half-dozen more drew close, breathing hard. The woman scanned the avalanche fan. "Who was inside?"

"Everyone," Garris replied.

"The wedding," a man nodded.

More dog drivers arrived, braking and anchoring, hurrying forward. "The Chief knows what to do," the woman assured him.

73

The hooded man passed the lantern to her and reached out his arm. Garris felt the Chief's mitted hand on his shoulder.

"How many?" the Chief asked.

"Forty or fifty."

"You were clear."

"Three of us were." Had he ever met the man? The Chief's hood hid his face. Only his eyes and teeth were visible.

"Let's unload," the Chief shouted. "I want lamps and kerosene here," he stamped his gumboot. "Blankets, bedrolls—by that sled. Tents, stove, food and coffee—at the edge of the fan." He was heavyset, with a barrel chest and thick arms. "We've got drilling rods," he told Garris, "long-handled brooms—things we can use to probe the snow. And lots of rope. Goose brought bandages. There will be doctoring to do. What's the matter?"

"My daughter's down in it."

The Chief's eyes met his. "We'll find her." He strapped on his snowshoes and faced the morass. "Where was the Mercantile?"

Garris turned to Butcher Peak, finding the cleaver, getting his bearings. "Over there," he pointed across the tumbled surface.

The Chief started forward. Garris followed.

"You can live for hours beneath the snow," the Chief said. "The trapped air's a big coat, keeping you warm. If there's a pocket by your head, you can breathe. If you're under a piece of wall or roof, you can move. Yvetta, isn't it?"

"That's right."

74

"There's a good chance, Garris. Ice numbs you. If she wasn't hurt, she won't be in pain. She may be able to hear us."

The Chief turned to face the rescuers. "I want lanterns," he shouted, "and a pole in every hand. You three," he pointed. "More snow could come off that peak. Every few minutes, whatever you're doing, look for movement. Watch for holes," he directed them all, "and keep an eye on each other. Call to those buried and don't stop calling. Alright," he nodded, extending his arm. "Spread out. When someone's found, I want a half-dozen of you to come running."

The rescuers hobbled forward, heading in different directions, calling out to the buried, moving planks and rocks, sounding the slide with poles.

"Yvetta!" Garris left the Chief's side. "Yvetta!"

He noticed Koopman between two blocks. The pastor was kneeling. He'd returned to Mattie.

Garris paused before a deep well. "Yvetta—"

He listened for an answer, praying she could hear. The great blue screw-thread in the sky above him spoke in a whisper now—an interior voice, filled not with panic and dread, but with hope and care. The fan glimmered, and so did the valley's slopes. It was as if the dawn of some other world had leaked into theirs. The blue light edged the searching rescuers. Their poles were made of turquoise glass, and their eyes were too.

"Yvetta," he shouted, stepping forward.

A woman cried out, "Over here."

Garris couldn't sleep. He lay faceup on his pallet, fretful, sticky with sweat.

Ned had risen the day after making his threats, expressed his disgust to the People and left on a hunting trip with Toluk and the One-Eyed Man. Koopman gave an impassioned lesson, encouraging the other Eskimo men to show up for work on the Meeting House. And they did. Jonas, because he trusted the rule of law, penned a letter to the Deputy in Nome, describing the friction with Astley and what the trapper had done to the natives' dogs.

Still, Garris was worried. No one knew when Ned would return. Jonas had asked Somebody to watch Bone Bag Creek, and he reported that the traps were there and baited. He found a weasel in one. The next day Somebody spotted him through the willows, skinning a fox. Ravens were gathered round, waiting for the carcass. The trapper was coming and going, and the black birds came and went with him.

Garris did his carpentry during the day, too busy to brood. But at night, the fears returned. When Mirabel was alive, they worried about protecting Yvetta. After she passed, he assumed her share and more. They had fled San Francisco to escape the crime and squalor, and the crushing memories. They were at the end of the earth now, a place without many comforts.

76

He'd imagined that here, at least she'd be safe. Did the trapper's presence change that? Was he in a stew about nothing?

That afternoon, the first bank of scaffolding was raised. Garris was up on top. Yvetta called to him as she passed, returning along the trail to the cabin. She had a ptarmigan under her arm, and she promised it would be cooked by the time he arrived. Two minutes later, he saw Astley and his dogs on the Creek, a few yards from where Yvetta had paused on the trail. Garris hurried back to the cabin. Yvetta was puzzled, but he didn't explain.

Now, as he lay alone with his thoughts, he rebuked himself. What was he doing?

Garris rose and crossed the cabin, the boards creaking beneath his feet.

He drew the hanging blanket aside and approached Yvetta's pallet. She was sleeping soundly, lost in dreams. He saw the photo of Mirabel on a section of log beside Yvetta's cot, and the look in her eyes urged him forward.

He put his hand on Yvetta's shoulder and shook her gently, waking her.

They sat at the little table, and Garris explained his concern.

Rightful was a shattered place, he said. It had been twenty years since Pike found gold. The handful of whites hanging on wanted things to be different, but their desires had no foundation. This was the land of the Eskimos, and they were a ravaged people. The life they had led was gone. Their leader was a bitter old man, looking for vengeance.

Yvetta nodded. She understood what he was saying.

Astley was sick, Garris said, and Ned had blood in his eyes. And the whites in Rightful had no control over either. The conflict could flare at any moment. If Bone Bag Creek became a battleground, they would be at the center of it.

Yvetta was silent. Then she frowned. She was still so naive about where danger lay, he thought. But her convictions were strong. Stronger than ever.

"Ned isn't the only voice in the camp," she said. "There are others who see the future more clearly." She spoke slowly, choosing her words with care.

"The People must see beyond the Great Death," she said. "Jesus isn't the answer. They need to believe in themselves."

"Are these John's ideas?"

She nodded.

"We're not safe here, Yvetta. I think we should leave."

"We can't do that," she said.

He was causing her pain.

Yvetta met his gaze. "We're in love."

At her age, he thought, love was a miracle. You imagined no one had ever felt that way.

"It will hurt," he said, "but in time—"

"You're wrong." She rose.

Garris looked up at her. His daughter's eyes were in shadow. She seemed to tower over him. She was judging him harshly, he thought.

"There's no one like him," she said. "He sees things others can't see."

She stood straight, her shoulders drawn back and her hands clasped behind her. It was the pose John took when he sang for the camp.

"He sees things," she repeated. "He knows things others don't understand."

Garris stood.

"Like the Flying Man," he said.

Yvetta looked away.

She wants to tell me, he thought, but she's afraid. She was worried she'd already gone too far. "What is it that John can see?" he asked gently.

Yvetta was mute.

"Please," Garris said.

A weighing stillness. Then she drew a breath and faced him.

"Everything has a deeper self," she said. "A Real Self. Animals, plants, the water and wind— Huge or tiny. Few or many. Real Selves can be silent. If they're hidden or cast aside, the hopeless feeling comes over us. When Real Selves are free to speak and sing, we feel their joy. Sometimes we're drowning in it. I've heard Real Selves. I've seen them with my own eyes."

Garris didn't react. This was a species of wood he'd never worked.

"I know John's Real Self," she said softly, "and he knows mine."

Her words brought him relief and sorrow: relief for her, that she was no longer carrying the burden for his happiness; and sorrow for himself.

"Three weeks ago—" Yvetta spoke haltingly.

Garris waited.

"The best day of my life," she said. "We were on an old Eskimo trail— Walking, not speaking. A butterfly—a large one, yellow and black—flew between us, zigzagging. John heard its Real Self speaking. It said to follow, and we did.

"We climbed beside a stream. The water was sliding from edge to edge, and the sun made it look like a stair of glass. Then it narrowed to strands, spinning together. The butterfly circled a bowl rimmed with rocks.

"Up the bowl's side— There were willows around it. Inside, at the bottom, was a green mat, like a bed."

Yvetta paused.

Garris said nothing, afraid of what he might hear.

"The bed was soft. Crowberry," she said. "There were cushions of azalea with red buds and tiny pink blooms, as small as snowflakes. We lay down with our heads on one. I couldn't hear them at first. And then, with John's help, I could."

Her voice was calm and self-assured.

"Bees were humming. Beside us, hoppers jumped. In the willows, the catkins were gold, like lit candles. 'Close your eyes,' he said. When I did, the wind rose and the willows shook, and the Real voices all spoke at once. The wind whistled 'freedom, freedom'; the hoppers snapped, hurried, impatient; the bees were preaching—to us and each other. I could hear the windflower petals, brushing, speaking of love, while the grasses trembled and sighed. Through it all was the water, drumming against the rocks.

"And then," she said, "the unbelievable thing. I heard

wings, fluttering. 'Open your eyes,' John said. Birds were bobbing on the rim of the bowl, flicking their tails. Their backs were as blue as my ribbon, and as I watched, they leaped into the air. They were flying around me."

A bead of tear, in the corner of her eye.

"They called my name," she said, "'Yvetta, Yvetta,' as if they had known me all my life. I laughed. John had to explain." She took a breath. "They were calling my Real Self."

Garris watched and listened.

Yvetta put her hand over her heart, eyes suddenly deep, pleading with him to understand. "I rose up," she said, "the smoky part of me. The other part—the hard part—was down in the bowl. My Real Self was free and flying. I was part of the sky, glowing and full of sun and wind. All around me were the Real Selves of birds and catkins and pebbles and streams, all speaking together. It was the voice of love—strong, but tender and sweet. The most beautiful voice I've ever heard."

Garris struggled to speak. "A day you won't forget." To his ears, the words sounded patronizing.

"Not ever," she smiled. "The birds are wheatears, my guides. They knew the Real Yvetta before I did."

He opened his arms, and when Yvetta moved close, he embraced her.

"You know now," she murmured.

Garris sighed. "This is a place of joy for you." He wanted to honor her new sense of who she was, but there was no forgetting Astley.

Yvetta read his unease. "I'll be fine," she assured him.

"Will you play me to sleep?"

Garris stifled his doubts and retrieved his guitar. He sat on the stool while Yvetta stretched out, and he played like he had since she was a child. Carefree and foolish, the music had little connection with the woman she was becoming. But he clung to its innocence, and she sang along, as if to soothe him. Bird feathers were tacked to the wall above her cot. As he gazed at them, his daughter's voice seemed to lift him out of a world he feared and could not comprehend, and return him to a realm of safety and understanding. He touched the strings gently, making them hum, weaving a cocoon for Yvetta's voice.

When she'd fallen asleep, Garris remained beside her, gazing at the photo of Mirabel on the section of log. So much life, so much beauty—

He rose, stepped past the blanket partition, leaned the guitar against his workbench and lay down. When he closed his eyes, the image of Mirabel came alive. Her smile was wistful. He could feel her longing. She was wearing her ivory blouse with the cuff collar, and as she drew closer, her eyes grew misty. A dangling lock tickled his cheek; and the parting of her lips and the charge of damp breath signaled the moment, that precious moment—of aching anticipation and naked desire—that preceded the splendor of the physical act.

It was the end of a long day when Garris drew up to Blinne's cabin door. Through the open window, he could hear her singing to herself—heartfelt words in a mournful tone. When he knocked, she answered and invited him in.

"What was that?" he asked.

"An Irish ballad."

"A sad one," he said.

"*Mo Chleamhnas.* 'My Match.' About a man who's with the wrong woman."

Blinne supported herself with a cane. As she spoke, she turned and hung it on the window sill. "When I'm loading the stove or making the bed, my leg likes the help." She motioned at a small table and a pair of caneback chairs.

Garris seated himself. She sat across from him.

"Can I ask how it happened?"

"A broken crate," Blinne said. "I was six, and we were playing hide-and-seek in a rubbish pile. Clayburn talks about getting a doctor to fix it."

"You won't find one here."

"Nope." She sighed and looked around. The shelves by her stove were loaded with cans, tea, jars of jam. A blackened ham hung on a hook. Pike was taking care of her.

"Bill's still with me," she said. "That's his jacket, on the peg. Every time I walk through the door, I see it." Her husband had been a market hunter. He'd been kicked to death by a moose the previous fall.

"I prefer Clayburn's place," Blinne said. "I like the smell

of his pipe and the light coming through his window. And there's always wood in the stove." She laughed. "'I'm spending tonight by myself,'" she mimicked. "'I'll bang till he opens the door. He doesn't know a thing about women."

"We can't do it alone," Garris said, "can we."

"You miss your wife."

He nodded.

"Ned's daughter has her lamp lit for you."

"She's an unusual person."

"Carrying a heavy load, with that father of hers."

"Maybe he'll put the business with Astley behind him." He narrowed on Blinne. "Yvetta admires you. Your honesty, your toughness."

"She's discovering what it means to be a woman."

"Quickly, it seems."

"She's got a friend in Sara," Blinne said.

"I'm not sure why. They're not much alike."

"Teenage girls," Blinne said. "They're both in love, and they're both trying to manage their parents."

"They talk about that?"

"Garris," Blinne laughed, "do you know what's going on? A storm has hit the Eisenhart place."

He shook his head, unsure what she meant.

"Somebody's fishing the water hole in the late hours," Blinne said. "Sara snuck out. She returned the next morning with her clothes soaked. She told them she'd slipped and fallen in, and Somebody saved her. Ruth is furious. Jonas is too."

"I see."

"Do you? Sara wants me to order a Davidson syringe for her. She doesn't want to get pregnant."

"That's why I'm here," Garris confessed. "Yvetta needs someone to talk to."

Blinne softened. He saw sympathy in her eyes.

"I want her to be free," Garris said. "I want her to follow her heart. I don't want her to be angry or resent me later. But— Yvetta's so young, so taken by John, so full of hopeful fantasies— She can't see the dangers."

Ned was gone for three weeks. He returned with a new perspective. After he divided the hunting bounty among the People, he proclaimed that the Meeting House needed a water supply, and he was going to build it. Some took him at his word. Pike was skeptical, and so was Kiachuk. But Ned picked a half-dozen men and began work on a large tank made of Eskimo drift. The water would come from snowfall in winter, and in the summer, the tank would fill with rain.

Three walls of the Meeting House were framed now, along with some rafters. Garris had drawn off the Mercantile's woodpile for that, but flooring, roofing and siding required new logs. He calculated the footage, and Jonas made arrangements with the drift cruiser, Rezkov. Ned and his men finished the water tank, and there was cheer all around when Lars christened it beside the Meeting House. It was Ned's way of reasserting his power, Garris thought. But the tank's front puzzled him. Ned and his men had carved a large crucifix there. It seemed unlike him to make that kind of concession.

Three days later, Garris was straddling a roof beam, swinging his hammer, cleating timbers. The valley was jade and emerald now. The snow had all melted. Willows along the river were thick with leaves, and dryas was blooming on every bench. The Eskimos gathered shoots and roots, and their drying rails were loaded with fish. The North, it seemed, would be kind for a while.

From his perch, Garris had a view down into the water tank. He was surprised to see it was full. Light flashed on its surface. The glitter of sun on the winding course of Bone Bag Creek had vanished. For a moment, Garris struggled for an answer; then, through the brush, he noticed a path of wooden culverts—hollowed logs connected one to the other—running from the head of the Creek to the tank's lip. Astley's traps were still there, but the animals were gone. Ned had drained the Creek dry.

Garris turned toward the Eskimo camp. And as if the fear had brought him to life, the trapper appeared, descending the slope behind the huts, headed for the yard.

Above the bloodstained pants, Astley wore a fur vest, and his hair looked matted. He was moving quickly.

Where is Yvetta? Garris thought. He couldn't see her. And then he could. She was mounting the river bank with the children, shepherding them toward the yard to hear Lars' lesson.

He descended the scaffolding quickly and hit the path running, the claw hammer in his hand, hoping to reach the

camp before Astley. At the bend, alder hid the view. The trapper would slow, he thought. Yvetta would find some cause to
delay. He pounded beside the river, breathless, praying for
time.

Then the camp appeared. Eskimos were collecting in the
yard. A few men were there, but it was mostly women and
children. Mattie seated herself on an overturned bucket. Was
the trapper still descending the slope? Garris couldn't see him.
Lars and John took their positions. A moment of silence, and
the lesson began. Yvetta was standing ten feet from John.

A shot rang out.

A voice bellowed over Koopman's, and as Garris mounted
the bank and headed across the bench toward the yard, he saw
Astley lurch through the seated Eskimos. He had a revolver in
one hand, barrel raised to the sky. The other held a club that
he drubbed against his thigh.

"Peel yer eyeball," Astley shouted. He swung his club over
nearby heads, flattening the crowd. "Tom teachin' now." He
leered at the pastor.

Astley's face had red spots. Was it blood?

"You're welcome to join us," Lars offered.

"Jess skin to me," Astley said. His tone was confidential,
as if Koopman was caught in one of his traps. He closed the
distance, raising his club.

Lars stood his ground.

Garris halted in the lee of a hut, his eyes on Yvetta.

Mattie stood. "Your soul," she cried to the trapper. "Think
of your soul."

Astley opened his arms and looked at the sky. "How you like it?"

A wispy cirrus lazed in the blue. The silence was absolute. No word from God, not a whisper.

The trapper snorted and swung his club. The blow folded Lars in two, and he fell to the ground. Astley stooped over him and clubbed him again.

The People rose as one. Garris saw dread in their faces, fear and hatred. A few seemed about to react. A woman had been cutting meat with a knife. One man had a machete in his hand. But no one moved.

Koopman wasn't defending himself. His arms lay limp, thinking no doubt that his god would approve. Astley's nostrils chugged. His spotted face shook, and as the club rose and fell, a tassel of beaks that hung from the haft rattled before each blow. A rock was bound to its top, Garris saw. If the club struck Lars' head, it would split it open.

He stepped from the lee of the hut, hurrying forward.

There was disbelief in the Eskimo eyes, rage, contempt— Women held their children. A man clenched his jaw, another bowed his head. One gripped the arm of another, stopping him.

"Come on," Astley croaked, as he brought the club down, "come on, come on." He was tempting the natives.

Mattie screamed and threw herself over Lars, trying to protect him. Astley kicked her aside. John Jimmy launched himself at the trapper's back, circled him and wrenched him around. Astley tore free and clubbed John in the belly. The young man groaned and sank.

Garris was striding through the natives, hammer in hand. Astley faced John again, raising his club. Yvetta screamed. As John pulled his knife from its sheath, Mattie cried out, reaching, gripping John's arm, trying to stop him.

Yvetta strode toward Astley, her eyes wild.

Garris reached the front of the gathering. "You," he boomed, raising his hammer.

The trapper turned.

Garris waved his daughter aside. Astley narrowed on him, recognizing his adversary.

"Father!" Yvetta cried.

Then an egg broke on Astley's chest, and the yoke slid down his shirt. Another struck his forehead. An Eskimo woman stood with a basket, hurling duck eggs at him. Astley laughed and drove his boot into Lars' side. Then he turned to Garris, grinned and shook his club.

"You," the trapper snarled. The promise of a future reckoning.

Astley dodged another egg, gave them his back and tramped away, returning up the slope behind the camp.

∧∧∧

Except for a window of seal gut, Ned's hut was like a cave. The earthen walls were dark and smooth, and the floor had a firepit at its center. The space was lit only by the coals in the pit and an oil lamp with a red flame; the air was smoky from smudges burning to keep bugs at bay.

Kiachuk stirred a pot with seal meat in it. Ned was explaining how he'd taken the seal in the old way, from a kayak. He sat cross-legged, with his younger daughter beside him. The speech was punctuated with sucking sounds—she was nursing an infant. The three were naked to the waist, and so was Garris.

"We have guns," Kiachuk translated her father's words, "but this is best."

Ned patted a spear on the wall behind him. Perspiration beaded his face.

"Family heirlooms," Kiachuk explained.

There were bludgeons on the wall, bows and slate-tipped arrows. Ned slid his fingers over a carved staff with an ivory blade.

"The elders' harpoon," Kiachuk said. "A symbol of leadership, passed from one man to the next."

"You'll give the harpoon to your son?" Garris said.

When Kiachuk rendered his question, Ned shook his head and answered.

"John's not a leader," Kiachuk translated. "The boy doesn't hunt."

She peered through the haze at Garris, spleen in her eyes. A rill of sweat coasted between her breasts. The younger daughter used a bird wing to fan her baby.

Garris faced Ned. "Does a leader stir feuds? Does a leader use craft and deceit to endanger his people?"

Kiachuk translated his words, but it was as if she'd said

nothing. Ned's gaze was vacant, and his dogged jaw just kept chewing.

The old man had imagined his ruse would make Astley a Rightful problem, that Garris and the others would rid the valley of him. But you're wrong, Garris thought. He and his daughter were going elsewhere. Yvetta would grieve. John would mourn her departure. The aborted Meeting House would stand where it was, and Ned could take the credit.

Mattie was with Lars in John's hut, tending the pastor's wounds. John was alright, but Yvetta insisted on staying with him. Garris wasn't going to leave her alone in the camp, so he accepted Kiachuk's invitation to spend the night. He'd arrange their departure the following day.

Kiachuk passed a bowl to him. It was full of berries drowned in oil.

Ned spoke again, mouth skewed, eyes shifting. Kiachuk translated, "She's attractive, don't you think. No little girl ever smiled so sweetly." Her tone was dull and indifferent.

Garris tried to make sense of Ned's words.

"He's talking about me," she explained. "He says I looked like an Eskimo when I was born, but every winter I got whiter."

Ned was still speaking. Garris could see the humiliation in Kiachuk's face.

"We are all like her now," she translated. "Whiter every year."

When Garris turned back to Ned, the old man was staring at him.

"Leading the People is a great honor," Kiachuk rendered his words. "But I have a special honor. It is for me to see the People die."

There was no reaction from his daughters. They seemed to be used to this kind of talk. In the silence Garris imagined Ned's forebears around the fire, chipping a blade, carving a fishhook, weaving a net. Kiachuk stirred the pot. There was the sound of the infant sucking. Then Ned faced him and spoke again.

"You have a pretty child," Kiachuk translated. "Where is your wife?"

"Death took her from us," Garris replied.

When he heard his daughter's translation, Ned lifted his chin with a knowing gaze, as if he saw in Garris another man who'd been robbed of his future. Then his words came quickly. Kiachuk struggled to keep up.

"We were merchants, traders, and not just for natives. Down the coast and across the sea—Yupik, Aleut, Russians, Chinese. Metal and stone, tools and fur, ivory and clothing. Whatever you needed, you could get from us. We lived at Sandbank. We were the People. Now we can't even pay our debts at Eisenhart's store.

"Forty years ago, we lost our caribou. The whites killed our whales and brought the Great Death."

Ned spread his arms.

"The People on the ground, and the dogs are eating them. Our children are orphans. Spring comes and the fish are here, but no one catches them. The People are sleeping, and they never wake up."

Ned stared at the fire, his skewed mouth chewing.

Kiachuk removed meat from the pot with a wooden paddle. Ned muttered something beneath his breath.

"You think I'm a fool," Kiachuk translated, "but what choice do I have? All my power has been taken away. The People did nothing to deserve this miserable end. Where is the justice for us? Where is the justice?"

Kiachuk handed the paddle around. Her nursing sister took a piece with her fingers. Garris did the same. When he put the meat in his mouth, it was rubbery, with a sharp taste. "The seal's heart," Kiachuk said.

Ned's temper seemed to change as he ate. The lines in his face smoothed. He straightened, faced Garris and spoke.

Kiachuk was silent. When Garris turned to her, she bowed her head.

"What did he say?" Garris asked.

Ned was speaking too, scolding his daughter.

"It's about me," she said dimly. "'You like Kiachuk?'"

Ned continued, waving his hand.

"She's no good to an Eskimo man," Kiachuk translated.

Garris looked at Ned, stunned. "You're her father."

"I have no children in me," Kiachuk explained. "A woman must be a mother before she can be a wife."

Ned was talking over her. Kiachuk closed her eyes. Garris could feel her shame and the roots of her darkness. It was as if she'd been deeply wronged or had made some surrender she shouldn't have made; and this was the explanation.

"What is he saying?"

Kiachuk shook her head.

"Tell me," he said.

"He's offering me to you," she said. "Stay here. Kill Astley and bring me his hide. Kiachuk's yours. Give Astley to me. You don't need children. You have Yvetta."

Garris turned back to Ned, seeing a bitter challenge in the old man's eyes.

Then the speaking was over. Ned returned to his food. There were only the sounds of eating and the infant nursing.

The younger daughter lay down. Ned stretched out, and then Garris did too. As he drifted to sleep, he heard Kiachuk humming. They said she had a wonderful voice, and it was true.

He dipped in and out of sleep, feeling the warmth of the smoldering fire, the odor of smoke in his nose, and then— The fragrance of hair.

Kiachuk had stretched out beside him. "Garris," she whispered.

He heard the distress in her voice. He turned onto his shoulder. Her face was in darkness, but he could see the lamp's glimmer on her braid and her ear.

"Forgive us," she said. "It was wrong. To use me as barter. To twist you that way."

He touched her cheek.

"My father has been a burden for the People. Instead of making things better, he adds to our grief."

"He can't help himself," Garris said.

"Astley will return, and the People will pay. John won't

sit by. He won't forget." Her voice wavered. "Sometimes I think—"

Garris put his hand on her shoulder.

"He wants it to be over," she whispered. "The last stroke— The end of the People. To see us dashed to pieces and scattered on the wind.

"Garris," she said. "I want you to stay."

"I have to think of my daughter."

"If you leave, she will suffer, and so will John. And the mission, and Rightful. And the People. We need you."

He was silent.

"You can see, how fragile life is for us."

Late that night, the wind mounted. It beat against the hut's seal gut window like thrashing wings.

Ned rolled over. "Sleep?" he murmured.

"No," Garris said.

"Wife, good. Good sleep."

"Good sleep," Garris agreed. "What happened to yours? You, wife."

"Influenza," Ned said.

The wind thrashed again.

"Wife good," Garris sighed.

"Wife good," Ned echoed.

Garris turned away.

At first light, he left Ned's hut to retrieve Yvetta from John's.

Mattie was dressing Lars. John Jimmy lay on a squirrel robe. A restless night had made his hair wild, and the turmoil inside him swamped his eyes. Astley's blow had only bruised his middle, but Yvetta was attentive, kneeling beside him with a cup in her hand.

"It's time," Garris said.

Yvetta began to cry. She dropped the cup and embraced John. It was really goodbye. John held her tightly.

Their naked devotion was hard to watch.

"No mercy from me," John said, eyeing Koopman over Yvetta's shoulder. Then, turning to Garris, "No forgiveness."

He'd learned nothing from the Bible about turning his cheek.

"We'll let the authorities handle it," Mattie said.

"He's a Swallower," John replied. "He's not from our world."

"Tell my father what you saw," Yvetta said.

"His mouth was open," John said, "when he struck me. The dog teeth were sharp, and his tongue was pointed. Stiff as a whale's erection."

"Astley's a man, not a devil," Lars said. "He'll be judged like the rest of us."

A few minutes later, the four were moving through the camp and along the trail. The morning sun glimmered on the Teeth in the west. Garris flanked Lars, crutching his arm.

Mattie was on the other side, one hand on his back, one on his elbow. Yvetta followed behind, tearful.

A barking rose from the communal team as they passed the pen. The lead had lost her nerve, but a younger dog had taken her place.

Mattie drew a breath and spoke. "Garris—"

Her hair was draggled. Her expression was glum.

"Lars and I— We want you to reconsider."

"My mind is made up."

Koopman faced him. "I prayed for guidance last night," he said. "I feel better this morning." His brow had a poultice, his chest and knee were bound. He laughed. "I don't scar. That's how God fashioned me."

"He heals quickly," Mattie agreed.

"And so with the injuries of life," Lars said. "They come and they go."

The framing of the Meeting House came into view, with the water tank beside it.

"Please," Mattie said. "So much depends on this. The mission's future. The welfare of the People. The charity of the Friends."

"We're not staying," Garris said.

"The Lord gives us strength." Koopman summoned his strength and gave a brief lesson. "Until the harvest, God asks us for patience. God asks us to deny wrath and fury for any end. The spirit must guide our lives—the spirit which calls us to live in peace with all people."

"Astley doesn't feel it," Garris said.

"This won't end in peace," Yvetta spoke out.

Garris looked at Koopman.

"Rezkov will be here tomorrow," the pastor mumbled. "Will you help him unload the logs?"

A sawing rig and trestles flanked the Meeting House. Nearby, a pile of drift logs had been stacked beside a low wagon. The dogs who'd pulled it were lying on the tundra, still in their traces.

Garris had helped with the logs, and as the Eskimo men departed, he stood talking to Andy Rezkov, sharing his thoughts about where he might land. Rezkov, in his early thirties, had a blunt nose and a dark beard. His eyes were clear and blue, but they dodged, and he kept them slitted. He was stocky and wide in the hips, and the way he handled his logs marked an uncommon strength. He wore knee-high rubber boots and a canvas hat. From the first word, it was clear he was unschooled and unread.

Sara had arrived with a sealed envelope. Jonas had penned a second letter to the Deputy, another plea for help. Rezkov was to carry it with him to Nome. He held the envelope in his hand, gesturing with it as he spoke.

"From Port Clarence to Nome," Rezkov said. "Logs from everywhere wash up on those beaches. Trees don't get started in the Arctic, but they all end up here."

"Strong dogs," Garris said.

"The strongest. We all need wood. Ain't it so? Build a home in good weather, build a fire in bad. White and Eskimo, Chinese and Canuck— We're appreciated. Without us, they would all have perished a long time ago."

"Us?"

"Me and Jook." Rezkov eyed the envelope. "You're leaving them with quite a mess on their hands."

"That's not my doing."

Rezkov waved the letter. "This won't help."

"There are laws—"

"Someone has to stand up to him." Rezkov put the letter in his vest and gazed at the Meeting House. "You're handing the victory to Astley."

"You know him?" Garris asked.

Rezkov shook his head. "I see his fires sometimes, when I'm passing the front range. Threads of smoke." He drew a corkscrew with his finger. "Setting traps in those peaks—" He smiled. "Hell of a dog driver, running a team up there."

"You'd go after him."

Rezkov nodded. "And I'd take a gun. You have one?"

"No."

"A man like Astley understands fear. From his trapline. A lot of those animals aren't dead when he finds them. Some whimper and foul themselves. Some panic. Some snarl. Some act helpless to catch him off guard."

"You think I'm afraid."

Rezkov made a simple face and nodded.

Garris laughed.

"Lars has an excuse for his meekness," Rezkov said. "What's yours?"

"When you've learned a little more about life," Garris replied, "you may see things differently. The wrong in the world is like a disease. It can't be defeated. You only put yourself in harm's way if you expose yourself to it."

"A man doesn't fight because he thinks he'll win," Rezkov said. "He fights because fighting's important."

"I have a daughter to protect," Garris said.

"Stand and watch while others get hurt. Is that what they do in San Francisco?"

"In the States," Garris said, "men like Astley wear white coats and tailored suits. Our president forced four million men to fight a war for no reason. He is everything I hate about mankind and the world. There's no getting rid of people like that."

"You're not in the States," Rezkov said. "You're on the frontier. It's just us and Astley."

Justice is in our hands. A simple prescription, Garris thought.

Rezkov removed his hat and used his thick fingers to comb his hair back. "A man uses trouble to measure himself." He spoke slowly. "In the winter we've got the cold. When it drops to sixty below, it's like Astley. The cold is watching you. It's clever and strong, and it wants to hurt you. If you take your mitt off, your fingers turn white. Work up a sweat and it freezes—you're wearing a suit of ice. You feel helpless. You want to curl up in the snow and pretend it's not happening. But you don't. You face it and fight it, and you feel some pride if you survive." He tapped his chest. "The cold wakes up the fire inside."

"Maybe you should go after him," Garris said.

"If he crosses my path—"

"Why wait?"

"He's harder to fish out of those mountains than you think. And I've got wood to deliver. But if Astley uses his chain or his club on man or dog when I'm around, I'll make him pay for it."

Garris smiled. "I like you. We might have been friends."

Rezkov returned the smile. "You never know—" He glanced at the framed-up Meeting House. "Astley will be pleased." He laughed. "The People may be better off without it."

Garris shook his head. Was the drift cruiser playing with him?

"Lars is an honest man," Rezkov said, "and I know he means well. I'm hauling his logs. But I don't like what he's doing."

He was enjoying Garris' confusion. "Always preaching to me. He can't stop himself. 'Andy, stop bartering with folks who don't have anything. Just give them the wood.' 'Charity,' he calls it. 'Good for your soul.' You know what I think?

"Jesus helped beggars because it made him feel like a million bucks. But they felt like hell. He took their pride, and they hated him for it."

"I know what you're saying," Garris replied. "Lars treats

them like cripples. But— Maybe that's what they are."

Rezkov regarded him. "There's a fellow in Juneau who got his legs cut off in the mines. He delivers mail downtown. Good man. Works hard, harder than the rest of us. Sets a fine example.

"My customers know: when the wood shows up, there's no credit, no charity. Jook and I worked hard to get that wood. If it's going to keep you warm, we want something in return. Fish or sourdock, a tool they don't use or a place to sleep, an old blanket to make shoes for my dogs— They get something they need, and so do I. Pride and respect. That's a life worth living."

He sighed and gazed at the logs he'd brought.

"We weren't put on this earth to get gifts," Rezkov said. "Lars has a good heart—the world needs more people like that. I just wish he wasn't so stupid."

"He knows how you feel?"

"Oh he knows," Andy laughed.

"May I meet your dogs?"

Rezkov smiled and led the way toward his team.

"Which one is Jook?" Garris said.

But he needn't have asked. At their approach, a large dog rose—a malamute with clear blue eyes and a dark widow's peak. One ear was tattered, and his muzzle was scarred.

"He's a native pooch, from Shaktoolik. I raised him from a pup. He puts on weight this time of year." Rezkov scratched behind Jook's ear. "He's the boss of this outfit."

Jook raised his snout, eyeing Garris.

"He's in harness year round," Rezkov said, "but he prefers the sled. That takes brains. Any dumb mutt can pull a wagon. You'd chase that bastard down," he said to his dog. "Wouldn't you."

"You'll think differently," Garris said, "when you have someone you care about."

"I have someone." Rezkov scrubbed Jook's ruff.

When Andy and his team had departed, Garris returned to the cabin. On his workbench, between an auger and his spirit level, was a revolver with a battered butt and a scratched barrel.

4

A cry had gone up. Garris was hurrying across the fan, shovel in one hand, shaking the other to restore some feeling in it. Beside a crushed cabinet, a pair of rescuers were stooped and digging. "A woman," one barked.

Garris knelt at the pit's rim and began shoveling out ice and debris, piling it behind him. The two men descended, clearing snow with both hands.

An ankle was visible, a sock-covered foot.

Garris saw the leg of an Eskimo woman appear, then her skirt and parka. The two diggers grabbed her and lifted her out. Her arms were stiff and splayed, as if she'd been struck from behind or frozen as she flew through the air.

They set her down on the snow beside Garris. One brushed the crystals of ice from her face. It was the woman

Garris had met at the Mercantile their first day in Rightful. She'd brought seal pelts to trade.

He waved for the Chief and knelt. The woman's lids flickered.

"She's alive," Garris said.

"Barely," the man touched her front. "Her chest has caved."

"Let's get her to the tents."

"It's too late," the other man said.

"Let me through." The Chief barged forward. He lowered himself beside the woman and put his hands on her arms and face, searching for pulse or breath.

His hooded head bobbed. There was little to see—the blink of eyes, his tongue shifting. Then the Chief stood, turned upslope and called for the sled. "Wish her a smooth passage," he muttered.

The two men returned to the pit. When the sled arrived, Garris and the Chief lifted the woman's body onto it, and the tower took a zigzag course up the slope toward a bench below the west leg of Butcher Peak. The Chief had chosen the spot as their morgue.

Garris thought of Yvetta. Was she breathing? Feeling the freeze? Was she calling for him, praying he'd hear? She wasn't panicked, he thought. Her mind was clear. She was strong in spirit, stronger than he was. She was telling herself to be patient. She knew how badly he wanted to reach her.

"There's another," one of the diggers shouted.

Garris swung toward the pit from which they'd pulled the

Eskimo woman. The loose crush was shifting. A small arm poked through.

He lurched toward the rim, falling to his knees. The digger had his hands beneath the struggling body. Garris reached, brushing the snow from around a small face. The child looked up and recognized him. With a moan, he grabbed her and lifted her out.

"What's your name?" she asked, trying to smile.

"Garris," he whispered, opening his parka, pressing the little girl against his chest. He began to sob.

"What's your name?" she asked again.

Garris touched her cheek, her shoulder, her sternum. Her little dress was damp, but she seemed unharmed. Her body wasn't chilled. Had her mother kept her warm? He rose to his feet, holding her close.

"What's your name?" she said.

He started up the slope. "Garris," he answered, kissing her brow.

"Look—" The little girl squirmed, pointing.

Twenty yards away, at the slide's western edge, a slab of ice had tipped up. On it, a man lay on his back, like a corpse on a cooling board, with the reflected aurora rippling over him. As Garris watched, the body seemed to levitate, hovering above the snow.

It was the One-Eyed Man. Rescuers were on either side of the slab, levering it up.

Across the fan, work stopped, faces turning to watch.

The One-Eyed Man looked frozen. His head was lopsided, crusted with ice. His arms were thrust out, fingers like claws, and the single eye was open wide.

He hung there before them, parka hooked on a jag of rime, stiff and insensible.

Without warning, his frame jerked as if an electric current had shot through him. His head bowed like a corpse peering into its tomb. Then it lifted, and from the hole of his mouth a hooting emerged. Was the ominous sound laced with words?

Garris turned to a native standing beside him. "What is he saying?"

The man looked frightened, baffled.

On every side the rescuers watched, listening to the terrible hooting.

Garris shuddered, cupped his hands over the little girl's ears and hurried among the petrified diggers, wondering what had happened beneath the snow. The One-Eyed Man had come back from the grave, but he'd come back mad.

A pair of warming tents had been erected at the slide's margin. Shortly after the rescue began, an Eskimo granny was found. Unscathed and clear-headed, she took charge of the tents. As Garris approached, the granny emerged, saw the little girl and hastened toward them.

At the sound of the old woman's voice, the little girl looked up, recognized her and reached out. Garris delivered her into the granny's arms, overcome with relief.

As he turned back to the fan, the One-Eyed Man's hooting stopped. And with his first hurried steps to rejoin the rescuers, his relief turned to dread.

There was a different world beneath the ice, and those buried and conscious were living a different life. Would the slide change Yvetta? Had it already? He had feared she was dead, or near death; now he felt a new fear. Who would she be if she survived? Would she emerge unchanged like the little girl? Or would entombment do to Yvetta what it had done to the One-Eyed Man?

He found his way through the rescuers. His pick was where he'd left it. A fresh hole had been started a few yards away. Garris joined the effort, raising his tool, driving it down.

The slide, he thought, was an infernal place. A place of suffering and torment. He had lived through a conflagration in San Francisco, a red fire that swallowed buildings and roared like a train. But it was nothing to the light in the sky above him now. Everything in the Rightful Valley—the avalanche fan, the dead river, the needled grasses and cobbled slopes—were glowing with scarlet reflections.

SEVEN AND EIGHT MONTHS EARLIER. SUMMER AND FALL, 1921.

In the end, it was Rezkov's words about the importance of fighting that changed Garris' mind. Maybe in the Arctic one man could make a difference. He had turned his back on life's ugly face. He was at the top of the continent now. How much farther could he go before he planted his feet and said, "No more."

His decision to stay healed the rift with Yvetta. She was once again proud to be his daughter. Lars and the others welcomed him back. Kiachuk's gladness was muted and somber, but Garris could feel how deep it went.

The army had taught him how to use a firearm. He bought shells from Jonas, set up some wood scraps on the Meeting House log pile and tested his marksmanship. Other villagers had weapons. They could band together and defend themselves. Garris talked to Jonas and Pike, and the three men agreed. Jonas sent Somebody to Nome for a fresh supply of shells and a pair of new rifles.

Lars led a service in his cabin on Sunday morning, treating the Harvest of Souls and the Great Dividing. As soon as it ended, target practice began, and the valley rang with gunfire till it was too dim to see. Overnight, Rightful became a different place. Everyone but Mattie and the pastor had a loaded weapon close by.

But none of them had the chance to put their firearms to use.

Tom Astley had disappeared.

Arnica sprouted around the Meeting House foundation. The blueberry hung pink bells, and the heather hung white ones. Moss campion covered the rocks upslope with magenta quilts. By mid August, the four walls were framed and sided, and there was still no sign of the trapper. Garris and his Eskimo helpers bucked logs and planked the roof. He listened while he worked, pausing to scan the scrub that bordered the plot. But his vigilance was reflexive now. His fears had faded.

Cloudberries appeared, gold and pink. Blinne badgered Pike, and with the nets they uncrated, scores of ptarmigan were caught on the tundra. For three nights, the villagers dressed the birds and loaded them into underground lockers for the winter.

That same week, the Eskimos busied themselves with packing and preparation, as if they were going on holiday. Tents, clothing and blankets, weapons and tools, and the camp dogs too. They left together under Ned's direction, headed for the coast. Summer's end would be spent on the shore or cruising in their *umiak*. They would net salmon, meet up with other natives and forget the white man. John went along, and so did Kiachuk.

"The mosquitoes will be glad to see them," Pike said. "With all that muskeg, the bugs own the place."

With the People gone, Yvetta spent most of her time with Sara. According to Blinne, the two girls told each other things they didn't share with anyone else. Sara, chafed by her mother's strictness, was increasingly defiant. The more laws Ruth laid down, the more determined Sara was to break them. Garris worried about how the strife was affecting Yvetta.

Two weeks after the People left, Yvetta got word that John was returning on his own to see her. She wanted to meet him midway, but Garris refused, imagining an encounter in the wilds with Astley. Yvetta seemed to accept his counsel. Then two days later, she disappeared. Where had she and John agreed to meet? Garris went to Sara and begged her to tell him. She said she had no idea.

Three days later, Yvetta reappeared. She said nothing to him. Garris was relieved but upset. He thought about confronting her, considered a reprimand, some kind of punishment. Then he decided against it.

Fall was a lonely time for him. The smell of dry earth and crisping leaves brought memories of Mirabel. The scents mixed with the chill of the river when he knelt to drink. The snuffing of life left a bitter taste on the tongue. He wondered if Kiachuk missed him as much as he missed her.

Ducks came and went with the cottongrass. The moss turned lemon and chestnut, the dwarf birch turned orange. The arnica tipped their heads down and vanished. Blueberries dotted the bushes, and for two weeks every tongue was blue. Then the morning freeze wrinkled the berries and plated the willows with tin.

The legs of the Peak turned red, as if the butcher had spilt blood on his nice green pants. The light snowfalls thickened, and the river's flow dwindled. At the end of the day, the sky was dark and the air was cold.

Garris was in Blinne's cabin, watching as she spooned berries into a pie shell. "Brace yourself," she said.

Yvetta had taken Blinne into her confidence.

She set down her spoon and met his eyes. "Your daughter's a woman now."

Garris had suspected as much, but the news still shook him.

"She knows what to do," Blinne said to reassure him.

He honored Yvetta's independence, but he was anxious for her.

"You can't be there with them," Blinne said.

Garris laughed. "I suppose not."

"They're so young. Who can tell the future."

In July, Yvetta had turned seventeen. Garris remembered the age as a time of infatuation, of shifting affections. She could wake up one morning, see John differently, and it would be over.

"The Eskimos say," Blinne licked her finger, "they were born on the same day."

"Yvetta started that," Garris said.

"I heard it from Sara."

"To be honest—" He stopped himself.

"What?"

"I wish the two girls weren't so close. Things seem to be coming apart over there. Yesterday she was sacking some rice for me. She started to cry. There was nothing I could do or say. She threw the scoop on the floor and ran upstairs."

"Ruth found the syringe I ordered for her," Blinne explained. "Ruth's torturing her, and Somebody too. She won't accept what's happening."

Garris saw the caution in Blinne's eyes.

"You don't want to be like that," she said.

With the People gone, Mattie harvested the mission garden herself, pulling up carrots, turnips, onions and potatoes. Lars was at loose ends. He visited the Meeting House daily to see how many nails had been pounded. As Garris worked, the pastor would stand on the boarded floor, pretending he was giving a lesson.

The completed building wasn't hard to picture. A single story, four walls with a steeply pitched roof, a gabled entrance, a five-foot clock tower at the rear, and a row of windows along either side. Garris hoped to get the tower up by Thanksgiving. In the heart of winter, he wanted to be working inside, with a loaded woodstove. He would fashion the furniture in the spring.

One morning, Lars arrived in an agitated state. When Garris asked what was wrong, Lars said that he and Mattie were reconsidering their living arrangement.

"We should be under separate roofs. It's in our contracts. But— We often work into the night, as you know. She fixes meals for us both. When it comes to maintaining a household, there's no one better."

"You're perfect together." Garris set down his hammer.

"We've talked about being wed."

"The Friends would allow that?"

"Yes," Lars nodded, looking around him, as if imagining the marriage might occur there. "It's what we both want. But not right now. That would be selfish. You see how things are. The mission consumes all our energies. The lessons, the schooling and nursing, counsel to those in distress, arbitration of disputes— We have so many duties to perform on God's behalf—"

"The People are gone," Garris pointed out.

"When we're wed, they'll all be present. They're a part of our lives. In the meantime— We're not setting a good example. Everyone in the valley knows. If word ever got back to Oregon— The responsibility, the money, the trust they've put in us— It would be easier if we were living apart."

"Easier?"

"Mattie can be very—" The pastor fumbled for words. "Cuddly," he said.

Garris laughed.

"We aren't decided, but if I move into an empty cabin, I might want you to do some carpentry. Just a little." He touched the planking. "This comes first, of course."

"Of course."

"It's the reality of it, I think." Lars eyed the rafters. "The dream coming true. With every new board, we feel a greater responsibility. And a deeper shame. We hope the Lord will forgive our misstep. We care for each other."

"Any god with a heart would understand."

When traffic at the store was light, Jonas would visit; and as the friction between Ruth and Sara mounted, his visits became more frequent. The Deputy had never responded, but as time passed, Jonas wondered if his letter had helped. Maybe the Deputy had crossed Astley's path in Nome and given him warning.

Once the roof and floor were done, Garris turned his attention to windows, a task he loved. What kind of hands made flawless joints? Hands like cat paws, strong and precise. The night sky continued to darken, and the hours of light grew shorter. The day before the first winter storm, the Eskimos returned.

Garris was up on the roof, framing the clock tower, when he saw the People enter the camp. Their hide packs were large and heavy, and the dogs wore bulging saddle bags. He climbed down and hurried along the path, surprised at the need he felt, the strength of his longing. He remembered Kiachuk's gentle hands, her careful lips. The perfect plait of her braids. Her arresting eyes, dark and bottomless.

As he entered the camp, he scanned the buoyant faces, looking for hers. When he spotted it, he hurried toward her, feeling his affection more than returned. Kiachuk was glowing. He opened his arms and embraced her, holding her close, smelling the sweetness of her breath as she touched his nose with hers. Neither cared who was watching or what they thought.

The People unloaded their nets and tools, the clothing and baskets they'd made, and a harvest of dried salmon. There was walrus meat too. The men had banded with hunters from other villages, caught a cow asleep on the rocks and divided the meat. Ned seemed in high spirits. John hurried to Rightful to find Yvetta. Lars and Mattie arrived with Pike and Jonas and the other villagers, and when the welcomes were over, the pastor led them along the trail, so the People could see how things had progressed.

At the sight of the Meeting House, there was surprise all around. Surprise and cheer, Garris saw. Kiachuk stood beside him with a quiet smile, encouraging him to feel the gratitude. Jonas explained to Ned that Astley had vanished, and when Kiachuk translated his words, her father laughed. "No traps?" he said. "No traps," Jonas affirmed.

"Ned's malice is gone," Garris observed.

"It's hard for him here," Kiachuk said, and she explained how the sojourn at the coast was, for her father, a remembrance of youth and happier times.

Then her voice softened. "I wished you were with me."

"I talked to you," Garris said, "every day."

"We were high on the slopes, picking berries, when the *sisuaq* entered the Channel. Beluga, perfectly white, gliding through the blue water. So graceful, so at home in it. I thought of you and your wood."

The next morning, the mission reentered the Eskimos' lives. Yvetta assisted Mattie with schooling and care for the children, and Lars' lessons resumed. Garris got his native helpers back, and in the two weeks that followed, they boarded and roofed the clock tower. The following week, Rezkov arrived with the stove they'd ordered, and it was set in place. Kiachuk visited the building site often.

Yvetta's attachment to John continued, but of the details Garris knew little. He didn't ask, and Yvetta didn't share. In the cabin, he felt the need for distance. He had a new dread of her nudity and what was boiling beneath. He grieved for her innocence and the closeness they'd lost. From time to time, she asked him to bring his guitar to the camp, and he would play while she sang for the Eskimo children.

Winter and serious cold descended. The Rightful River hardened to ice, the storms grew thicker, and the snow didn't melt. By late October the land was white. Garris saw now the value the Meeting House would have for the mission. The snow and the cold prevented Lars from giving lessons to the collected camp. The need for shelter drove them into a hut, and the largest held only a family or two.

Garris offered to make Yvetta a pair of snowshoes. She liked the idea, so he set about the task, working at night by lantern light. He bent birch for the frames. Kiachuk gave him squirrel hides for the webbing. The project was shaded with meaning. It was a nod to Yvetta's independence, a blessing of her desire to make her own way over untraveled ground. When the snowshoes were done, it pleased him to watch her by the cabin door, strapping them on. Then, ignoring the trail, she'd shuffle through the powder, headed into the spotless hills—for a tryst, no doubt, with John.

A light snow was falling. A small wood fire burned near the Meeting House stoop. Natives were caulking the exterior walls. Garris stood beneath a tarp, planing a lintel for the entrance. His vice held a span of bleached spruce, and as the blade slid over it, a shaving curled up. Through the veil of snowflakes, he saw Kiachuk approaching. She was in a fur coat, moving quickly along the river trail.

At the bend, she turned and approached him.

Garris set down his plane, stepped forward and embraced her.

"You never stop working," she said.

It was a compliment, so he smiled.

Kiachuk looked aside. "I have something on my mind," she confessed. "I've been thinking, and I've made a decision. I've come to talk about that."

"Alright."

"Get your coat. I want to walk by the river."

Garris doused the fire with a fistful of snow and put on his coat.

"Will you play for the children tonight?" she asked as they started along the trail.

"If Yvetta likes."

"They can't get enough of her. They compete for her attention."

"Strange little gnomes," he said. "If mankind has a soul, they're its truest expression."

She regarded him. "Only children are entitled to live in a child's world." And then, "I love your music. You've written more serious things, for adults?"

Garris shook his head.

The prints of a fox appeared in the trail's powder. The breeze whistled past. Garris could hear the river sliding beneath the ice. In the distance, the Teeth were white.

"I brought you a treat." Kiachuk pulled a small parcel bound in cloth from her pocket and unwrapped it. "Tomcod with *kopatuk*. Sour sorrel." She handed him a piece.

"I like it," he said, touching her sleeve. The fur was lush, dark and silky.

"Mink," she said.

"A lot of them."

"It was a gift from my father years ago."

"A fine one."

Kiachuk laughed. "'No man's going to keep you warm,' he said, 'but you'll have a good coat.'"

Garris wasn't amused. "That's not right."

"Does what's 'right' matter so much?" She studied him. "The world is full of wrong. Will it ever live up to your expectations?"

"Why should he care that you can't have children?"

"Our ideas are foolish, aren't they."

He was silent. He could see the pain in her eyes.

"It's a terrible thing for him," she said. "'Kiachuk' is a lazy version of *qatiqaaq*. Our word for 'white.'"

Garris wasn't following.

"I'm another injury your race has dealt him," she said.

"You're his daughter."

"I am, and his slights anger me. But I'm sorry too. Sorry he feels so much shame, that he's so helpless—"

"You're too understanding," Garris said.

"Am I? When I was young, it wasn't like it is now. The People were tougher. We didn't dwell on our misery or curse our lives. Things changed when my father took charge. He's a fine hunter, but he isn't an *omelik*. He isn't a leader."

"You think Ned knows?"

She nodded. "So do the People."

His boot heels crushed the ice of the trail. Her mukluks stepped softly, quietly.

"They have a high opinion of you," she said.

"Because of Yvetta."

"Because of the Meeting House."

"I get paid for what I'm doing."

"That's not how they think of it. In the old days, Sandbank had a Meeting House. We called it *kazgi*. A big hut, big enough for everyone. A place for feasts and dances, a place of power for men— A place where spirits gathered."

"Spirits."

"During the Great Death, the Bureau pulled it down."

"The government," Garris said.

Kiachuk nodded. "They pulled down our *kazgi* and drove out our *angakoqs*. Men like my uncle, the Flying Man. The Bureau had good reason. The Great Death made the *angakoqs* crazy. But we had our own faith; and after, we had none.

"Those who speak English know what a Meeting House is. But those who depend on John's translations hear '*kazgi*.' That's how my brother interprets Koopman's words. They don't think you're building a church, Garris. For them it's a place of reunion with those they love, alive or dead.

"Having our *kazgi* again— It's like having our history returned and our honor restored. It's our identity, our feeling that we are one—not just individuals, hoping the next scourge of disease will strike the neighboring hut instead of our own. Do you understand?"

He considered her words. "It's a pleasing idea, but— No. I don't understand. In the world I'm from, there is no *kazgi*. The cities are full of strangers. We have a Union that preys on us. There are so many people, one life doesn't matter."

His words seemed to sadden her.

"We aren't brought together," he said. "We are divided and consumed."

"In some ways," she said softly, "you are like my father."

"That's not a compliment," he guessed.

"No, it's not." Kiachuk looked away. "My father is bitter and alone. He doesn't believe we have a future."

Where the river bank was shaded, hoar had sprouted like beds of white flowers.

"You miss your wife," she said. "Mirabel."

He didn't answer.

"Mattie said a cancer killed her."

"A mole on her hip."

"I remind you of her," Kiachuk said.

He shook his head. "You're nothing like her. Not physically, or in temperament. She was young for her years."

"And I'm old for mine."

"That's not what I meant."

"What did you mean?"

"You're a thoughtful woman. A wise one. You understand that life is a struggle. You'd be a good wife."

"You're right, I would."

She halted and faced him. "Shall I be yours?"

Garris was speechless.

"You're the man I want for my husband," she said.

"That was Ned's idea."

"I made up my mind the day I met you." Her dark eyes were humorless. "Do you think about me that way? Sleeping together. Being inside me."

She was a black-and-white woman in a black-and-white world.

"I have, at times," he replied.

"Under one roof. Taking care of each other."

"This is sudden," he said.

Kiachuk nodded to herself.

"I've made something for you," she said, opening her coat. "Something you'll need." From a sealskin sack by her side, she drew out a pair of Eskimo mitts. "I measured your hand that night in our hut, while you were asleep."

Garris pinched a thumb, feeling its softness. Fate had been kind to him.

The wind began to blow and the snow fell thickly, so Kiachuk headed back to the camp. He put on the mitts and watched her go.

Garris needed materials from Nome, and Pike was providing the funds. He went to Pike's cabin to review the list, but Pike wasn't there. Garris found him at Blinne's.

When he knocked, the old man opened the door.

"We're going to settle this," Blinne said, grabbing Pike's shoulder.

"Don't threaten me," Pike warned.

Garris took a step back.

"Come on in." Pike pulled him across the threshold and kicked the door shut. "Cherry's sour this evening."

"I'm going back to the States," Blinne announced.

"No you're not."

"Andy's hauling me to Nome."

"Let's have some tea. Garris is here."

Pike pulled out his pouch and loaded his pipe.

"I've got my ticket," Blinne said. "You can wave to me from the dock."

Pike eyed Garris, spouting his lips in mock distress.

"They're fast these days," Blinne said. "I'll be gone," she snapped her fingers, "like that."

It was time, Garris thought, for the scales to weigh love's deserts. But Pike acted like Blinne's upset was nothing. He opened the stove door, huffed at what he saw, then closed the door and put the pipe in his pocket. He crossed the room and grabbed her coat. "It's chilly in here," he said. "Let's go to my place. Garris will come."

Blinne was fuming.

"My fire's lit," Pike smiled. "Somebody left the Monday papers and a jar of preserves. I'll read while you make us a pie."

"I'm not wintering here on my own."

"You're not on your own." Pike made an obvious face.

"I'm not spending my nights in this freezer alone."

"We've talked about a different arrangement."

"It's all talk and no arrangement."

"Cherry girl," Pike opened her coat and held it toward her.

"I'm lying to myself," she swore.

"Don't be like that," he said tenderly.

"'Just head on home,'" she mimicked, "'head on home.' How many times will I come crawling back?"

Blinne moved toward Pike. In the quiet, her bad leg dragged on the planking. He seemed not to notice. She reached for one of his suspenders. It was sagging, and she tightened it. She brushed the tobacco ash off his shirt. Pike raised her coat, and she turned and slid her arms into its sleeves. "Brace yourself, Piker."

"For what?"

"To wake up and see me beside you."

"That's what I want." He folded his arms around her.

Blinne closed her eyes and kissed his cheek. Then she limped toward the door, opened it and stepped outside.

Pike shook his head. "A man can't get a proper rest with all that kicking and squirming."

"These items I need—"

Pike waved his hand. "Go ahead and order the stuff." And he turned to escort Blinne to his cabin.

Garris headed for the Mercantile.

As he mounted the porch, the door swung open. Somebody strode toward him, breath short, lips trembling. At the sight of Garris, he set his jaw and raised his arm, as if he meant to push him out of the way. Then he grinned and shook Garris' hand.

"'Evening," Garris said, baffled.

Somebody laughed and hurried away.

When he crossed the threshold, Ruth was in the kitchen, bent and sobbing with her head in her hands. Jonas' voice sounded upstairs, rebuking Sara, then pleading with her. As Jonas descended, Ruth stamped to the foot of the stairs.

She clenched her fists and shouted. "The answer is no. No, no, no."

"We all need to calm down." Jonas sighed and held his arms out to Ruth.

"Don't touch me," she said, jerking away.

"I'm sorry," Garris muttered.

Jonas noticed him standing in the entry. Garris folded the list in his hand and turned to leave.

"Wait outside," Jonas said.

"I gave that girl my best years," Ruth lamented.

Garris backed through the entry and closed the door behind him. The voices were muted now. The sun was sinking in the south, darkening the Teeth. Yvetta would have returned from the camp.

Jonas emerged from the Mercantile and stepped beside him.

"Somebody's asked us for Sara's hand," he said.

The news surprised Garris. But it shouldn't have, he thought.

"It's been going on for a while," he said.

"That's the problem. Their minds are made up." Jonas shook his head. "It was a mistake to hire him. They're so close in age. I could have sent him away, I should have. I still can, I suppose." He regarded Garris. "I could say no. You have a daughter. What do you think?"

"She wouldn't forgive you," Garris replied.

"No," Jonas said. "There's no reasoning with her. Or with Ruth. My wife is— I don't know what's wrong. Maybe it's worry for Sara. Ruth was married before we met. She was Sara's age. When he died, Ruth went to pieces."

"I'm feeling sorry for Somebody."

"I know. We all like him. He just isn't the kind of fellow you think will be joining your family. He has all these grand ideas— You know what he told me? 'I'll want the key to the store. Once we're married, I'm going to have a hand in running things.'"

Garris laughed. Jonas did too.

"Good for him," Garris said. "He's honest, and he means well."

Jonas nodded. "I was a buffoon at his age. It takes a while to stand on your heels."

"What will you do?"

"What can I do?" Jonas replied. "She says she's in love. She's not a child. I want her to be happy. Sara's a commoner, like myself."

"You're thinking about giving your consent."

"I'm thinking about how to handle my wife," Jonas said. "She's as upset with me as she is with Sara. What do you need?" He looked at the list in Garris' hand.

"It can wait."

On his way back to the cabin, Garris tried to imagine how he'd react if something similar happened with Yvetta. He passed the water hole, frozen over now, remembering Somebody's midnight angling. Yvetta knew about Sara's plans, no doubt.

As he passed Mattie's cabin, Garris noticed a lamp was burning in the vacant shack beside it. Through the window, he could see Lars alone, folding his clothes.

Yvetta would be fixing dinner, he thought. And as he drew closer, he saw smoke puffing from the cabin's stovepipe. Garris reached for the door grip.

Then he saw it.

He was puzzled at first, unsure what it was. Mounded, like something fresh-cooked for a banquet— The light from the window glimmered on it. Steam twisted from its surface. When Garris knelt, a foul odor rose into his nostrils. Entrails. The insides of some animal had been piled in front of their door. Not long ago, only minutes perhaps. With Yvetta inside.

Garris looked from the entrails to the window, then he stood and circled the cabin, seeing the signs in the snow. There were paw prints and tracks made by sled runners. And deep impressions from a pair of hide boots.

/\/\/\/\

"I should have expected," Rezkov said, "you'd be the first to know. I met a family in Iron Creek. They're acquainted with your trapper. They're from the Endicotts, in the east. Astley's summered in those mountains for the past three years."

"Making trouble," Garris said.

Rezkov nodded.

The morning was cold, and their breath fogged the air. Yvetta had left for the Eskimo camp. After dumping a fresh load of timber at the building site, Rezkov had anchored his rig beside the cabin. The eighteen-foot tow sled was empty now, but the driver's basket was piled with stove wood.

As they hauled wood into the cabin, they hashed over Astley's intentions. Garris had said nothing to Yvetta about the entrails he'd found the previous night.

"Trying to give you a scare," Rezkov said.

"He's done it," Garris admitted.

The two men added the wood in their arms to the stack beside the stove. When Rezkov straightened, he peered at Garris. "You need to be prepared—mentally ready. With a man like Astley, you don't hesitate."

Garris was silent.

"That day in the yard," Rezkov said, "when he was beating Lars— I heard the story from Mattie. You had a hammer in your hand."

Garris nodded.

"What Astley was doing— It made you angry."

"Of course it did."

"You need that," Rezkov said. "The anger, the emotion. No pause, no thinking. Look the beast in the eye. When he strikes, you strike back. Crazy or not, he's flesh, like the rest of us." The drift cruiser turned and stepped toward the door. Garris followed.

The wind had picked up. As they passed through the entrance, a cape of snow lifted from the shoulders of Butcher Peak.

"Wouldn't you know," Rezkov said.

Garris could barely hear him over the wind. The two stepped back inside.

"Our first blizzard." Rezkov laughed, as if pleased by the prospect. "I'm going to build you a fire." He knelt and began feeding fuel to the stove. "I'm like Jook—winter suits me. Sit down. You're done for the day. You can't work in that blow."

Garris lowered himself and knelt beside him.

"We're the same about wood, you and me," Rezkov said.

"Are we?"

"The only difference is— I'd rather burn it than build with it." He turned a twig over the coals, watching the kindling take. "It's a miracle, wood turning to fire. It's hard and splintery, then it's dancing flames." He looked at Garris. "Fire is life: that's the faith of a backward man.

"You're running down a trail, getting close to a camp. You see the smoke first. There's a tent or cabin, a hut or a lean-to, but it's behind a rise or down in a gulch. All you can see is the blue thread. Or a gray flag waving over the willows. Your heart leaps. 'That's Garris,' you think, 'in the middle of all this ice and snow.'" His eyes gleamed. "'He'll be glad to see us,' you think. 'What a fine place we've made this world.' I say that to Jook. 'We gathered this wood to keep Garris warm, and we're hauling it to him. We're hauling it, boy. Astley brings the cold and darkness. But you and me—we're bringing light and heat.'"

He put his hand on Garris' shoulder and squeezed it. "We work hard, and we deliver. But sometimes we have to fight. Things will be right, my friend, when you make them right."

Garris wasn't inspired. He was feeling cornered. It was summer when he'd embraced the idea of defending himself. Wind gripped the cabin and shook it. Beyond the rattling windows, the sheets of blowing snow cracked.

"In weather like this, we'll be helpless," he said. "I can't pursue Astley on foot, and we won't have any way to escape."

Rezkov nodded. The problem was real.

"It would be different," Garris said, "if I had a sled and some dogs."

"It would," Rezkov allowed, "if you knew how to run them. It's not as easy as it looks."

"You could teach me. I'd be a good student."

"You're strong and nimble, your carpentry's proof of that. But—"

"But what?"

"Arctic dogs aren't like boats or automobiles. They're smarter than most people you know. They were born here, and they savvy this land better than we do. They need respect and the freedom to make their own decisions."

"If I had a dog like Jook, I wouldn't get in his way."

"They want devotion. If they feel it, they'll protect you, the way you protect your daughter. Where is she? At the camp?"

Garris nodded.

"If there's danger around you," Rezkov said, "but you don't see it, the boss of your team will smell it and hear it. She'll make your safety—and your daughter's—her business."

"She?"

"I was thinking of Zoya, Jook's little sister."

"She's as smart as Jook?"

"Maybe smarter," Rezkov said. "But she has dreams right now that I can't fulfill. She wants to lead." His expression softened. "Whether you're a man or a dog, someone has to believe in you."

5

THE FAN, PITTED AND TRENCHED. APRIL 23, 1922, 5:17 A.M.

*G*arris paused to catch his breath, leaning his pick's haft against a blue block of ice, removing his left mitt. It was soaked, and the thumb notch was torn. He thought of Kiachuk—the day she'd given the mitts to him, the night she'd answered, *"Nuliaq."* The memories brought a floodtide of feeling. He stopped himself, pulled the mitt on, grabbed his pick and returned to the trench he and two others were digging.

The auroral drape was bright above them. Its scarlet hue was gone, but Garris carried the hell in his head. Seeing the confinement, the bedlam the slide had made for its victims, the borders it put on their unlucky lives—

Still no sign of Yvetta, and the rescuers had dug in many places.

The area downhill of the store's razed foundation had been thoroughly plowed. Most of the wreckage was there; and so far, most of the victims. Of those they had reached, all but three—the Eskimo granny, the little girl and the One-Eyed Man—had died beneath the snow or in a warming tent after being exhumed. Yvetta was everywhere Garris looked. Under a raft of wall, beneath a cake of ice— But when the dog teams dragged the boulders and walls aside, she wasn't among those who were found. Upslope from the store's remains, the digging was hopeless, as the blocks were imbedded and the crush had fused. But one man had a saw, and another a pry bar, and with Garris' help, they did things the picks and shovels could not. They found a dead native woman, but not Yvetta.

As the rescue wore on, they dug deeper. Garris' emotions spiked and sank with the uneven pace. The search was hurried, but as soon as a body was found, things slowed. Was the victim alive? A circling trench had to be dug to prevent collapses, the ice and rubble cleared with care.

Removing a buried corpse wasn't easy. Frozen parts had to be bent—a spine flexed or a limb, a head turned on a neck. The rescuers did their best to keep them intact. Those wounded, damaged by debris, were rusty and blackish. Victims who'd been smothered were ashen or blue. Those who had died from the cold were white as wax. No matter how they'd expired, most were found with their eyes open.

In the morgue below the west leg of Butcher Peak, the dead lay in the snow. Garris looked up from his digging, seeing another corpse being sledded there. Anguish, dread and despair; and the knowledge that time was passing. Then a cry would go up—a buried body had been spotted—and hope would return.

For some reason, the diggers with him had stopped. The Chief had halted the work. Rescuers were standing, facing the river.

As Garris turned, he saw dog teams approaching, and mushers behind them, riding their sleds. Word had reached a nearby village, and reinforcements had come.

When the sleds were anchored, the Chief addressed them all.

"Some of the Pleasant folks need rest. The fresh teams will spell them, six at a time. There may still be a few alive," he said. "In a protected spot. If they're not too cold. If they can breathe. They might be too weak to cry out. They might have blacked out or fallen asleep. We've saved three, and we hope to save more. But— Most will be dead. Be braced for that."

Those from Pleasant were silent. As the death toll rose, a distance had grown between them. Morbid images walled them off, Garris thought. Like ghosts, drained of feeling, detached from life. A shepherd of doom directed their efforts, with his black hood, his grim voice, and eyes that glinted through rimey holes.

"How many still under?" a woman asked.

"About twenty," the Chief replied. "And there are two who were up on the mountain." He looked at Garris.

"Rezkov was caught," Garris said.

Groans and curses.

"We'll look for them later," the Chief said.

He assigned tasks to the new arrivals, and six from Pleasant were sent to the warming tents. As Garris was returning to work, the Chief grabbed his arm.

"You need some rest," he said.

Garris replied, "I can't do that."

The Chief seemed unsurprised.

As he started back to the trench, Garris noticed Koopman at his elbow. Where had the pastor been? He was shivering in his blankets, face gritty, hair like a bird's nest.

"I dug her out," Lars said.

"Mattie?"

"I proposed," Koopman said. "All I had was her hand, but I proposed and she accepted. Then I dug her out."

Garris put his arm around him.

"It's what we wanted," Lars said. "But—"

There was bafflement in the stricken man's face.

"It isn't Mattie." Lars peered at him. "Come see."

"Yvetta's still missing."

"You know Mattie," Lars said.

"My daughter—"

"Please," Lars begged him. "Please come see."

Koopman led him through the heaped and tumbled diggings, back to the place where they'd found Mattie's hand. Lars had dug a broad pit, and on the surface beside it, a body lay. It was Mattie, Garris saw. But he could understand Lars' confusion.

Her spine was crooked, and her flesh was blue-gray. Mattie's luxuriant hair was a frozen knot, and her eyes were lifeless. The arm she'd raised above the snow was rigid and fisted now.

"Is it her?" Koopman said.

"I believe it is," Garris replied.

"Her lids won't close," Lars said.

Garris grasped Lars' shoulder and pulled him closer, his brow to his friend's. Garris remembered his wife on the hospital bed, silent, motionless. And the wounded soldiers who'd gone to sleep in the barracks and didn't wake up.

"I put the mission first," Lars said.

"She loved you, and you loved her."

"She was reaching for me," Lars lamented.

Garris recalled: Mattie had opened her hand before she died. Trying to grab hold of something, or clawing for air—

"She was reaching for me," Lars said, "and I wasn't there."

The truth in the grieving man's words shook Garris.

"She died alone," Lars said.

The real Mattie, Garris thought. In her final moments, she knew who she was and what she wanted.

FIVE MONTHS EARLIER. NOVEMBER 11, 1921.

After Rezkov departed, Garris hiked through the blizzard to warn Lars, Pike and Jonas about the calling card Astley had left by his cabin door. He expected violence, and he was committed to standing his ground. But there were so many questions. Would he wait to be attacked, or would he fire at Astley the first chance he got? He might not have many. When and how would the trapper appear? He seemed to enjoy surprises.

Yvetta's safety was paramount. He shared the new cause for concern with her, and the need for vigilance, and she understood. But when it came to being closely watched and her trysts with John, she was far too confident, convinced the young man would protect her.

A few days passed. Rezkov returned with Jook's sister, five other dogs and a sled with a small basket. Andy spent the afternoon with him, but mushing didn't come easy. Balancing on the runners, turning the team, controlling the basket, finding an understanding with Zoya— The sled gave him a way to escape, or to run for help. But he was barely stable at slow speed, and his nemesis was a master.

Abruptly the air grew colder. Storms left two feet of diamond dust around the cabin. Would bad weather matter to Astley?

To his union suit, and worsted shirt and pants, Garris added the mitts Kiachuk made, a pair of mukluks, seal leggings and a squirrel skin parka lined with wool. With John's help, Yvetta was similarly suited. Near the stove, where she slept, it was warm, but on the other side of the blanket the cabin was freezing, so Garris slept with his furs on, imagining the confrontation. Could he react in a heartbeat, without deliberation? Would his aim be steady? It had better be, if he was going to protect her.

Dawn passed to dusk with no day between, and the sky lost its blue. It was pink and peach, amber and lilac, and then it was dark again.

While Garris mulled the next crossing with Astley, the villagers went on with their lives. Blinne moved in with Pike. Did her threats change Pike's mind, or was he worried about her being caught alone by the mad trapper? The day after he carried her things to his cabin, she announced she'd be staying the winter. Big news, for them and for Rightful. Garris was there with Yvetta for the celebration, but it was all he could do to control his disquiet for an hour or two.

The Eisenhart stalemate was broken by Jonas, who gave Somebody his consent to marry Sara in the spring. But instead of relieving the tension, his decision made everything worse. Ruth refused to talk to her daughter. Garris heard about it from Yvetta, who took Sara's side. "She's not a child," Yvetta protested. "It's Sara's life."

Jonas came to the cabin one night and shared his troubles. "She's trying to scuttle the wedding. She's furious with Sara, and she's blaming me."

Garris heard the trouble in his words, and he saw deeper trouble in Jonas' eyes. But he paid it little attention. He wondered that people could make a crisis of nothing, and ignore that a real crisis was coming.

It seemed that the weight of the threat rested solely on

him. He was watchful day and night for the trapper; and watchful, as well, that Yvetta was close to him or in the company of someone who could defend her. Kiachuk continued to visit the building site. She brought seal liver, rockfish, berries in oil, and an unspoken faith that he would somehow prevail. They talked, they laughed, they said odd things to see how the other would react. She knew that his mind was on Astley, but they avoided the subject.

When Astley's strike came, it came at night. And his target was the Eskimo camp, not Garris or Rightful. The trapper parked his sled at a distance and entered the camp on foot, silently, waking no one.

Garris found out the next morning. He was at the Meeting House, loading the stove, when Ned and Kiachuk appeared. The trapper had crawled into a hut, she said, and forced himself on a woman while her husband and children watched. Astley's dog teeth were like a salmon's, one of the children claimed.

"Toluk heard him leaving," Kiachuk said. "He looked out and saw Astley pass a fish rack. The spears and netting went right through him. Toluk started after him, but Astley's feet left the ground, and he vanished into the sky."

"He can fly," Garris said.

Ned released a torrent of Inupiaq curses.

"Father wants to make a window out of him," Kiachuk said.

The cabin needed firewood and fresh water. It could all be done in an hour or less, but Garris plotted the errand carefully. Yvetta didn't know how to use a revolver. He would carry it with him. An early departure would be safest.

He rose before dawn, while she was still asleep, harnessed the dogs and headed downriver. When he reached the mouth, where the Rightful met the Sinuk, he loaded firewood into his sled from Rezkov's cache. On the return, just before the village came into view, he filled his empty barrels with water from the overflow they kept open. It wasn't until his team was directly below the village, climbing the slope, that he saw a sled parked in front of his cabin.

Garris called to Zoya, hurrying her, fearing the worst. He reached his hand into the kitbag that hung from the handle-bow, fumbling for the revolver.

The visiting sled had a strange appearance. There were things attached to the rails, dangling on threads and thongs. And the frame of the basket wasn't weathered wood. It was white as bleached bone.

The cabin door opened, and Tom Astley emerged, dragging a large sack over the threshold. He lifted it, swinging it forward, banging it against the sled. Garris heard the clang of metal, then he saw the sack wobble and bulge. Yvetta was struggling, shifting inside. Astley dumped the sack in his sled basket.

"Hike," Garris urged Zoya. The team pulled hard, but the sled was heavy with water and wood. A veil of windborne snow hid Astley. A moment later he appeared through a tear in the veil—not his head or his face, but his fox parka. It was open, and along one side was a row of white buttons. The trapper seemed larger, much larger than Garris remembered.

The parka turned. Had Astley seen him? Through the veil of ice dust, the man yanked his anchor and yelled to his team. The sled shot forward.

Following fast, Garris raised his revolver, hand shaking. The target was too far away, appearing and disappearing. Gauzy swirls, a foggy shape— Suddenly a sharp image jumped through the blur: a white cap settling on the crown of a head. Then both cap and head disappeared. It was as if the sled was driving itself, bearing Yvetta away.

As Garris passed the cabin, ravens perched on the eaves flapped into the air. Others sprang from the snow or left off circling to follow.

He cried to Zoya, inept and helpless. What did he know about driving dogs? He was already falling behind. Rage rose inside him, rage and fear. Legs balanced on the runners, one hand on the bow, raising the revolver— Were the dogs pulling with all they had? Couldn't they go any faster? The bumps shook the gun's muzzle, and so did his unsteady hand. Through the shifting veil, he could see Astley's sled and his seven-dog team. The sled swerved, and the driver came into view, his parka flying behind him as he left the trail. Where was he going?

Zoya made the turn at high speed—it was all Garris could do to hang on. The trapper was crossing the river ice, gliding up the far bank. The ravens croaked overhead, keeping pace.

For a moment, Garris saw the sack in Astley's basket. Yvetta was struggling.

Zoya was lunging, the sled careening around an islet of willow. Garris lurched to the side, avoiding a spill, losing sight of the trapper. Then his sled reappeared, climbing the slope. Garris raised his gun again, but the whole world was shaking. With Yvetta so close to his target, he dared not fire.

The slope was steep, but the gap was still growing. What was Astley doing? His sled rails were gliding on a cushion of fog, as if he was leaving the earth, bearing Yvetta into some other realm.

It's hopeless, Garris thought. I'm losing my daughter.

Astley seemed to hear him— Through a porthole in the blowing snow, the trapper's face appeared, looking back, magnified and baleful. A grin drove its points into his cheeks. Wind roughed the ermine cap on his crown, and the flattened heads of two winter weasels clapped at his ears.

Garris roared, and his team gained speed. Their tongues were trailing like red ribbons. Their breath sheathed his sled in a tube of fog. But when Astley's sled reappeared, it seemed still farther away. Garris cursed himself and the gap between them. With the veils flying and the ravens croaking, the trapper's sled disappeared over a rise.

Garris lowered the gun, heart sinking as his sled slowed. What could he do? Could Astley's track be followed? Could a good driver with an empty sled catch up to him? How long would it be before snow covered the track? How could he ever have let this happen?

Zoya was still pulling. As they approached the top of the rise, Garris saw Astley stooped over his sled, trying to right it. Nearby, Yvetta was doubled in the snow, the open sack caught on her leg.

Garris shouted to Zoya. Astley looked up.

The trapper hurried to Yvetta, circling her with his arms, lifting, trying to get her back in the sled. She kicked and clawed at his face. Garris raised his revolver, aimed at Astley and fired a shot. The trapper fixed on him. Was he hit?

Garris fired again.

Astley drove his boot at Yvetta's face.

Again Garris fired, but the shot must have missed. The trapper was leaping onto his runners, and the sled was pulling away. A cloud of powder rose, and Astley disappeared behind it.

Zoya halted before Yvetta. Garris hurried to her and sank to his knees. She lay huddled, motionless amid a scatter of carpentry tools. He saw blood on the snow, on her arm and her face. Zoya nuzzled her, and Yvetta shifted.

Garris sobbed with relief, drawing a folding knife from his pocket. Her ankles were bound. He cut the thong and gathered her up. As he lifted, her eyes opened. There was terror in them, and disbelief. She was shuddering, chilled to the bone. Her dress was torn, her pale skin and chemise showing through the gap.

He carried her to his basket and set her in it. She turned away, trying to close her dress. He removed his parka and put it over her, feeling her fright keenly.

Then he drove his sled back to the cabin, thinking, *Why had he left her alone? How could he have been so careless?*

When they arrived, Garris helped her to her cot. He spoke to her gently, binding her wounded arm to halt the bleeding, examining her hands and feet for frostbite. Was she still cold, or was it fear? She was bundled in blankets beside the stove, but she was still shuddering, staring at the space before her without speaking, as if he wasn't there.

Somehow she'd freed herself from the sack. Had her arm caught on a sled rail when she threw herself out? The flesh of her chin was torn away. Her shoulder looked like it had struck a rock or been gashed by one of his tools. A chisel or the blade of a plane. Astley had cleared his bench, and the hammers and saws, the vices and drills, were in the sack with her.

Garris stoked the stove and added another blanket, embracing Yvetta from behind, kissing her crown. He didn't want to leave her, but he had to get help.

Mattie answered his knock, grabbed her satchel, alerted Lars and returned to the cabin with him. When they entered, Yvetta shrank with dread, as if she feared the trapper had returned. Mattie inspected and dressed her wounds. Lars arrived with Blinne, and when Blinne sat beside her and began to speak, Yvetta seemed to recognize her.

Blinne asked her what had happened. Yvetta looked at her but didn't reply. Garris faced Lars. The pastor sighed and put his arms around him.

Two hours passed. Pike appeared, then Sara and Somebody along with Jonas and Ruth. Somebody was sent to the Eskimo camp. Yvetta was more lucid now, and when Sara took her hand, Yvetta spoke.

"When I got free," she said. "I could see the heads of those he'd killed. They were hanging from the rails." Her gaze wandered. "They bucked and swayed. 'I'll be one of them,' I thought. 'He's going to do that to me.'"

Sara touched Yvetta's cheek.

"He was taking me somewhere far away," Yvetta told her. "'Don't let him do it,' they said. 'Don't let him.'"

Garris motioned Mattie and Blinne aside.

"This isn't Yvetta," he muttered.

"She's in shock," Blinne said.

"She's seen the face of evil," Mattie told him.

"Give her time," Blinne said.

The door opened and Somebody burst through, John and Kiachuk behind him.

Yvetta stood. When John stepped toward her she held out her arms. He embraced her, and she began to cry. Would the tears, Garris thought, bring her back to herself? Yvetta's focus shrank, as if she was no longer aware there was anyone else in the cabin. He and the others stood silent, watching.

John opened the blankets and pulled them more tightly around her, smoothing them over her hip. The movements revealed his familiarity with Yvetta's body. She was speaking now, to him alone, in the People's tongue. Her eyes grew wide, as if with some wild speculation.

146

Garris turned to Kiachuk. "What is she saying?"

She shook her head.

"Tell me," he insisted.

"'When he tied me,'" she whispered, "'he used his dog tooth like a knife.' Maybe he files them for the purpose."

A helpless fury boiled inside him. He felt himself drowning in it.

Ruth had heated cider on the stove. She began to serve it up, using the cups she'd brought. Somebody tried to help her, but she elbowed him aside.

"She's talking about the ravens," Kiachuk whispered. "Shadows of those he's taken. Stolen souls."

Ruth offered Garris a steaming cup. Kiachuk took it and shook her head.

Blinne had turned to speak to the group. "We're going to crush that louse."

"You should know—" Pike drew a breath. "Before molesting Yvetta, Astley raided our cabin. He made off with three slabs of bacon."

"He sacked our place as well," Jonas said.

"Flour, sugar, and all the tobacco," Ruth said, glaring at Somebody. "Casanova was down by the river, charming the duchess."

Tobacco, Garris thought. These people were as slow as pigeons.

"Astley's been watching us," he said. "From the boulder bed or the Butcher's knee, or high on its backside. He knew when to strike."

The villagers agreed to secure their doors. After collecting his tools from the snow, Garris fashioned wooden slide bolts and installed them on every shelter. A rotating watch was posted. Pike vowed to get the Deputy involved, whatever it took.

In the days that followed, John visited Yvetta often. Garris made him welcome, and they tried, each in their way, to restore her clarity and confidence. John was as galled as Garris about what Astley had done, but mixed with his hatred was an arrogant poise, as if he was her sole protector. Garris gave them their private time in the cabin, but when he came and went, he heard hints of the young man that only Yvetta knew. Native prophet, spirit diviner—

Delusions, Garris thought. He'd had enough of his own. He had little skill with a dog team or a revolver. The trapper was a lot more than he could handle. He hoped Jonas was right about the law, and when Pike got word from Nome that help was on its way, Garris allowed himself to suppose that justice might be done.

The Deputy was a portly man with a trimmed mustache and a nervous tic. They were gathered before the Mercantile when his sled arrived. It was a long one with twelve dogs to pull it. His shoulder shrugged with each hand he shook, and when the introductions were over, he opened his parka and showed them his badge. A large revolver was holstered to his thigh. He refused to do anything until he'd had a bath and something to eat. Somebody carried his duffel to the lodgers' room where he would spend the night.

When he was ready, the group gathered around the kitchen table.

"How is the young woman doing?" the Deputy asked.

"Recovering," Garris replied.

"She got quite a scare," the Deputy nodded.

"She's in Mattie's cabin," Koopman said. "My partner in the mission." He wore his new sense of propriety uncomfortably.

Garris volunteered, "If you need to speak with Yvetta—"

"Let's not disturb her." The Deputy waved his hand. He looked around the table. "Tell me what happened."

Garris began to speak. The Deputy glanced at Blinne and winked at her.

Garris halted mid-sentence, glaring. Jonas grasped his arm.

The Deputy's shoulder shrugged. "Please, continue."

Jonas took charge. Astley's recent attacks had started with the rape of the Eskimo woman, so he described that. The Deputy looked confused. "Were there any witnesses?"

"The husband and three children," Lars said.

The Deputy shook his head. "I mean the abduction of the girl."

"I saw the whole thing," Garris said stiffly.

"We're all concerned about Yvetta," Lars said, "but this family will never be the same. The woman and her husband would like you to hear—"

"Does anyone know where he is?" the Deputy asked.

The group was silent.

Finally Pike spoke. "In the Teeth, most likely."

"That's a lot of geography."

"He's a dangerous man," Garris said, trying to control his contempt.

"You need to find him and lock him up." Blinne's eyes were cold.

"You could nab him in Nome," Pike said. "There's an Aleut trader, Ungak."

The Deputy nodded.

"He buys Astley's furs," Pike said.

"That's worth remembering," the Deputy agreed.

"What will it take to arrest him?" Garris said.

"A warrant. I don't have the authority to issue one. I need a judge for that."

"So get a judge—"

"We only have one," the Deputy said with a reflex shrug. "He doesn't bother with warrants for anything short of murder. There's no time for cases like this."

The words ignited Garris' rage. "So why are you here?"

"I had to run up north for a body," the Deputy sighed. "It's outside, in the sled. You were on my way back."

"If you enlisted the Eskimos," Jonas said, "they'd find him."

"I wish I could."

"He's a kidnapper and a thief," Pike said.

"And a rapist," Lars protested.

"He's watching us," Ruth pointed out.

"We have to wait," Blinne explained to the group, "for Astley to kill someone." She turned on the Deputy. "What's wrong with you?"

The Deputy didn't reply.

"God will judge what we do here," Lars said.

Pike pinched his ring, rotating it on his pinky. He leaned toward the Deputy and fingered his fur. It was thick and chestnut in color. "That's not weasel," Pike said.

"Siberian sable," the Deputy told him. He knew Pike was playing him, and he played along, lifting the hem to show off the lining. It was black with gold stars.

"We're law-abiding people," Jonas said.

The Deputy nodded. "I know you are."

"Astley is dangerous," Ruth said.

"I'm sure he is," the Deputy replied. "I'm sorry. Really, I am. I cover all of western Alaska, from Iditarod to Barrow. Just me. No wife, no girl, no family. I live on the trail, and the few pleasures I take," he patted his fur, "are all I have. There's a lot of crime in my patch—far more than I can handle."

Jonas looked startled. "We were counting on you to help us."

The Deputy rose. "I know you're upset." He gazed at Garris. "If it was my daughter, I'd feel the same way. I've got a long day tomorrow, so please excuse me."

He crossed the kitchen. A moment later, they heard him climbing the stair.

Garris felt the silence closing around him.

"All great ambitions suffer setbacks," Pike said. "Rightful will have its own police someday."

"We can't wait for that," Blinne muttered.

Pike set his palm on the table. "During the rush, men were shot down in the street. You'd step over their bodies to get your groceries."

He rose, coaxing Blinne up. With his arm around her, the two of them left.

"Hell's waiting for him," Koopman said.

"For all of us," Garris answered, "and we don't have to wait. Look around you, Lars."

Garris picked up his daughter at Mattie's cabin, and they walked in silence to theirs. The moon glowing behind knots of cloud looked like a prowler had passed and left his fingerprints on the silver.

In the cabin, he stared at the tools on his bench. Then he crossed the floor, picked up a box of plane shavings and tossed a handful on the kindling. They curled like lamb's wool. Yvetta watched without speaking.

Garris cursed the Deputy and his callous judge. He cursed the country and its worthless laws. He cursed the fools he'd made his bed with, and he cursed himself—for endangering Yvetta, for his feeble mushing and his faint-hearted aim. But most of all, he cursed Tom Astley.

∿∿∿

He rose the next morning before Yvetta and fixed her something to eat.

Before they'd finished, there was a knock on the door. It was John, but he wasn't alone. The One-Eyed Man stood beside him, holding a native spear.

John entered, greeting Yvetta in his usual way, embracing her with deep emotion, sparing Garris nothing. And she responded with a warmth she showed no one else. Then John faced Garris and asked to speak with him privately on the river trail. The One-Eyed Man, John said, would protect Yvetta with his life.

The armed native looked like a fierce adversary. John, insistent as he was, had Yvetta's silent support, so Garris agreed.

Fifty feet from the cabin, John began talking.

"We need her," he said. "I need her, and so do the People. Yvetta is our *kao*, our sunlight." He peered at Garris. "Do you have any idea what Astley is thinking?"

Garris met his gaze. "Do you?"

John looked down the trail. "He's like the ravens who follow him—to eat what he's skinned, to pick apart creatures caught in his traps. The world is Astley's corpse."

He shared Garris' hatred, but his tone was measured.

"We have to protect Yvetta," John said, "and the People, and the whites in Rightful too. He's treating us like the animals he traps."

Garris stared at his boots, listening, not speaking.

"I'm no weasel," John said. "You're not a mink. But we're acting helpless, waiting for the snare to choke us or the jaws to snap. We have to make an end for Tom Astley."

Garris looked in John's eyes. He could feel the young man's fear and hatred, and it mixed with his own. He remembered the moment in the yard, when John had attacked the trapper.

"We have to act now," John said.

"We can't just sit here waiting, can we."

John shook his head. "He must be destroyed."

His determination was like a tonic to Garris. Naivete made the boy strong.

"We can find him," John said.

"Can we?"

"I know the Teeth as well as he does," John nodded. "I lived there, with my uncle."

John didn't care about the law. He was a hothead, with a prophet's zeal. But his vehemence no longer seemed reckless or rash. Being passive would lead to something disastrous.

Things will be right when you make them right, Garris thought. Going after Astley called for someone more seasoned, more sober than John. Someone Garris could trust. Like Andy Rezkov. No one was better with dogs.

The Meeting House came into view. The walls were closed up and the clock tower was done.

John halted. "This building will change things," he said. "For the People, for Yvetta and I, and for you. Our hopes, restored. The harmony we dream of. You're framing our future."

ʌʾᴡʌ

Garris got word to Rezkov, and they met in the cabin. After Andy had stoked the fire, Garris poured whiskey into a pair of graniteware cups, and they sat at the little table and talked. Yvetta lay on her cot, quiet or sleeping.

"I want to make things right," Garris said, "but I need your help."

"What do you want?"

"John thinks we can find him in the Teeth."

Rezkov cocked his head. "Astley knows those mountains."

"John does too. That's what he says."

"John's a firebrand," Rezkov laughed. "I like the boy. You trust his judgment?"

Garris shook his head. "I trust yours. The judgment will come from you."

"Me and Jook," Andy corrected him.

"You and Jook."

Rezkov swallowed the whiskey and set the cup back on the table. Then he squinted at Garris and raised both hands, as if he'd been awaiting the request and was growing impatient. "Let's track him down," Andy said.

The next day Garris got Pike and Blinne to watch over Yvetta while he and Rezkov secured supplies from the store. It was late afternoon and Garris was on his way back to the cabin when he saw Kiachuk hurrying toward him. Her expression was troubled, and she was out of breath. She's gotten wind of the plan, he thought.

Kiachuk opened her arms, turned her head and embraced him.

"No," she said. "Please."

"A madman's declared war on us."

"Not with John," she said, meeting his gaze. "He's out of his head."

"He's right to be. Astley has to be stopped."

"You don't know," she said. "You don't understand." She stopped herself and drew a breath. "My father's responsible. John's imagining he's a hero. Not Ned's kind of hero. Not a hunter far out at sea, standing on an ice floe with a harpoon in his hand. A spiritual hero. A savior."

"Right now, I'm seeing a lot to admire in him."

"My brother has his own gospel. We don't understand who we really are. The 'self' you wake up with and carry around— That's not your 'Real Self.'"

Garris nodded.

"You know about this," she said.

"A little. Plants and birds have Real Selves." He shrugged. "So do rivers and clouds. Yvetta told me."

"It's not the sweet story you think. Our Real Selves aren't bound to life here on earth. They have lives of their own, in a different world. They can't be destroyed. It's a dangerous belief—inspired by John's memories of our uncle. Garris—" Her eyes were like bottomless wells.

"The Flying Man was an *angakoq*," Kiachuk said. "A sorcerer. The People believed he could travel to other worlds, where things invisible on earth could be seen and known. The cause of illness. Cures for bad hunting. The plottings of witches and demons."

A dark window was opening. Through it, Garris glimpsed a bygone mind, frightened, believing, before the triumph of reason.

"He's always had one foot in another world," she said. "Now, because of Astley, the lunacy is surfacing."

"What lunacy?"

"John imagines his beliefs will protect him. He thinks he has special powers." Kiachuk pursed her lips and looked aside. "He's been preaching his own gospel during the lessons."

"What?"

"The words coming out of John's mouth were once about Jesus. Now he's teaching his own religion. Mattie and the pastor have no idea."

"How long has this been going on?"

"It started after Astley beat him. The mistranslations were cautious at first. Now they're shameless. I don't think he cares if he's found out."

Yvetta is part of this, Garris thought.

Kiachuk nodded, reading his mind. "She's kept John's secret, and so have I. Without knowing— You're at the center of John's new faith."

"What are you talking about?"

"We will be judged," she said. "Soon, very soon. Maybe tomorrow. We will be separated. Those who don't know their Real Selves will be damned and lost, and those who are one with their Real Selves will enter the *kazgi* together."

Garris was speechless.

"Our Real Selves will be united with the Real Selves of our departed relatives and our ancestors, who we desperately miss. According to John, you're building the earthly version of our heavenly home. And you're Yvetta's father—the man who brought her to the People."

"Yvetta knows that's nonsense."

"Does she? John sees a purpose in your coming. His belief sweeps logic away."

"I'm surprised," he admitted. "And concerned. But John's right about Astley. We have to get rid of him."

"Astley won't be the end of it. There's a new abandon among the People. John's in a frenzy about what Astley did. It was our cousin he raped, and poor Yvetta— But the sickness goes deeper. The homelessness, the disease, the future we've lost—

"The Great Death was a time of madness. Misery and despair— Our *angakoqs* ate the spotted mushroom. They flew to other worlds, and when they came back, they brought fear and hatred. They saw devils wherever they looked. They turned the People against each other.

"My uncle was a kind man. He could be hopeful, inspiring. But he was frightening too. He did crazy things. Terrible things. When the officers chased him into the Teeth, John went with him. They lived there together, in a secret place. John worshipped his uncle. He flew with the Flying Man, and he's proud of that.

"Garris— There's someone inside my brother, someone nobody knows. No one except Yvetta."

Mysterious John, Garris thought. Did Yvetta really believe he had magical powers, that he could fly to another world and mingle with Real Selves?

"What does he say about Astley?" Garris asked.

"'I'm not afraid of him. I have the Flying Man's wisdom, and his tricks. When Astley is dead, our fate will change. The People will no longer be plagued by devils. Our pride will be restored in the *kazgi*, and our ties with the past will be renewed. Our Real Selves will mingle and join, and our hearts will no longer be sad.'

"It's foolery, Garris. Hopeful madness, the dream of a child— You can't trust John. He has no magic. Don't risk your life. Don't go with him." Kiachuk closed her eyes. "I'm sorry I asked you to stay. You're in danger here," she said, "and the People are beyond repair."

Garris folded her in his arms and put his lips to her ear.

"You don't want me to leave," he whispered. "And I don't want to go."

6

*T*he aurora dissolved and the sky brightened quickly. The buttons on a rescuer's coat could be counted from ten yards away. Seven more had been removed from the slide, none of them living. Yvetta was yet to be found.

There were no answers, but as Garris swung his pick and hurried his spade, the questions harried him. Had she retained her calm? Was she thinking about her father? Was she dreaming about the future, about having her own son or daughter, about growing old with the man she loved? Too much time had passed, even if she could breathe, he thought. Even if she was in a protected space. The cold had claimed her body, and the darkness her mind.

A flash of sun appeared to the south. Having harrowed the surface at all locations, rescuers had returned to the spot downslope of the store. They were deeper now, six feet down, eight feet, ten— Diggers nearby were uncovering personal effects, things Garris recognized. A crushed basket, Sara's hand mirror, a pillow Ruth had embroidered. They picked them up and tossed them aside like scavengers at a dump. He looked away, breath ratcheting in his throat. His right thigh was bruised, his back was aching and both hands were cramped. His mind was like a failing engine, racing wildly, then sluggish and numb.

A dozen yards away, two teams of dogs were pulling a dark slab of rock. As the slab moved aside, an icy hollow appeared and a moan rose from it. A woman, crying out.

Garris lurched forward. "Here," he shouted.

When he reached the hollow, he knelt and peered down. Amid the blue blocks and the white cement, a clothed shoulder was visible.

Rescuers were running from all directions, Koopman among them. "Stay to the side," the Chief ordered, "keep your weight off," then he fell to his knees at the hollow's edge.

Garris pointed at the green fabric on the woman's shoulder. It was Ruth's gown. Through a shell of ice, he could see the side of her head.

"The Eisenhart woman," the Chief recognized her. And the others did too. Everyone knew the couple who ran the Rightful store.

"You three," the Chief turned. "Shovels only."

Garris and two others clambered into the hollow and began clearing snow from around the trapped woman. She continued to moan.

Then another sound surfaced, a low wheeze beside her. Garris moved his spade carefully. The resisting crystals squealed like mice. A man. He could see the bushy crown of his head. It was Jonas. They'd been buried together.

The warming air softened the snow. The two digging with him removed it quickly. Ruth's arm was free now. A span of ice had jackknifed around her. Garris began to chip away at it, and the man beside him joined in. "Her husband's right here," Garris said. The digger grunted. He could see the body and hear the wheeze.

The third digger had uncovered Ruth's knee. She was still moaning.

Jonas' voice warbled, and Garris shuddered. Was he struggling to breathe, trying to speak? Could he hear his wife? He was under a heavy load, with a smaller airspace and no room to move. But he was close enough—

And then Garris realized—there were syllables in Ruth's moan, Jonas' wheezing had shape. The two were speaking beneath the ice. What were they saying?

Ruth's face appeared. The snow was clear around it, but she wore a mask of ice condensed by her breath. Garris used the haft of his shovel to crack it open, and all at once, her moan became words.

"Torture," she cried. "My love, my love—"

Her face was white as marble.

"Is she free?" Garris gasped.

"Ruthie," Jonas wheezed. The digger beside Garris had cleared the crush from the storekeeper's face.

"Torture," Ruth shrieked, "torture—"

"Ruthie—" Jonas' voice was slurred, as if he was drunk.

The ice cracked across her front, baring her green gown. A violent shake, and Ruth shrieked again, words emerging— hysterical words: "Daniel—save me, save me!"

The shovel trembled in Garris' hands. The digger at his elbow was mute.

"Daniel," Ruth pleaded, "don't go, don't go."

Ruth wasn't speaking to him, but Jonas was listening.

"Ruthie," he rasped, "Ruthie—"

This wasn't the Jonas that Garris knew. There was a stranger inside his body, frightened and helpless. The stranger had taken the storekeeper's heart and mind.

"Lift her out," the man beside Garris said in a hushed voice.

Garris got his arms beneath Ruth's shoulders. The other two diggers circled her waist and legs, and together they heaved her up. Those on the rim caught hold of her.

"Here," the Chief said, and she was set down on the surface. The Chief knelt beside her.

Garris could see Ruth's face. It was scratched and bloody. In her icy hair was the tortoiseshell comb Jonas had given her. She was twisted half around, and when the Chief tried to straighten her, she convulsed. As Ruth was covered with blankets, her lips parted, she convulsed again and was still. Garris looked up to see Lars watching. As he met the pastor's gaze, Lars turned away.

Garris and the other two diggers attacked the ice around

Jonas. The airspace by his head had kept him alive, but the rest of his body was locked in place, as if a vat of plaster had been poured over it. One arm, extended toward his wife, had frozen stiff. He was no longer speaking or moving. Suddenly a large ball of snow tumbled out and Jonas shifted. The diggers dropped their shovels and struggled beneath him, supporting his legs. Garris grabbed his shoulders and pulled, and the cold body slid out. The three of them boosted it over the rim.

The Chief turned Jonas over as Garris climbed out.

Dawn cast a peachy light on the waxen face. The shop-keeper's brows had wrinkled with shock, and the cold made it permanent, like a photograph preserving a fleeting thought. His jaw was clenched. Blood had flown from a cut in his temple into his eyes and frozen them shut. His attention was fixed on something nobody else could see or feel.

"He's still with us," the Chief said, motioning for blankets.

What had he wanted from Ruth, Garris wondered. A kindly whisper, some simple solace. He had struggled for breath a few feet away, carrying her curse. Alone in the cold. His head rested on a pillow of snow now, a halo of tea tins and jam jars around it.

The frozen lips parted. Jonas' hand rose and clutched the Chief's coat.

"Take him to the tents," the Chief barked.

A half-dozen rescuers descended on Jonas and lifted him up. Garris saw the puzzle in every face. No one knew who Daniel was.

As they bore him away, the Chief stood. No wind, no

voices. The silence was jarring. Garris thought of Mattie and her naked hand.

Koopman stumbled forward with a load of Ruth's dresses in his arms. He'd found the remains of their bedroom. No one had a better idea, so they wrapped Ruth in her dresses and sledded her to the morgue.

FOUR MONTHS EARLIER. DECEMBER 10, 1921.

Ruth and Jonas had offered to care for Yvetta in Garris' absence. She seemed more like her old self when Sara was with her. And the news that he had joined with John to hunt down the trapper seemed to brighten her.

With some misgivings, anxious about leaving her in others' care, Garris escorted his daughter to the store. Sara was waiting on the porch beside her father. She hugged Yvetta, then the two girls linked arms and disappeared inside.

"How's Ruth this morning?" Garris asked.

"No change," Jonas said. "We're making the best of it. Here's some news. There's a fellow in Nome who's going to lend me his Edison and some cylinders. We'll have a waltz for the bride and groom. 'Somebody's tall and handsome, somebody's fair to see.' You know the song?"

Garris laughed and nodded.

"I've never seen you dance," Jonas said.

"I may not come back."

"You have to come back," Jonas replied. "I need you to play the wedding march."

"I don't know one."

"You could write one for Sara." Jonas raised his brows. "Somebody wants her to have a tune of her own. The ceremony's in the front room. We'll march from the store, between the grain sacks and bolts of cotton."

Rezkov carried provisions in his sled. John rode in Garris' basket.

In the dim light of dawn, they crossed a frozen lake and followed a streambed that wound through the foothills, all smooth and rolling, unmarked by trails. Sled tracks appeared—old ruts, drifted with snow—and the tracks led to a pass. When they reached it, the first jagged ridge rose before them, crowned with cusps—the front range of the Teeth. Beyond and on either side were lines of prongs and needles, spindles and flints, pale Teeth in an amethyst sky, dark Teeth slicked with ice, strands of fog trailing like spittle between.

The rutted path turned, and they followed it, passing mouth after mouth, ravine after ravine, each bounded by bristling ridgelines. Garris was still making mistakes, and when he confused the dogs, they would look over their shoulder to see what was wrong. The sled track wound into a ravine entrance, and they made the turn with it, climbing. These ruts, too, weren't fresh. Garris mushed behind Rezkov, doing his best to mimic his moves. Boots far back on the runners, legs flexing smoothly, swaying as his team flew over each rise. The drift cruiser rode the sled as if it was part of his own anatomy.

As they ascended, the ridges converged, and the closer they got, the more jagged and broken the Teeth appeared. Bad winters had bent them, split them to pickets, raised hooks and burs on their tops and sides. There were shattered stumps on the jawlines, gaps and empty sockets, swathes of grit spilling down the white gums. The teeth on his saws, Garris thought, were designed to serve him. These Teeth served no one. They'd been riven by ice and sharpened by storm. John's head turned, scouting the ridges.

Where the snow was deeper, Garris followed Rezkov's lead, leaving the runners, jogging beside until the team picked up speed. When the incline grew steep, he jockeyed the sled and shifted his weight, balancing on the downhill side.

They drove as high as they could, anchored the teams, and the three of them scrambled up to an embrasure between two teeth. As they reached the gap, the vista opened: a sheer drop, ranks of fang, and the icy expanse of a frozen sea curving over the top of the world. They scanned the foreground, looking for a fresh sled track or a twist of smoke, seeing nothing.

They returned to the teams and continued. The scrub on either side was broomed and frayed, crusted with snow. As calm as it was, the signs of storm were all around them. And the signs of animals too. John pointed and called them out. Weasel, fox, mink, wolverine— In the crusted snow or on dusted ice, prints could be seen. A fox had left a channel in the powder, and it led to a tumble of rocks. A den, John said. A trapper knew where his victims went for safety and sought them out there.

Garris kept a weather eye on John, mindful of Kiachuk's warnings. But nothing he did raised any doubts. His senses were keen, his judgment well-grounded.

Darkness forced them to halt, and they set up a tent. Rezkov grabbed a pair of tarps from his sled. "I'll be over here," he said. He spread one of the tarps on the snow and called Jook to him. The team followed their leader. With Jook at his head and the others curled against his back and belly, the musher pulled the second tarp over them.

In the tent, John lay down and covered himself with a blanket. Garris, stretching out beside him, slept as he did in the cabin, pillowing his head on his parka hood, drawing his arms out of its sleeves and crossing them over his chest.

He shivered and slept in fits and starts, thinking of Astley, wondering if he was near. He thought about the wedding march to distract himself. Garris pictured the corridor where the march would occur and came up with a name. "The Rice and Cotton March." But a melody didn't follow. The specter of Astley loomed between him and the emotion from which music arose.

The next morning was colder. The wind blew, stirring the powder, and the sky was steel gray. They scouted the remaining ravines in the valley, then circled to the west and entered another, checking between each line of teeth for signs. The next day they crossed a gravel bar and climbed a third valley.

It was there, in the late afternoon, they found his trail.

Rezkov and John inspected it closely. The surface had been packed by snowshoes. Sled runners and paw prints came after. There was nothing to identify the track as Astley's, but who else would be breaking trail here in the middle of winter? It had been days since snow had fallen, and the track was crisp and clear.

Andy turned and gazed up the valley. The thought of a looming encounter rattled Garris. Rezkov looked sober, determined and ready. John was still on his knees, eyeing the track. His hand dipped into his parka pocket and drew something out, silently, covertly. Garris watched him set the object on the grooved snow—a dark rock covered with bone-white eyes, like a sprouting potato. John passed his palm over it, as if the motion conferred some control.

He returned the rock to his pocket and rose with a knowing smile. Conscious Garris was watching him, he turned away. In the cold, with his ruff up and his bone goggles on, he looked like the hero he imagined he might soon be, destined for a victory remembered by generations.

When they returned to the sleds, Rezkov loaded his rifle. Garris checked his revolver and shells, placing both in the kitbag beneath his handlebow. Then they started after him.

The trail led around the hip of a peak and into a narrow gorge. Garris thought he heard barks and squealing, but there was nothing to see. They passed from the gorge to a canyon, then into another. As they emerged, the trail rose to follow a gum line, winding among giant teeth, then plunging, crossing a saddle. As the sun was setting, the track turned west and descended to a streambed. Along the shore, pink light glittered on the tromped snow and the paw prints and grooves. The trail wound through islands of scrub, and the shadows of the naked boughs were like nets cast before them.

The temperature dropped. Beneath the sled's weight, the crust broke like crockery. Then the snow grew firmer and the dogs moved faster. Rezkov paused by a frozen pond to light the lanterns, but the prospect of catching up to Astley in the dark was troubling, so they spent the night there.

They found one of his traplines the next morning.

John spotted frozen entrails on the snow. He circled the area on foot, stopping before a hand-sized depression. Rezkov broke off a bough for him, and when John poked the depression, a hidden trap snapped. He lifted the bough, and Garris saw Astley's tool.

It had two rusty jaws that were closed by a spring when a leg stepped between. The trap was secured by a chain, with the entrails as bait.

John pointed at a line of paw prints inches away. "A fox with a home nearby."

They followed the trapline up the canyon, finding Astley's ruses and contraptions along the way. Leghold traps—dainty for minks, larger for foxes—with aisles of gravel to guide the prey in. Snares pinned to alders, wire nooses hanging between rocks where the tracks of an animal ran. His scent was masked by fish oil. A noose left the prey hanging, a trap's chain insured it couldn't escape.

The sled track led them into a gully. It was late afternoon and the wind had died. Not a sigh or a whisper. The traps they'd seen—at some point, Astley would return to check them. Garris listened for runners, a bark or panting, but the gully was deathly still. The white slopes were crossed by dotted lines, fox tracks scribed on either side. Jook followed the trail through an alder thicket. The trunks were hidden, buried in snow. Only the limbs were visible, twisting this way and that.

A hiss sounded among the branches. Rezkov slowed.

Garris could see him searching. Then Rezkov halted, grabbed an ax from his sled and started through the alders.

Garris stopped his team, and he and John followed.

Amid the branches, a moose antler was frozen in the snow. Beside it a female fox lay curled, her leg in a trap. Her snout was puckered and there was terror in her eyes.

The three men gathered around. Rezkov raised his ax and delivered a blow to her head. She relaxed, her eyes turning glassy as the fear faded.

John knelt and sniffed the antler. "Fox pee," he said. "She couldn't resist."

"He carries it with him?" Garris wondered.

"You cut out the bladder," John said.

Rezkov knelt, shaking his head. Garris sank beside him.

"Their coats are fine this time of year." Andy stroked the fox's side.

The two men looked at each other, then stood.

John remained on his knees. With his knife, he cut off

the fox's forepaw. Rezkov saw what he was doing but seemed neither surprised nor troubled.

Darkness was settling when they found a place Astley had camped.

In a huddle of boulders a fire had blazed, blackening the rock and leaving a bed of ash. On either side were wasted pyres of scrub. "Camp lights," Rezkov muttered. John pointed.

Garris saw the tops of the boulders were lathered with blood.

"Skinned his animals," Rezkov said, "and fed them to his dogs."

"Or his birds," Garris said.

"He left one for us." John was staring at a knee-high slab a few feet away.

The three stepped closer.

"A weasel," John said.

It was a frightening sight. The animal's skin had been removed. Its flesh was red and gleaming. The weasel was life-less. Had it been dead when Astley stripped it? There were tufts of fur, tags and edges, where the blade had passed. Everything else looked stiff and enameled. Without its covering, Garris thought, the animal was reduced to its fetal state, staring but sightless, curled as if trying to return to the safety it knew before entering the world. "An ugly business."

"Men were meant to wear skins," Rezkov said. "We don't have fur of our own." He pursed his lips at the naked weasel. "Not my kind of work."

John was silent, but Garris saw the hatred in his eyes. Was he thinking of the weasel's Real Self? He wondered what John would have said to Yvetta.

The young man turned, took a few strides, then knelt by a flat spot and ran his fingers over the tundra. "He slept here last night or the night before. In a tent." He raised a curl of grimy cord.

Rezkov exhaled. "That's enough for one day." He turned to his team and unclipped a dog's tugline.

Garris regarded the bloody rocks. "I'm not sleeping here. Let's follow the track a little farther."

"Jook is beat," Rezkov said. "They need food, and so do we. We'll make our bed over there, away from all this."

In the tent, after Garris lay down, John hunched over a plate of rock. Through narrowed lids, Garris saw him take the fox's forepaw and the grimy cord and set them on the rock together. Then John puckered his lips and blew on them, muttering *"nayek"* between each breath. *"Keoo,"* he said. *"Azit naozok."*

How much of this had Yvetta seen, Garris wondered.

That night, his dreams were the dreams of a trapper. Bait and jaws, chains and snares, sweat and urine, and tracks in the snow. Finding a catch, strangling or clubbing it, stripping its skin and resetting the trap. When the images relented, he found himself lying in a close place, with blood all around him—on his hands and arms, on his chest and back, and smeared on his face. He could smell it and taste it. The air that flowed down his nose and throat was wet and warm.

They followed Astley's trail the next day and the next, expecting to overtake him. But the trapper remained out of reach. Up canyons, over saddles and shoulders, rock piles and talus, and through the cusps. Winds blew ice dust into the tracks, fog hid the view. Astley had no power over either, but at times, Garris imagined he did. The Devil of the Teeth. Here, the phantom trapper had dominion.

Devil or no, the tension continued to mount. The dogs felt it. At dawn, when Garris clipped Zoya into the gangline, he saw a strange intensity in her eyes. The chase, the fear and the danger, was stirring something inside her. John was in his own world, sharing little. When they stopped to eat, he filled a pail with water and sat staring into it. "What are you doing?" Garris murmured. John didn't reply. Rezkov was mute and watchful, awaiting the moment when Astley would appear. The low arctic sun made ghosts of them, half murky peach, half in blue shadow.

They came upon a second place where Astley had slept. John inspected the ground.

"He's making cold camps now," he said. "No fires, no smoke."

Rezkov replied, "He knows we're close."

The trapper had slept in a rocky hollow. Whatever he was eating, it was dried or raw. On a slab, they found another skinned animal. This one had a message on it. Astley had written on the carcass with his knife—not words, just lines and points. John touched the glossy flesh, eyeing the marks as if he understood them.

Kiachuk was right, Garris thought. Her brother had some of Astley's madness.

A snap startled them. When Garris looked down, he saw the toe of his boot had been caught in a trap. No pain, but he could feel the pressure, as if something alive had its jaws locked on him.

"I think we're supposed to laugh," Rezkov said.

John wasn't amused. Garris shuddered.

There were more grisly gifts farther down the trail. Stomach, lungs, intestines and bladder—he'd inflated them like children's playthings and hung them from the alders. Astley knew he was being hunted. That should worry him, Garris thought. But it was they who were worried.

New traps appeared. Traps for them.

At the mouth of a canyon, Rezkov sank suddenly. Garris halted, and he and John helped him out of a snowbank. A wire had been strung between outcrops on either side of the track. It had caught Rezkov's shoulder and thrown him off his footboards. Beneath his parka and shirt, the flesh was torn and bleeding. If he'd been facing forward or moving at higher speed, the wire would have taken his head off.

They bound the wound and continued, Rezkov still in the lead. John twitched his head from side to side, as if he was watching two things, trying to keep both in sight. The track jagged to the left, plunging into a chasm. Jook read the deceit and stopped at the edge. An hour later, loose snow hid a pit-fall, and Jook sensed that too. Could he smell the pit, could he hear the wind in it? How did he know?

Once Astley had them thinking like prey, he began to toy with them. He put a line of rocks across the track, and they stopped to examine it. Finally they agreed—they were nothing but rocks. Rezkov spotted what looked like another wire, but this one was sewing thread. He was showing he could frighten them.

As they returned to their sleds, John put his hand on Garris' shoulder. There was a surprising softness in the young man's eyes. He sees I'm rattled, Garris thought, and he's imagining he's my protector.

A frost fog baffled the sun, and the light turned chalky. Everything—men and dogs, the frozen slopes, and the Teeth themselves—looked disembodied, lifeless as plaster. Then through the fog, a strange sound reached them. *Screeks* and *cucks*, as if someone was wiping a window.

"*Tulugaq*," John said. "Stolen Selves, returned from the dead."

Garris searched the swirling air. John answered the sounds, whispering, snapping his fingers, freeing squeaks from his throat. The cries mounted. Garris heard bill clacks, blowing and croaking.

John was speaking to Astley's ravens in their own language.

They appeared all at once, zagging, banking, swooping and diving, wings spread or crushed to their sides, tumbling and flapping. Garris felt their arrival like a contagion, and as

177

they clattered and shrieked, the contagion spread. Fear, spite, hatred, contempt— Their rasps were insistent, demanding.

John was fixed on the way ahead. So was Rezkov.

Forward, through a break, amid a rank of bristling spines, a smooth shape appeared. Pale gray, it was as tall as the Teeth and shaped like an egg, with its tapered end up. The Egg was hollow, its top was shattered and the jagged edges were varnished black.

Rezkov halted. John was looking around. Garris could feel his keenness and his concentration. The fog was clearing.

Snow had melted and refrozen on the Egg's curving sides, glazing them with ice. The gaps in the fangs around the Egg looked deeper now, and as the wind rose, the cold whistled through them.

Rezkov pointed.

Fifty yards farther along Astley's track, the fog had parted around a cairn. Beyond it was another, and another. The cairns were evenly spaced, every half-dozen yards. There was an animal's head on the summit of each.

What did it mean? Was the trapper leading them toward something? Did the heads mark off a boundary? Did they enclose a space? Astley was speaking to them, but what was he saying?

The ravens' croaking continued to mount.

And then Garris saw— Below the weaving birds, standing on a stage of rock, was a monstrous creature, larger than a man, with reddish fur and a craning head, snouted and glaring.

Transfixed, heart racing, Garris watched the head crane forward, farther and farther, as if it would detach from the body.

A spook, a demon— The madness in Astley was declaring itself.

Rezkov cried out to the specter, challenging it.

John Jimmy was speaking native words in an intimate voice, as if he was luring Astley, as if he intended to absorb the demon or swallow him whole. John's knife was in his hand, and he was taking slow steps toward the scud of fog that stood between them and the stage of rock.

Rezkov's dogs were moving forward, pulling his sled. "Got your gun?" he called.

Garris didn't reply.

Zoya followed Jook's lead, entering the fog. The sled slid through it quickly, blindly. Garris reached into the kitbag and clasped the revolver.

John's shoulders appeared, then Garris could see Rezkov's dogs, motionless. Beyond them, the stage of rock swam into view. Andy was standing beside it, holding his rifle.

The monster had vanished. So had the ravens.

Garris braked and stepped off his foot boards, striding forward with his gun in his hand. John had reached the stage.

Rezkov bent over and picked something up. The head of a fox, stuck on a branch.

Garris gazed at the flat rock, then at Rezkov. The musher shook his head.

Astley had opened his parka wide, hitched it over his brow and pushed the stick through the parka's neck, moving the fox's head from below.

Garris was speechless, struggling to reconcile the horror he'd felt with the evidence of Astley's trick. John was peering at him, seeing his state.

"He's married to the Stolen Selves," John said darkly. Astley had removed his mask for a moment, and so had John. "They plague him, but he keeps them fed, using magic claws and the dog with seven heads."

John's notion of Astley was madness, and he was crazy to use the knife in his hand. "He's a man," Garris said. "Just a man."

"Why do you think he's here, so high in the Teeth?" John challenged him. "The trapping's easier lower down."

"He's addled," Rezkov said.

"Why?" Garris asked, wanting to know what John would say. "Why is he here?"

But John had turned his back on them both.

/\/\/\

In the tent that night, Garris dreamt he was Astley, fresh from slaughter.

He was driving the trapper's sled, wearing the trapper's parka. It was open to the night and flew back on the wind. Garris was full of music—night music, with the wind howling through it and the dried heads jumping on their strings, shaking and nodding and singing along. All the frantic voices, the severed spirits of creatures he'd killed, shrill and raving, deranged and euphoric—

He woke in darkness, shivering, feeling a hopeless degeneration. The refuge he'd sought, the distance, the separation— It was too late to ward off Astley's sickness. Its jaws were closing around him.

Out of the darkness, the hollow croaks reached him.

Garris held his breath. It was no illusion. Somewhere beyond the tent, raven wings waved and the black beaks spoke. He found his revolver. He was reaching for Rezkov's shoulder to wake him, when the croaking came again, nearer, insistent.

Garris threw back the tent flap and rose into the freezing air. The sky was clear, the moon almost full. No one near the tent— No birds in the rocks or on the ground. And the dogs— Rezkov's were curled and covered with snow, and his were too. Except for the swing dog who was nowhere in sight. And Zoya who stood rigid in the moonlight, facing a line of teeth.

Through the dimness, Garris saw a shadow move.

He hurried forward, cocking his gun, seeing the shadow more clearly. A giant hunched raven; or a man, stooping and rising. The croaks grew louder as Garris approached.

The rock beneath him was crumbling. The teeth were ground down to the jaw. Ahead, cusps rose, iced on one side, black on the other. A sled and a dog team were parked beneath them. The shadow swung around. Foot sounds, and Astley reached his sled, leaped onto the runners and shouted to his dogs. Garris was pounding forward, but the sled was moving away.

He halted and raised the gun, training the muzzle on Astley's back. The trapper lurched from side to side. Garris tensed on the trigger and squeezed. The shot blared in his ears, and the recoil jolted him. He heard Astley grunt, and he saw him sway. But the sled didn't slow. As it passed a rotted tooth's stump, moonlight washed Astley's back. A dark flower had bloomed beside his hip. The sled took a bend, and the trapper was a silhouette. Then the silhouette misted in a puff of snow and the sled disappeared.

Twenty feet from him, he saw the ravens. Between two teeth, the snow was cratered. The birds were perched on the rim or flapping, rising and descending into it.

Garris stepped closer. The crater was soaked with blood. Within, a butchered dog lay on its side. His swing dog. A few feet from the dog's muzzle was the carcass of the trapped animal Astley had used to lure the dog away from the team.

Garris waved his arms, scaring the ravens into the air. Then he knelt, seeing what the trapper had done. He hadn't just killed the dog. He'd skinned its head, leaving the fur of its face rucked around its shoulders.

Foot sounds. Shouts. His shot had roused Rezkov and John. They were hurrying toward him. The ravens were razzling, circling low, waiting to mob the dog and resume their pecking.

As Rezkov drew close, he fired his rifle. A raven fell out of the air, and the others departed. Andy lowered himself beside Garris as the razzle faded.

They stared at the mutilation together.

"It's my business now," Andy said. His fury was palpable. "She slept in my lap when she was a pup."

John was standing behind them.

"The People have a story," he said, "about a hunter in a storm. He takes shelter in a cave. Inside he sees the body parts of all the creatures he's killed."

Garris turned. John was holding his hands up on either side of his face, as if his mind was the hunter's, crowded by hauntings.

It was starting to snow. In the moonlight, the flakes of ice gleamed as they fell.

Rezkov was eyeing Garris' gun.

"I hit him." Garris touched the back of his hip.

"He's got an artery there. Maybe you killed him."

Garris didn't reply. John looked away. It was too much to hope for.

Before they crawled back into the tent, Garris and Rezkov knelt beside Zoya. Garris hugged her. Rezkov pulled on her ears. She pushed her forehead against them both. "She knows what's happened," Andy said. He gazed at Zoya. "Don't you."

When they rose the next morning, the snow was still coming down. It lay thick on the ground, covering the tracks. The silence was absolute. They dug out the sleds, roused the teams and clipped them into the ganglines, all without speaking. As they ate, the shadow of a row of teeth rose to meet its counterpart on the opposite slope.

There was no tracking Astley now. The chase was over.

If Garris had hurt him, would that be the end? Or would Astley strike again?

They didn't want to leave the dead dog in the Teeth, so they wrapped his body in a tarp and hauled it back.

$$\wedge\!\wedge\!\wedge\!\wedge$$

Kiachuk helped Garris bury the dog. They put him beneath a mound of rocks on the backside of Butcher Peak. The snow was light, but it was still coming down.

He was quiet and morose, glad that she was with him. He'd been trying to dodge the thoughts and feelings his encounter with Astley spawned, but burying the dog had stirred them up. They sat by the mound together, facing the Teeth.

"Talk to me," Kiachuk said.

He faced her, uncertain how much to share.

She sensed that and took his hand.

"I'm afraid," Garris said.

"For Yvetta."

He nodded. "I wanted to protect her and I failed." He let go of her hand. "And I'm afraid for myself."

"You're afraid he'll come after you?"

"I am. And—" Garris shook his head.

"And what?"

"We were hunting him, thinking the way he thinks. I've

never wanted to kill a man." He tracked the cusps of a ridge in the distance. "I'm afraid he's turning me into someone I hate. Maybe he's already done it."

That won't make sense to her, Garris thought. But he was wrong.

"We all have an Astley in us," she said.

He saw the gloom in her eyes. Instead of avoiding it, he joined her, finding comfort in her bleakness. Garris recounted his dream of blood, the night he imagined he was Astley.

She listened, and when he'd finished she kissed him. Then slowly, she began to speak.

"We're not children," she said. "I've been through a lot, and so have you. We should be braced for things like this. But we're not. We're too hopeful. There's something inside us that refuses to accept.

"If only the whites hadn't appeared. If only we still had our home on the coast. If only things hadn't changed, and our lives were like they were." Her eyes softened. "It's no use for us to be bitter. There's no future in that. We have to continue. And we can't continue without accepting what's happened."

"Accepting's too painful," he said. "Who can accept Tom Astley?"

"He can," she said. "He explains everything he does to himself."

"It's a curse to live in a world like that."

She nodded. "It is. The world has no conscience."

"Not an ounce of it," he said.

"It must come from us."

185

"Conscience?"

She nodded and put her lips to his ear. "Speak yours to me, and I'll speak mine to you. No one else needs to hear."

That night, when Yvetta lay down on her pallet, Garris sat on a chair beside her, with his guitar in his lap. As she fell asleep, he composed the wedding march. It was a cheerful melody, at odds with his gloomy state—a rollicking thing, like the songs he'd written in his daughter's youth.

Guitar in hand, Garris knocked on the Mercantile door. Joy and assurance—that's what a wedding wanted. He hoped the tune would suit the occasion.

"Let yourself in," Ruth shouted.

When he entered, she was standing by the kitchen table, bent over an old suitcase, struggling with the latches.

"Let me help with that," Garris said, leaning his guitar against the table.

They sprung the latches and opened the suitcase together. A faint odor of mold rose from the clothing folded within. Ruth's face was lined and drawn, a gray lock draggled across her forehead. "Here it is," she sighed.

She lifted a yellowed wedding gown from the suitcase, and as it unfolded, a handful of withered petals fell to the floor. Ruth's lips parted. When she looked at Garris, her eyes were large, and there was too much in them—memories, things long forgotten. She used her shoe to sweep the petals aside.

"What's the point of tying the knot with him?" she said. "We can't afford to give her a decent wedding. As for this—" Ruth scowled at the gown. "It won't fit her. We aren't built alike. Anyone with eyes can see that. You'll find out soon enough: when your child grows up, it's a kind of death."

Jonas emerged from the corridor. When he saw the guitar, his face brightened. "You finished the march?"

"It looks like you're busy," Garris said.

"No, no," Jonas insisted, "I want to hear it." He glanced at his wife, then he motioned Garris toward the store.

Garris picked up his guitar and followed.

"That gown has a curse on it," Jonas said as they stepped past the sacks of grain and bolts of cotton. "Ruth would be happier if Sara wore overalls. We could find a dress in Nome, but Sara won't let it be."

"She wants a marriage like her mother's."

"I suppose." Jonas halted at the counter and turned to face him. "It's more involved than it looks. This isn't just about Somebody."

The shopkeeper needed someone to confide in.

"My wife is a complicated woman," Jonas said, as if he'd been struggling to understand Ruth for years and was still trying. "There's envy in her upset. Jealousy."

"About what?" Garris set his guitar on the counter.

"Sorry. I want to hear that march," Jonas assured him. He peered at Garris. "Ruth has regrets, some hard feelings, about our wedding. It wasn't what she hoped for. I barely had a nickel to my name. She wore the same dress she'd worn at

187

her first wedding, to Daniel, her first husband. She wanted a new one. And a tortoiseshell comb, so she could put her hair up. It was 'so common' to wear it down."

Jonas reached into his pant pocket. "I bought her this."

He opened a velvet pouch and drew out a comb of carved tortoiseshell. "I'm going to give it to her the morning before. It will be a special day for Ruth too."

Jonas spoke with resolve, but Garris could see the uncertainty in his eyes.

"You knew her, when she was married to Daniel?"

Jonas shook his head. "I saw him for the first time in his casket. My family was acquainted with his. Ruth and I met at the funeral. We were married the following spring." He returned the comb to its pouch. "Honestly, Garris—

"If Yvetta wants John for her husband, be thankful. That boy has a future. Somebody—" Jonas rolled his eyes. "He thinks he's J. P. Morgan. I've rented a tux for him. You know what he said this morning? 'I need your watch and chain.'" He laughed. "We're sending out formal invitations."

Garris smiled. "He was telling me."

"Typeset, on little cards."

"It will be a fine affair," Garris said.

"Lars wanted it the Friends' way—no dancing. 'It's a bad example for the People,' and Ruth agreed. You can imagine how Sara reacted."

"Lars will be reasonable," Garris said.

"He's giving a lesson before the vows. The less festive the ceremony, the happier Ruth will be."

7

*T*he walls of the tent were dripping. Someone turned off the primus stove, and the purr sputtered out. On a bed of heather, Jonas lay on his back, his body motionless now. Garris was kneeling beside him.

The storekeeper's suffering was over. He'd breathed his last. His blood-stained lids had loosened and parted, and the shock that flickered in his desolate eyes wouldn't return. Garris folded the lifeless arms across his chest and drew the blanket over him, hiding his face.

He pictured the man, well-meaning and hopeful, removing the tortoiseshell comb from its pouch. What had he done to deserve the hell he'd endured? In her final moments, Ruth crying for Daniel, with Jonas listening. She had a husband, a child, and the store. But that wasn't enough.

What did Jonas really know? How conscious was Ruth

189

of the secret inside her? Barely aware, Garris guessed. Like Mattie, the real Ruth had been buried and abandoned—so starved for love, so pained by the loss, that she had waited till the end to declare herself. And the woman who rose and spoke condemned the Ruth everyone knew, and Jonas along with her.

Secret selves, disconnected selves, hearts closed and sequestered.

Garris helped strap Jonas' body to a sled, then he slung the tow rope over his shoulder and hauled it to the morgue. It was midday now, and the air was warm. The slide's surface was blazing, inescapably white. It dazzled the eyes and seared the mind. Like death, there was no hiding from it. As dazed and bleary as the rescuers were, the glare isolated them more.

When he'd placed Jonas' body among the dead, Garris descended the slope to rejoin the team. The Chief saw him and approached, moving beside him. Garris described how the storekeeper had passed.

"He had air," the Chief said. "It was the cold that killed him. He was down there too long." He paused, as if choosing his words carefully. "We've plowed the surface thoroughly. Anyone who's still under is buried deeply enough that the cold would be fatal. We're going to continue, but— It's unlikely we'll find any others alive."

Garris saw the meaning in the Chief's eyes.

There was no hope left. His daughter was gone.

His shoulders sank, he bowed his head. He turned away, his feet still moving, sending him stumbling across the fan.

Garris closed his eyes, giving his mind and senses to the fierce light. In this vacuous state, grief took hold. The sun ached for Yvetta. The wind searched for her, speaking her name. All creation mourned her disappearance, unable to understand it.

The wedding march he'd written was echoing in his ear. It was a dirge, a song for the dead. He'd ushered them out of life, and he was still playing it, like a musician at a street wake after everyone's left. He was drenched with sweat, humming his dirge and spreading his arms, knowing Yvetta's lifeless body was buried somewhere beneath him.

"Garris—"

A hand clutched his shirt and shook him. Garris peered through the heat, seeing Lars, face smudged, clothing soaked. His Bible was under his arm. The cover was gone, and the spine was broken.

"Is this God?" Lars said.

Garris lowered his arms.

Koopman scanned the slide and the weary rescuers with a glazed look. "I believe it is," he said. "This is His doing."

The search continued through the afternoon. Garris gave what energy he had. But as the Chief predicted, they were all corpses now, and Garris felt only dread. Images of Yvetta unharmed and sane were replaced by frightful ones. Yvetta gray or blue, frozen and staring, brittle as glass. Yvetta disfigured, mangled, rusted and black. But he still felt compelled to find her. He wanted to hold her in his arms again. He wanted to know how she'd gone, how she had spent her last moments.

Across the fan, a woman cried out. "It's Pike, Pike!"

Garris hurried to the pit she and two others had dug.

They were down in it, clearing snow from around someone's head and shoulders. Inside a shell of ice, Pike's brow and his matted white hair could be seen; and below, the tailored coat he'd worn to the wedding. Then one of the diggers cracked the shell, and the lower part of Pike's face burst into view, smiling like the young man in the photo who'd posed with his gold.

He'd been dead awhile.

"There's someone else—" The woman chipped at the crusts.

Garris descended into the pit to help, reaching with both arms, scooping loose ice away. He recognized the blouse and the cherry brooch, perfectly silver and winking light. She'd polished it before the wedding, he thought.

At first it seemed they'd been tangled together. But as the ice was removed from around the pair, Garris could see it was a conscious embrace. Blinne too had a shell of ice over her face. Her eyes were open, staring, her head resting on Clayburn's shoulder. Both of his arms were wrapped around her. There was no way to separate them now. They would have to be pulled from the pit together.

One of the diggers straightened and called for the Chief.

The woman looked at Garris and tapped Blinne's mask. The fiery colleen was like a mannequin seen through a shop window. The two had been alive for a while. Had they heard the rescuers searching above? How long had they held each other? If they spoke, what did they say?

The Chief descended into the pit. He grabbed Pike's shoulder and tried to move it. "His joints are frozen," he said. "Get the ax," he directed a man on the rim.

"Let me try," Garris said.

Before the Chief could reply, he grabbed the woman's pick and began cutting ice away. There was a small space by Blinne's shoulder that he was able to open quickly. As the support came loose, her weight shifted, and the blue hunks around her waist ground and slid. The crush hissed, then a *clang* sounded and black metal appeared. The slide had tumbled the Eisenharts' cast iron stove down the slope. Blinne's good leg had been pinned beneath it.

Garris continued to chip while the Chief and the others watched. The ice was delicately balanced. Garris watched the puzzle for signs of collapse. Another *clang* and a *hiss*, and the stove rocked aside, freeing Blinne. Overhead, a passing cloud made the sun strobe, and the strobe pierced the mask of ice, reflecting in the dead woman's eyes.

Garris felt Blinne's presence.

There were no signs of panic around her. She seemed to have passed calmly. Her features—lips and jaw, the flesh around her eyes—looked relaxed, as if she'd been resigned to her fate, content with it even. Her hands were like Mattie's—fisted with cold—and one arm was frozen against Pike's shoulder. Pike's pinky band was on Blinne's ring finger.

The snow around Pike was looser and came away easily. His pant leg was torn, and his leg was bloody, but he hadn't been trapped. As Garris swung his pick, drapes of snow fell at

Pike's rear. A channel appeared, and to his surprise, when he edged into it, Garris saw traces of digging by hand. There was lodged debris: a pair of ceiling beams and the kitchen table had created a tunnel through which Pike had squirmed. The ice was gleaming, polished by breath. Garris leaned in. There was a window frame Pike had crawled through. Could he have made it to the surface? Pike had no way of knowing. There was tunneling to do and obstacles in his path. But he didn't tackle them. The digging halted beyond the window.

Blinne was trapped. Pike had a path of escape, but he hadn't taken it. Garris imagined him crawling back, feeling his way to Blinne in the dark, touching her shivering body and embracing her.

"Garris?" the Chief barked.

"I'm here."

A foolish old man and a shanty girl, tangled in a web of falsehoods— But unlike Ruth and Jonas, their love was real. When the slide stripped the lies and delusions away, they discovered who they were.

What had he known of the two? And what had they known of each other? In the hour of death, they were like they had never been in life. They had seen a deeper, truer version of themselves and each other. Real Selves, Garris thought. It was as if Yvetta was whispering in his ear.

They roped the pair and used the dog teams to pull them out. As he helped bind the couple in canvas, Garris thought: if he'd been under the snow with Yvetta, and she'd been unable to move, he would have stayed with her.

He straightened, gazing downslope, thinking of Kiachuk. In this blinding light, her somber eyes would have given him shade. Where was she? So many dead, so many of her people. Garris tracked the frozen bed of the river to where it disappeared around the bend.

"Rezkov and the other—"

Garris turned to see the Chief at his side, eyeing Butcher Peak.

"I've sent a team up there," the Chief said, "to see what they can find."

ONE TO TWO MONTHS EARLIER. WINTER AND SPRING, 1922.

Despite their failure to bring the trapper to ground, Yvetta honored the attempt. She was grateful Garris had joined arms with John. Not for herself, but for the People. Garris mentioned John's strange behavior, but she wouldn't hear it. "He's wiser than you think," she said.

And more devious. Garris attended a lesson and saw for himself how things had changed. John spoke his "translations" with a new command, eyes burning, arms spread wide as if to gather the People. Some looked circumspect, but many were swept up, inspired by his message. Yvetta stood a few feet from him, attention unwavering, beaming and proud. Koopman was oblivious, energized really, pleased by the Eskimos' new engagement without understanding the cause. Mattie was more suspicious.

In Lars' cabin one evening, Garris heard her voice her concerns.

"Something's wrong with John," she said.

Koopman shook his head, disagreeing.

"What's troubling you?" Garris asked.

"He's always been so inquiring, so studious," Mattie said. "He and Lars used to spend hours preparing for a lesson."

"It's a sign of his grasp of scripture," Lars said.

Mattie looked at Garris. "He's abrupt with us now. Impatient."

Garris thought of sharing what he knew, but he didn't have the heart to disillusion Lars. And the disclosure would have meant trouble with Yvetta.

Her confidence seemed to mount daily. Her questions about Astley betrayed a hopeful bent. How bad was his wound? Bad enough that he'd snuff the feud? Bad enough that he'd leave them in peace? Garris didn't believe it. He imagined Astley in his sled, talking to his heads, plotting revenge. He woke in the dark, thinking he could hear the trapper circling the cabin. Kiachuk did her best to allay his fears, but not a day passed when the threat was forgotten.

Garris took Yvetta with him whenever he could. Elsewise he trusted to Pike and Blinne, and John Jimmy too. Despite his concerns, he believed John would do anything to defend her. Gradually, for others in Rightful and the Eskimo camp, the tension abated. February came and, for a few hours midday, the warmth of the sun returned. There were no reports about Astley from villages nearby, and Rezkov heard nothing of him in Nome. Was he on the mend, trapping in the Teeth? Had he wandered south or east?

"Gangrene rotted him," Pike said. "He starved. Maybe he froze. Astley got his due."

"I hope you're right," Garris said.

"Put him out of your mind. Forget him."

The Meeting House was nearing completion, and Lars was in high spirits. He was writing an inaugural lesson. Mattie was making curtains on her loom. At the start of Holy Week, everyone gathered to hear Koopman's service. The Meeting House was still without seating, so they all stood. Afterward Ruth and Jonas handed out gifts of sugar and tea. When it was over, Lars and Mattie pulled Garris aside. They knew he was troubled.

"God is good," Mattie told him. "We're very grateful."

"He'll be judged," Lars said. "But not by you."

Perhaps the danger was past. The sun waited till 6 p.m. before it vanished. Breath steamed, and the cold air made your skin feel stiff. But the sky was blue. And there were nights when you could see the stars.

From the first day of construction, Garris had looked forward to making the furniture, and after months of anticipation, the time had arrived. He loved tables and chairs. Each required precision and care, an attention that would be keenly felt by others. It was the same for a jeweler, he thought, laboring over a ring or a necklace. The chosen wood sensed its special future. The grain might be dense, reluctant, fighting the plane. Then all at once, it understood. It relaxed and softened, accepting the carpenter like a lover. The shavings gave freely and the sawdust sighed, emitting the fragrance of warm earth and sunlit leaves.

Kiachuk sensed his growing calm and applauded it. She appeared one day as the sun was sinking, with a blanket in her arms. They ate the food she'd brought, and by then it was dim. She retrieved an oil lamp from her sack, and Garris stoked the stove. When he closed the iron door and turned, Kiachuk was kneeling, using both arms to sweep the wood shavings closer. Together they lay the blanket over them.

"I have something for you," he said, retrieving an oblong object from his pack.

She took it, turned it in her hands and opened the end.

"A needle case," she guessed.

"*Keeoa rong*," he said, which meant something like "sew this, please."

"You're learning."

"You're a good teacher." He touched her waist. "What's the word for 'hip?'"

"*Sipeeak.*"

Garris touched her elbow.

"*Igoosik*," she said.

He put his finger to her ear.

"*Seeun*," she laughed.

He kissed her brow.

"*Kabloot*," she said.

He touched his tongue to the lid of her eye.

"*Eesee*."

Garris drew back. "How do I say 'wife?'"

Kiachuk met his gaze. "*Nuliaq*," she replied.

Garris touched his nose to hers, and they held each other while the wood sizzled and snapped in the stove.

"It's warm," she said. "Can we see the night?"

Garris rose and stepped toward the door. When he opened it, the icicles hanging from the eaves were dripping. Beyond the wet curtain, the dark sky appeared, stars glittering. He returned to the pallet they'd made, and Kiachuk removed her parka and her sealskin leggings. He did the same. She didn't turn away, show him her back or side. She removed her hide pants and shirt without modesty or cheer. Her face showed no emotion, but that wasn't because of its absence. Garris knew her now.

Her younger sister had a milky smile for her infant, and it was served all around. Kiachuk didn't smile like that. Her delight, when it surfaced, came with shadows. But as their intimacy grew, the hope in her nature had ripened. She had a new cheer, and at times it seemed the darkness inside her had been forgotten. Naked now, she motioned him toward her.

Garris shed his union suit, imagining what she might look like, not in hide or furs, but in a cotton dress. He rubbed her nose with his, then he kissed her lips as his fingers slid over her ribs and around her waist. Always the carpenter, he prized a body that was flawlessly smooth, without checks or knots. And hers was.

She whispered Eskimo words in his ear, things he didn't yet understand, while her hands spoke to his physical need. Her light was magnetic, and so was her darkness. Along with her hope, he embraced her sorrows, feeling them clapping around him like the leaves of a tree. And he offered her what he knew she wanted—the strength in his arms, a home for her heart, his heedless desire. When dissimilar woods are dovetailed, their scents combine at the joining.

They lay entwined for what seemed a long time, listening to the dripping eaves and the crackling wood.

Kiachuk took hold of his hand and raised it before her. The back had a pleasing scatter of nicks. "It's rough," she said, "but precise."

"When I'm working, I imagine the nerves grow from my fingers. They're as sensitive as the seed-hairs of a dandelion. Are your feet cold?"

"They are," she said.

Garris slid down her side, using his hands to rub the warmth back into them.

"What are you thinking?" she asked.

"I'm being thankful," he said. "You're still a puzzle to me. You've lived through the Great Death and your father's failure. You're an outcast to most of the People. But you've accepted it all. You're not bitter or vengeful. You haven't given up on mankind."

"We're different, aren't we."

He looked up at her. "I don't want that to matter."

Her eyes grew deeper. He could see the darkness leaching into them.

"Why do we think our misfortunes are undeserved?" she said. "Is it because we come into this world so fresh and so pure?"

He didn't reply.

Kiachuk looked aside.

"Maybe we are meant to be hurt," she said. "By luck, by mistrust. By others' pride and indifference." She wiggled her toes and looked at him. "You will laugh at me," she said. "Am I stealing you?"

"What do you mean?"

"I want you for myself, but you're married to someone else."

"I am?" he laughed. "Who am I married to?"

"To Yvetta, and her innocence."

Garris shook his head. That wasn't true. Kiachuk didn't know what it was like, being a parent. The fear of losing Yvetta—

"Injuries," she sighed. "We load them on ourselves and each other." She spoke from her darkness now. "An ugly reflection that catches you unaware. Suspicions dressed up as kindness. Disinterest when you're on fire. Admiration when there's nothing to admire."

She held her arms out, as if pleading with him. Garris slid between them.

"Are you angry at life?" she said.

"I don't want to be," he replied.

"Neither do I."

On Easter morning, the storms returned. Indoors, there were times when the roaring and shrieking was so loud they couldn't hear each other talk. Outside, the cold hardened the drifts and the fierce winds scoured them—keels and prows, claw marks and gouges. All hints of the river vanished. Its bed and banks were lost beneath the blasting and plaster, and the shoreline willows disappeared.

The violence ended with a cloudless sunset. The cabins were piled with snow to the eaves. Garris and Yvetta dug a chute to the surface.

He was returning from the Mercantile in the dark. As Garris turned to descend the chute, he saw flames spouting out of the Meeting House clock tower.

A moment of shock, numbness, disbelief. Then he was hurrying to the nearest cabin, banging on Lars' door. They rousted Jonas and Pike. The blaze was spotted by a woman in the Eskimo camp, and people came running from both directions. The building was already gutted, and flames were eating through the siding in a dozen places. The river was frozen solid, and a bucket brigade using the water stored in barrels would have done nothing. So the gathering crowd just stood on the trail and watched their Meeting House go up in flames.

Garris, too, was motionless. The long hours, the careful

thought, the fretful precision— His skin prickled in the cold night air, but his insides felt loose, as if his bones had dissolved. He was yielding, laughing inside—grimly, viciously—amused by the appalling futility of his labors.

The People were speaking in their native tongue, but you didn't need a translation to know how they felt. Their fury was palpable, and so was the despair beneath. The Meeting House was a lie, their bitter looks said. Another promise broken, another hope dashed. They'd been gulls to believe it would ever be real.

Yvetta was in tears. When John Jimmy arrived, she went to him. The two stood apart, the young man more sullen than any of the others. John called out some Inupiaq names, and the faces of his kinsmen turned. He spread both arms, as if to render some verdict or cast some spell. Then it all seemed too much for him. He clasped Yvetta's hand and turned, heading back along the river trail.

Lars was standing a few feet from Garris, watching the blaze. The man who often had so much to say was mute. The sight of his dream turning to smoke had robbed him of speech and thought. Mattie had her arm around his waist and her lips to his ear.

Garris felt a hand touch his. Kiachuk was beside him. Ned stood a few yards away, chewing his jaw at the fire while Pike and Blinne exhorted the natives nearby. The crackle and roar swallowed most of their words, but Garris heard "Astley," and "Astley" again.

His name spit through the air, the hissing red tapers like the tongues of trapped animals, returned from the dead. Despite the months of himself Garris put into the building, it wasn't the time or care that pokered his hatred and tugged his insides. It was the thought of the man who had ignited the blaze.

Was he going to stand there watching till there was nothing but ashes?

He met Kiachuk's eyes. Then, without a word to her or anyone else, Garris turned and headed back to the cabin.

The night was a long one, without sleep. Yvetta didn't return.

As soon as there was light, Garris followed the trail back. The skeleton of the Meeting House was spindly and smoking. In the place of the clock tower was a charred spire, like a canine filed to a point. He circled the ruin. The conflagration had melted the snows around it, but he found the path Astley had used. And if the paw prints and runner tracks weren't enough, the trapper had left a crucifix where he'd parked his sled. It was made from two splintered chair rails and a hide thong with a duck-head tassel.

Garris returned to the trail and started along it, thinking of Yvetta. The Meeting House had risen from his labors. She'd left without saying a word to him. Were her thoughts only of John? Anger. Resentment— He had never felt those emotions with her, but he felt them now.

As he approached the Eskimo camp, he saw Kiachuk on the path, hurrying toward him. There was fear in her eyes.

"It's happening," she said.

Garris shook his head. What was she telling him?

"Discord, malice," she said. "Wounds that won't heal. The end of the People. John is the cause. His followers have taken up arms. They want blood—from Astley or the whites or each other. Those who believe in Christ are blamed. Two families have already left."

"Where's Ned?"

"In the hut with my sister, repairing a net. Pretending it's nothing.

"Astley's a demon," she said, repeating her brother's creed. "John is promising the People a battle. A triumph of the spirit. We will have our vengeance, and our miseries will fall away. Our Real Selves will fly to the heavenly *kazgi*, and we'll live forever with those we've lost."

"I don't want Yvetta in the middle of this." Garris stepped forward, continuing along the path.

"She won't leave John," Kiachuk said, following.

A fog hung over the camp. The huts, with their ropes of smoke, seemed to have been lowered from above, idling on earth for a time, pale and insubstantial, until it was time to be drawn back up. The place looked abandoned. The schooling and washing, larding and weaving, had ended. Then the wind pulled at the fog, and a corner of the yard came into view, crowded with people.

Garris drew closer. He heard a man speaking in the Eskimo tongue.

John Jimmy stood on a sealskin robe, with natives gathered around him. His face was painted with wavy lines above and below his eyes. His upper lip was black, and the lower was red. He looked stern, proud, in command, but his voice was a high-pitched gabble. The speaking voice came from the One-Eyed Man, who was by John's side, addressing the crowd.

"What's he saying?" Garris asked.

"It's about our Real Selves."

Ten feet from John, Yvetta stood on her toes, hands fisted against her breast. As John gabbled, he looked her way.

"The vest belonged to my uncle," Kiachuk said.

John's front was dark and feathered.

Garris halted at the crowd's perimeter. No one seemed to notice him. Old and young, the People were rapt.

The space around John was marked off by stuffed mittens, standing straight up, like hands emerging from the frozen ground. John tittered like an insect now, voice strangling at the top of his throat, in the midst of some kind of struggle. His trunk quivered, his lips twitched, his eyes clenched then opened, shocked by what he was seeing or feeling.

John shook his head as if denying, his tongue juddering in his throat. There was pain in his face. His mouth gaped wider and wider. Was he going to shout, was he about to scream? Or was it a proffering? He was opening himself—hesitant, fearful, but opening— As if some invisible presence hovered in the air before him, and he was inviting it in.

Garris shivered. John was in another world, and Yvetta was with him. As he jabbered, her lips moved and her tongue darted, miming along, feeling what he felt.

Kiachuk spoke in his ear. "He's eaten the spotted mushroom."

Women covered their heads, some with their parka hoods, some with their hands.

All at once John's falsetto was consumed by a rushing, a deep exhalation. He lost his footing, falling forward into the arms of the One-Eyed Man. Another hurried behind him, raising John's legs. He was prostrate now, and his breath turned rhythmic, filling his chest.

A third man approached and straightened John's arms, extending them stiffly before him. They were bulging, muscular, strangely enlarged.

Yvetta stepped forward, entering the circle of mittens. There was an object on the fur stage with a grass mat over it. She removed the mat, revealing a carved figure, dark with age. It was prostrate like John, with a grotesque face—a thick muzzle, heavy jowls and a gaping mouth, with ragged teeth and top shells for eyes. The carving was armless and a diminutive body tapered behind.

Garris whispered, "What is that?"

"The Flying Man's Guide," Kiachuk replied.

John's breathing was violent now. His whole body shook. Yvetta grasped one of his arms and tore it free. The natives gasped, and Garris gasped with them. Startled faces, wondering looks— The One-Eyed Man was still speaking, but his voice had calmed. It was as if he stood on a high place and addressed the observers far below. Yvetta removed John's other arm and stepped back out of the circle.

John's inhalations ceased, and a ghostly drone rose in his

throat. His neck locked and his eyes slitted, as if he was plunging forward.

A hiss, air escaping under fierce pressure, then a shriek like an angry wind, as if John had released something, set something loose. As if the way was opening before him. Garris imagined him flying through the air like a spear.

"Far, far," Kiachuk translated the One-Eyed Man's words, "through swarms of birds and clouds, above a city of lost souls, over a black abyss and a boiling sea—"

The One-Eyed Man's travelogue faded.

John was in motion; and then, in a heartbeat, he was perfectly still.

The natives were motionless, silent.

"Our destiny," Kiachuk whispered.

Garris heard a word he recognized. Was it John speaking, or the One-Eyed Man?

"*Kazgi, kazgi,*" the word moved from mouth to mouth, echoing through the crowd, confirming John's vision.

Then John's eyes closed. He went limp.

The two men let go of him, and he fell to the ground.

As one, the People closed their eyes.

"We can't look," Kiachuk whispered.

Her tone acknowledged the foolishness, but she was turning aside, and the grip on his arm urged Garris to do the same.

Then it was over. The natives were talking to each other.

When Garris turned back, John was gone. Yvetta had her arms wrapped around her middle, as if she'd been with John on his spirit flight and was rediscovering her earthly self.

Garris loosened Kiachuk's grip and strode toward his daughter. She saw him coming and stood her ground.

He halted before her. "What are you doing?"

"Raising the Meeting House—"

"John can't stop Astley with magic," he said.

Her expression was stony. "This isn't your business. It's up to the People to find their future. There's nothing left for you here. No work to do. I don't need you to look after me." She turned her back on him.

Garris was stunned, speechless.

He stood watching as she crossed the yard. A child's fantasy, he thought. Witchcraft and sorcery. Rosy madness.

Garris turned on his heel. He saw Kiachuk at the corner of his eye, but his heart and mind were churning so, he didn't signal or pause to speak.

The snow on the river trail crunched beneath him. As he approached the site of the Meeting House, the odor of smoke filled the air. A breeze wove through the quiet, piping, murmuring, rustling in his ear.

"She's so different," Mirabel whispered.

His dead wife was walking beside him. "The little girl we knew is gone," he said. "Yvetta is nothing like her."

"She's still there," Mirabel disagreed. "Our little girl."

"I can't see her," he said.

Mirabel was silent. When her voice came again, it was troubled. "What is she doing in the Arctic?" Mirabel asked. "Why have you done this?"

Then the wind died, and there was only silence.

Garris continued along the trail alone. When he reached the village, Jonas was leaving the Mercantile. The shopkeeper fell in beside him, and together they walked to Pike's place.

"An awful thing," Jonas sighed.

Garris didn't reply.

"Our future. All that painstaking work—" Jonas looked at his boots as he walked. "I gave Ruth the comb," he mentioned, "and she's calmed some. At least there's that."

At his knock, Blinne answered and invited them in.

Garris wasted no time.

"When would Astley come down from the Teeth," he asked, "to sell his furs?"

"Soon," Pike said.

"Before the weather gets warm and spoils his pelts," Jonas agreed.

"We'll be waiting for him," Garris said. "That fur trader in Nome—" He fixed on Pike. "When Astley shows up, we'll get that bastard."

"Get him?" Blinne cocked her head.

"I'll shoot him dead in the street."

"They'll hang you sure," Pike said.

Garris unmuzzled his scorn. "No assay's being done on Astley." He eyed the photo on the wall with contempt. "Your scales aren't working, old man."

Pike stiffened. "What does a carpenter know about—"

"It was luck," Garris said, "and your luck has run out. Rightful is finished, and so are you."

"Whoa." Jonas put his hand on Garris' shoulder.

He swiped it off. "Peddle your rubbish to someone else."

Pike was shaking his head. Blinne glared at Garris as if facing up to Astley was a younger man's business.

A knock on the door.

When Jonas opened it, Mattie stepped forward with Lars. She was holding his arm, steering him, as if he'd lost track of where he was.

"We were up all night," Lars said, "wondering why He would do this. The Meeting House was a perfect expression of His will—the sort of thing He wants us to do here on earth." He looked at Mattie. "What can we tell the Friends? Our gift is in ashes."

Mattie tightened on his arm, pulling him closer. "What's happened is a test of the People's faith, and a test of our own. This is our moment," she said, "to prove ourselves to God and each other."

Lars nodded. "We received His guidance at dawn."

"The Meeting House is a material loss," Mattie said. "Our spirit is unshaken. We must come together and pray—all of us, white and Eskimo—"

"And re-chart our course together," Lars said.

Garris laughed. "You don't know a thing about your flock."

Mattie peered at him.

"They haven't heard a Christian lesson for months," Garris said. "Your translator has his own religion."

Lars looked confused. "What are you saying?"

"John wants a Flying Man's vengeance."

"He's upset right now—"

"John's not waiting for God to judge Astley," Garris said.

"It may look like he's strayed," Lars frowned, "but I know that boy's heart."

"You're an idiot," Garris said angrily.

"That's uncalled for," Mattie snapped.

"Your 'teaching' has gone the way of the Meeting House," Garris told Lars. "And your charity is a sham. You lavish the natives with it, while this poor woman goes begging."

Mattie shuddered. She began to cry.

"God sees all," Lars said, closing his eyes.

Another knock. Then rapping, insistent.

When Jonas opened the door, Kiachuk stepped through, breathless, distraught.

"John and Yvetta," she gasped. "They're gone."

"Where to?" Garris asked.

"Into the Teeth. To get Astley."

"You didn't stop them?"

"I didn't know what they were doing," she said. "Father gave John the dog team. They're headed for the Flying Man's shelter."

"Where is that?"

"Only Ned knows." Her eyes brimmed with fear. "John took the harpoon."

"This miserable place," Garris turned on Pike, waving his arm as if he would sweep the valley away. "I wish I'd never set eyes on it."

He strode through the doorway and along the path. Kiachuk hurried after him.

8

*T*he sun was past its peak, but Garris was still on the fan with the others, swinging his pick, fighting the gloom. Since the noon hour, none of those found had been found alive. The Chief had been right—

"The bride," a cry went up, "the bride, the bride."

Garris turned. Thirty feet from him, a man stood waving a twisted veil. Another was kneeling, holding up objects—a handmade basket, an embroidered scarf. He hurried toward them. The Chief descended from up the slope, shouting, summoning others.

"The groom's here too," the man announced. "We can see his leg."

The Chief marked off the trench. The snow here was already four feet below the surrounding fan. Garris and the

213

others began to dig. A few gifts were found—a necklace of trade beads, a carved pipe in a pouch. Remnants of the cake appeared. A piece of stairwell and the sideboard on which the buffet was spread had wedged together, forming a barrier around which the snow had plowed. A span of roof sealed the pocket, holding the crushing cement above the couple. A dark-panted leg was visible and the hem of a gown. When the trenching was done, a half-dozen rescuers lifted the span and moved it aside. Sara and Somebody appeared beneath a shell of ice.

The Chief halted the workers, edging around the couple with an ax in his hand. He used its blunt end to crack the shell and then a group of rescuers removed the pieces.

The two were frozen, Garris saw, but they'd been alive and together for quite a while, long enough for the warmth of their bodies to create the glassy cocoon. And the ridges and pits in the snow around them weren't random. They'd been able to move. How long had they held each other—

Then he realized: they were dancing.

Sara's arm was crimped by the sideboard, and Somebody's right thigh had been crushed. But the postures were unmistakable. Hands clasped, her head on his shoulder— Garris looked around. Others could see it.

The Chief directed a pair of men to remove the planking beside the couple, and as the boards were lifted, the Edison phonograph appeared intact on the sideboard, its black tulip horn facing up. The last plank, it seemed, was caught in the machine's armature. As it was freed, to the rescuers' amazement, the interrupted waltz resumed.

No one thought to stop it. They stood facing the wedded couple, listening, honoring their last intimacy while the cylinder turned.

The music was upbeat and buoyant, like the two who danced. It was as if, at the final knell, all that remained of their joyful natures had been released. Deeper, more profound—But their Real Selves were no different than the kids Garris knew, perhaps because they had not yet been tangled by life.

Sun beamed into the pit, bathing the couple in light. Their eyes were closed. Somebody's face was white, pale and smooth as polished marble. Sara's gown glittered, the hem swept to one side, as if it had frozen as she turned. She was smiling, blissful to be in his arms. Somebody looked proud, grinning to the last at having made his big splash.

The waltz slowed as the spring unwound, then it reached its end.

There was silence all around.

The Chief scanned the solemn faces and issued directions. Rescuers descended and began to remove the frozen bodies.

At the same time, two weary fellows made their way through the crowd. The Chief saw them and turned. They'd returned from searching Butcher Peak's west flank.

"We found a sled," the first reported.

"Just one?" Garris asked.

"Just one," the other said.

"Was the frame made of bone?" Garris asked. "Were there animal parts, strange decorations?"

The man shook his head. "Just a mess of snapped runners and broken spars. No sign of the driver. The dogs were caught in their harnesses. We dug far enough to see if any survived."

"All dead, except for the lead," the other man said. "The tugline snapped. The dog might be deeper, beneath the sled. With the musher."

Garris looked at the Chief. "It's Andy."

The Chief nodded. His silence was full of resignation. He turned and stepped closer to the pit. Garris followed, swallowing his breath, trying to ward off the feelings brewing inside him.

The rescuers were easing the wedding couple apart. Garris climbed down to help, wrapping his arms around Somebody's thighs. Something glittered at the dead groom's waist. He was still wearing Jonas' watch and chain.

Garris remembered the couple standing before Lars. He shivered, thinking of Yvetta, feeling a chill around his heart. She and John Jimmy had been seated at the front of the gathering. Had they died together? Were her final moments like Sara's? He prayed they were. All his doubts and fears about John were nothing now.

He scanned the margin of the pit. When the dance started, how close were Yvetta and John to the waltzing couple? Were they somewhere near?

It seemed the Chief had similar thoughts. He was ordering rescuers to expand the trench on either side of the wedding cocoon. As the bodies of Sara and Somebody were lifted out, Garris grabbed his pick.

EIGHT DAYS EARLIER. APRIL 16, 1922.

With Kiachuk in his sled, Garris mushed to the Eskimo camp. It was clear and cold, and the trail was fast. If he expected to catch up with Yvetta and John before they reached the Teeth, he didn't have long.

The yard was empty, but threads of smoke rose from the crude dwellings.

Garris braked before Ned Jimmy's hut.

Kiachuk got out and crawled into the earthen tunnel. He followed, moving the drape of fur aside.

Inside, the fire was going. Ned sat by it, poking the coals. His younger daughter was beside him, infant in her lap. It was like a sweatbox, and they were stripped to the waist.

Garris and Kiachuk knelt. She leaned forward.

"*Alapah?*" Ned smiled at her.

Kiachuk nodded. "He asked if it's cold," she told Garris.

"Where has John taken Yvetta?" Garris said.

Kiachuk rendered his words for Ned.

Ned made a puzzled face.

"Ask him again," Garris said angrily.

Kiachuk did as he said.

217

Ned looked mystified and shrugged. He leaned forward, picked up a spoon and made circles in the stewpot with it.

"Where is the Flying Man's shelter?" Garris demanded.

"Let me talk to him," Kiachuk said.

"Where?" Garris insisted.

She delivered his question.

Ned stared at Garris without speaking, defying him, refusing to answer.

The old man's flesh was gleaming, his face wreathed with smoke. Sweat dripped from his daughter's chin, and the shadows of both wavered like phantoms on the wall behind them. "He's playing with me," Garris said.

Ned was silent, motionless.

Kiachuk spoke to her father. Her tone was imploring, and when he didn't respond, her voice grew harsh.

Then Ned spoke, slowly, grimly, his eyes on Garris.

Kiachuk seemed to wither. His lips parted, then she bowed her head.

Ned laughed and waved his daughter away.

"What did he say?"

Kiachuk didn't reply.

"Tell me, damn you," Garris raged.

She faced him, fear in her eyes. "I'm burning a lamp for John," she rendered Ned's words. "The white girl is worthless."

Garris hurled himself through the smoke. He caught hold of the old man's hair with one hand, while the other reached for the wall, dashing heirlooms aside. Carved hooks, feathered hoops and rattles—the claptrap of a Stone Age world. Garris grabbed the seal club and pulled Ned across the coals. The old man flailed, crying out. His sweat hissed on the fire, and then Garris was in the passageway, dragging Ned behind him out into the cold.

Before Ned could get his feet beneath him, Garris brought the club down on his chest. He grunted, and Garris struck him across the jaw. "Where is my daughter?"

Kiachuk was shouting. She grabbed Garris' arm. "Stop, stop—"

"Where?" Garris roared, and he struck again.

Kiachuk knelt by the old man's head, shaking his shoulders, wailing to him in her native tongue. Garris grabbed Ned's arm and pulled him from her. Silent Ned with his burden of shame. Garris walloped his back. "You'd send her to slaughter." He kicked Ned onto his side and raised the club. "Where are they?"

Kiachuk was sobbing, hugging his leg, trying to pull him away. Her sister stood wide-eyed, with her parka on. Ned's jaw was bleeding. The old man was freezing, shivering with cold. The commotion had drawn the natives from their huts.

"This is all your doing," Garris said. "Your precious honor—"

Ned's eyes were wide, like a man with a secret who had just been found out. He turned his head as Garris brought the club down.

"Please, no," Kiachuk screamed. But Garris hurled her aside and struck Ned's face. Other Eskimos were watching. "*Pinagu*," a man cried. "*Naga, naga*," another joined in. Were they going to help their elder? No, Ned had no honor left. He'd lost the last of it. They just stood there, breath steaming, seeing their fallen leader curled on the ground.

Kiachuk was sobbing hysterically, fists to her ears.

Garris brought the club down again. If Ned wouldn't speak—

"*Mannik*," the old man groaned.

"What is he saying?" Garris yelled.

"*Mannik*," Ned whispered.

Garris raised himself. Kiachuk was mute, shaking.

"What is *mannik*?" Garris demanded.

There was a larder box at the hut's entrance. Kiachuk's sister reached into it and held up an egg from the mission coop.

Garris stared at the egg. Then he dropped the club and hurried toward his sled. The People watched him, but none dared to move.

As he sprang onto his footboards, he glanced back. The two sisters had both knelt beside their father, but Kiachuk was facing him. When their gazes met, she turned away, as if repelled by something profoundly ugly.

Born a beast, or made beastly by a vile world— What was the difference.

Garris pulled his anchor and whistled to Zoya, and with a curse for them all, the sled tore out of the camp.

/\/\/\/\

Cold kept the Teeth sharp. Frost cracked and serrated them, and the rasp of storm winds filed their edges. The jagged front range rose before Garris, little changed since they'd followed Astley in December. Spring was yet to come, and the cusps were still white. Only a few dark tips and faces were showing, enameled with ice.

He'd made good time. The track of the Eskimo dog team was fresh, and Zoya knew where she was going. They'd been through this maze before. They entered the first valley, ranks of cusps on each side. Lower down, the air had been clear and the wind had been calm. But here, fog ruled. The jagged silhouettes were etched in it, cracked and leaning. In places the spines were continuous, a wave that would never break, an angry crest that threatened the sky.

He imagined John, frenzied, breathless— Plotting revenge. The hero in a warped fairy tale, oblivious to the peril he was putting Yvetta in. And she—so blinded by romance, so devoted to the People's cause—thinking the two of them would somehow call Astley to account.

Deep in a ravine, Garris saw the sun to the south, poised over the bristling ridge. As he watched, it seemed to burst like a yolk, orange and gold pouring through the embrasures. He recognized the gulley ahead. Zoya turned up it, the fangs so near he could see their scratched faces, crosshatched with snow. The pointed ridges were swimming in fog and murk. Below, the snowy white gums sank into the valleys.

Astley had made his life hell. If he found the man, he'd

shoot him through the head, strip his hide from his flesh and nail his pelt to the cabin wall. He imagined the trapper's face hanging there, flattened and wrinkled.

The track turned as it ascended, and a line of teeth rose into view, with the giant gray Egg at its center. The shelter of the Flying Man.

At the Egg's tapered top, through the shattered opening, a cord of smoke twisted into the air. Someone had driven a hollow log through the opening. Whoever was inside had lit a fire.

The croak of ravens reached him. Garris swung around, scanning the track ahead and behind, searching the nearby rocks. The birds were turning in the air above him, wheeling over the shelter.

He called to Zoya. The sled moved forward slowly.

Garris could see the Eskimo dog team now. The animals were curled in the snow at the foot of the shelter. John and Yvetta—were inside.

What were they doing? Their track was easy to spot. Anyone could have followed them. The dogs and the sled were in clear view, and the smoke signaled their presence. Astley was no stranger to traps. Did John imagine the Flying Man's magic would help them?

Garris braked and dropped his anchor. He pulled his revolver from the kitbag and slid it into his parka pocket. The gun was for Astley, but he'd use it on John if the boy stood in his way. Yvetta could hate him for the rest of her life. He was getting her out of that Egg, whatever the cost.

He glanced at Zoya, braced himself, and started up the slope, winding between snow-crusted boulders toward the shelter. The ravens' razzle echoed from the rocks, as if the Teeth were shifting, squealing against each other.

He was fifty feet from the shelter when he spotted another dog team in a nearby ravine. Garris froze. He could see the bone-white frame and the dried heads hanging from the rails. He drew the gun from his pocket and checked the cylinder. His hands were shaking. All the chambers had shells.

Where was the trapper? Was he somewhere outside? Or was he in the Egg with them?

Garris continued up, watchful but hurrying now.

The entrance was a crack in the Egg's shell. Garris slid through it, and the light dimmed. He held the gun in his right hand, feeling forward with his left, moving into the shelter's cold interior.

Beneath his hide boots, the rock was choppy and dark. Tipping, fumbling, listening and squinting to see— The way twisted. He was entering a confined space, like an anteroom. Shadowed, dark. But somewhere beyond, in the depths of the Egg, there was a pit fire that was casting a glimmering light on the walls around him.

A face loomed out of the rock. Garris faltered, his heart in his throat.

A motionless face. A mask, painted and feathered.

Below it, a pair of sealskin rattles.

All around him, on the uneven shelves, stuck in niches— Masks carved from wood or bone, eyes empty, mouths gaping or closed. Anklets, a staff, carved charms, pipes made of stone. He was in some kind of sanctum—a chancel, a dressing room. Here, Garris thought, the Flying Man made himself ready. From his shelter in the Teeth, he had taken wing, departing the world and returning to it.

Garris steadied his weapon and continued forward.

A quilled cape. Bone batons, bracelets of teeth— The *anga-koq* put on his costume and spread his wings, and with the help of the spotted mushroom, he rose into a world of dreams. Where did he fly to? What did he see? The source of life for beasts and men? The world we go to when this one ends? Or a place between, where desperate spirits are redeemed in battle?

Where was John? How far had he followed the Flying Man?

Ahead, the antechamber narrowed to a slot. A curtain appeared, worn and dusty.

Garris remembered the moment of terror, his first glimpse of the fox monster. It had stood on a slab in sight of the Egg. Had John come to wrestle a creature like that?

Quietly, carefully, Garris drew the worn curtain aside.

The Egg's interior came into view.

Its walls were black. A fire burned at its center.

A few feet from the fire a tall figure stood—John, with a giant mask on and both arms raised. The wooden face added two feet to his height—ugly, with a grin that stretched up the side of its face and three giant teeth sticking out. A small wooden skull was pegged to its brow.

John was shaking and twisting, his seal gut parka crackling as he moved.

Tom Astley was stepping toward him, a wire noose in his hands.

Where was Yvetta? John's parka was sewn with wooden tags, like windy currents meant to carry the wearer aloft. By his foot, Garris saw the carved Guide with its gaping mouth and its armless body tapering behind.

Astley lifted the noose. All at once the crackling and shaking stopped. John stood perfectly still. Astley slipped the noose over his masked head.

Garris aimed his gun.

Astley jerked the noose tight. John's raised arms quivered.

Then, from behind, a terrible screeching.

Astley whirled, leaving the noose hanging. His eyes were giant, wild and black.

Yvetta, in native rags, ran toward the trapper with an axe in her hand.

Astley pulled a knife from his boot, and Garris fired.

Then nothing made sense. Astley faltered, blood appeared on his thigh. The masked figure behind him collapsed, and Yvetta screamed.

The mask belonged to a scarecrow, its arms stuffed with straw. The real John was crouched on the floor with the elders' harpoon in his hands, ready to deal Astley a fatal blow. But he was wounded and groaning. The bullet had passed through Astley's thigh, into John's calf.

The trapper straight-armed Garris, staggering past. Yvetta fell to her knees beside John, sobbing. The harpoon slid from John's hands.

Garris whirled. Was he going to let Astley escape? The trapper was lurching past the curtain, into the antechamber.

Garris raced after him.

Beyond the dressing room, the Egg's stony threshold was splashed with blood. Down the path Garris stumbled, gun in his hand. More blood, on the rocks and snow. He could see Astley now, scrambling down the ravine toward his sled and team.

The trapper passed behind a boulder. When he reappeared, Garris fired. Astley made a snarling sound and turned, his giant eyes wolfish. He'd smeared circles of soot around them. Garris took aim. The trapper reached his sled and was pulling the anchor, he sprang onto the footboards. A second shot— Garris fired and missed. Then Astley was returning down the trail he'd broken.

Above, the black birds croaked through the fog, flapping after him. Garris stood watching them, realizing what had happened. They had set a trap, Yvetta and John. And he had sprung it.

He made his way back to the shelter's entrance, his daughter's screech echoing in his ear. An alien sound, a sound he would never have expected to hear. When he reached the inner chamber, she was on her knees, tending to John.

His face was painted with wavy lines, as it was in the yard. Garris could see the scarecrow's insides, and the sticks John

226

had used to move its hips and shoulders. Yvetta used the dummy's shirt, binding it around John's calf to stop the bleeding. She slid the Flying Man's Guide into a pack and slung it over her shoulder.

Without a word to each other, Garris and his daughter helped John through the shelter. He used the harpoon like a staff to support his leg.

Outside, the weather was changing. The wind whipped and the sky was leaden. If a storm was about to break, they belonged in the Egg. But John's wound couldn't wait. They had to return.

Garris descended the slope, clipped the communal dog team in with his own and hitched the Eskimo sled behind. Then he and Yvetta struggled John down. He refused at first to lie in the attached sled. But Yvetta insisted. She put the Guide beneath his wounded leg. As she climbed in beside him, Garris noticed a black daub beneath her ear, a tattoo perhaps. A paw with four toes, like a print in snow that a fox would leave. John held on to the bloodless harpoon, while Garris bundled them together in the basket. Then he mounted the footboards, called to Zoya and they set off.

The wind picked up immediately. Beyond the first switchback, it started to moan, and the Teeth on either side disappeared in a flurry of snow. It was suddenly colder, much colder, and the dogs' breath was white. They crossed a spineless plateau and skirted a caved-in molar. Then a giant cusp rose, and the track sank below it. Garris felt the ice spicules rasping his face. A line of giant fangs rose ahead, and the wind whistled between. Zoya followed the gum line, winding through them, on the level where she could, then plunging to a saddle and starting across it.

The surface rippled with washboard dunes, then it fuzzed. The point dogs put their muzzles down, trudging forward, trusting Zoya to steer. Garris watched the track. It blurred and sharpened, and then the blizzard thickened, and it vanished completely.

He stopped the team and put hide socks on their feet so they wouldn't freeze. Was Zoya alright? She seemed unconcerned, more composed than he was. Behind them, the towed sled was invisible. Silent.

As they started forward again, the winds blew harder. The snow beneath the dogs disappeared. All Garris could see were their backs. The track had vanished for him. The only guidance was Zoya's nose.

Their progress slowed. Time passed, far too much of it; and as the hour grew later, the blast grew colder. The wind cut through his parka and leggings. It was as if he was wearing nothing at all. A buffet threw him off the runners. The sled spilled, but the team didn't halt. They were dragging it forward. Garris caught up, set the anchor and righted the basket. He checked the towed sled to make sure it hadn't dumped the two inside. John was beneath the blankets with his eyes closed. Yvetta's were open. When he tightened her parka hood, she looked at him like he was a stranger.

He pulled the anchor and they continued forward. The wind was howling now, hissing and shrieking. He was crusted with ice, and so was the sled. For endless moments, the blast was so strong he couldn't breathe. It was as if the cold had been waiting. It saw its chance, and it was closing in quickly. Garris was numb and shivering, and a deeper cold threatened. Its voice blew in his ear—an exhalation that had no end, an expiring sound from an infinite chest. And deep in its throat were clicks and whistles—things being plotted in secret.

He could see only the two wheel dogs now. His intention, his purpose— It was a knot falling out of a board. There was nothing but a hole. Garris gripped the handlebow, facing the void. But the wind bit his face, so he lowered his head.

Were they moving forward? For a moment, he imagined his team and his sled were suspended in space. He tried to open his eyes, but his lids were frozen shut. He was in a world that could only be felt and heard. Garris gripped his right mitt with his teeth and pulled it off, using the warmth in his fingers to melt the ice on his lashes. Steam rose from his fingers, as if the cold was dissolving them. He put the mitt back on quickly. A lost mitt meant a lost hand.

Were they moving forward? he wondered again. The din was deafening. The wind seemed to be lifting them, raising the sled and dogs and sending them through the air. Were they still towing Yvetta and John? Garris looked back, but he saw nothing. He had to check.

He braked and dropped the anchor. Then he stepped off the runners, fighting the wind, tramping back far enough to make sure the sled was still there and the two were inside. When Yvetta saw him, her lips tightened. "We're lost," she guessed. Did he hear contempt in her voice, or was he imagining that? He struggled forward again, passing his basket, feeling his way up the gangline, touching each dog, trying to reassure the animals and himself. One whined and folded its fores, ready to curl in the snow.

Zoya seemed perplexed. She pointed her muzzle one way and the other.

He knelt beside her. Where were they headed? Had she lost the track? Was she finding her own way over the crusted ice?

She faced the blast, ears turning as if to question his delay. He clutched her ruff with his mitts. She gazed at him through slitted eyes, then shook herself free.

Garris returned to the sled and stepped back on the runners, and the dogs continued forward. Zoya was fighting the blizzard on her own terms, but he hadn't a clue what those terms were. When Rezkov told him to trust her, Garris hadn't understood what that meant. But he understood now. They were going wherever she took them.

Trust, he thought. A little breath, a little faith, a little calm. He was alone now, with no sense of direction and no control. He had to focus on harboring his warmth and holding on. Trust wasn't urgent or frantic. It was a kind of postponement, an abeyance, a waiting. Kiachuk had trusted him, he thought. Would she ever trust him again?

Lantern lights pierced the dimness and the whirling snow. Garris could see the silhouettes of buildings, but it all seemed unfamiliar, as if they'd taken a wrong turn and had arrived in a foreign town. Something whisked his leg, making him start. A willow thicket. They were running on a trail. Garris could see ruts in the ice between his legs. Zoya veered to the left, and he saw the Mercantile on a rise, still rooted firmly.

Garris cried out—with relief, to hail someone, to comfort Yvetta—he wasn't sure why. Then he settled himself and called to his lead, taking charge, directing Zoya to Mattie's cabin. It was her they needed.

Garris banged on the door and shouted, wondering if anyone would answer. The door opened, and Mattie's face appeared with a lantern beside it. When he led her to the sled, Mattie lifted the blankets. John was on his back, his leg covered with blood. With her help, he and Yvetta carried John into the cabin. They made a pallet for him and lay him beside the stove. With a kitchen knife, Mattie cut away John's pant leg. Then she retrieved her medical satchel.

"I shot him," Garris said.

Yvetta had knelt by John's head and was caressing his cheek.

"A lot of blood," Mattie said. "Let's hope the bones aren't badly fractured."

Garris looked from his daughter to John, feeling helpless. The body was a mystery to him. Bones he could understand. But the rest—muscle and nerve, soft organs with blood pulsing through every part— It was not the work of a carpenter.

"Leave him here," Mattie said. And then to Yvetta, "Can you help me by staying the night?"

Garris stepped behind his daughter. She was staring at the

bloody wound. He thought to speak, then held his tongue and kissed the top of her head. He drove the team back to his cabin alone.

As soon as he braked, the dogs collapsed in their harnesses. He stumbled from the sled and sank beside Zoya, hugging her, burying his face in her ruff.

9

AT THE FAN'S TAIL. APRIL 23, 1922, 6:42 P.M.

*T*he surface before him was heaped and buckled. Garris was stooped, digging a sounding hole by the boulder bed. At the end of its run the slide had piled against the rocks, filling the fissures. He was far from the store, but this was a place that hadn't been plumbed. Yvetta and John might be here.

When he raised his head, the snows around him were vacant. Up the slope, rescuers were trudging toward the tents, blotched with sweat, picks over shoulders, dragging their poles. The Chief was descending toward him.

"What are you doing?" Garris demanded.

The Chief shook his hooded head. "They have to be fed. Some need sleep."

"Why now?"

"They're the only two left," the Chief said, choosing his

words. "We're not going to find her alive. And— I don't know where else to look."

"She's farther east," Garris said, turning. He pushed past the Chief, stumbling over the rucked ice. When he reached a frozen wave, he returned to his task, digging alone.

Time passed, however long. When Garris stopped to mop his face, the One-Eyed Man was standing beside him, studying the pit he'd dug. The strange fellow nodded, as if approving of Garris' work.

"They're going for Rezkov."

The voice was behind him. A hand touched his shoulder. Garris turned to see Koopman's earnest face.

"The Chief wants you to bring Zoya," the pastor said.

Before Garris could reply, Koopman looked at the One-Eyed Man with a puzzled expression, as if seeing him for the first time. "Is it you?"

"I'm not leaving—" Garris' voice broke.

Lars wasn't listening. He bowed his head, thumbing the pages of his torn Bible. "Lazarus was His message to us."

Garris drew his shovel out of the crush, trying to collect himself.

"I've lost the Gospel of John," Lars muttered. He sighed and looked back at Garris. "Rezkov," he remembered. "Shall we pause?" he asked the One-Eyed Man.

A half-hour later, the search party was climbing the west leg of Butcher Peak. As they crossed onto its western flank, Garris thought of Kiachuk. Was she still in the camp with Ned? Why hadn't she come? She seemed impossibly distant.

He remembered her scream, the feel of the club in his hand, the way Ned cringed and shook as he brought it down. "Are you angry at life?" she'd asked. And she'd gotten her answer. Her absence from the diggings seemed like a sign of his sealed fate. He'd raged to save Yvetta; now his daughter was gone, and he'd lost them both.

The Chief and the others had reached Rezkov's broken sled and were gathering around it. The right side had buckled, Garris saw. The runner had cracked, and the braces had all stove in. The handlebow was clear, but the crushed basket and nose were buried. So were the dogs in the point and middle positions. He stood with the search team now, looking down at the shallow hole. All you could see were dogs' limbs and patches of fur.

"What is she saying?" the Chief asked him.

Zoya's ears were perked, her snout pointed down, taking the dead dogs' scent.

"Nothing yet."

The group went at the ice with picks and shovels, removing the dogs' frozen bodies. All but Jook had died in their traces. Once they had trenched around the sled and freed it, they dug deeper. But there was no sign of Rezkov or Jook.

"He might have been thrown clear," a man said.

"They're buried higher up," a woman guessed.

"Or the slide carried them down to the river."

Garris turned, scanning the slopes below.

The valley had never been so peaceful. The sun was warm, just a whisper of wind, and the spring thaw, with all its trickles and gurgles, was yet to come. An alder thicket strung purple webs on a blue horizon. Powdery blue, like Andy's eyes. Brave eyes, Garris thought, keen with resolve to make things right. Could a man give so much out of simple friendship?

"This didn't snap," the Chief said.

He was down on his knees, examining Jook's tugline.

"The dog chewed through it," the Chief said.

Garris grabbed Zoya's rope and strode toward him, imagining Jook searching for Andy, ears up, tail waving, tines of steam jetting from his nose. He loved the musher, Garris thought.

When he knelt, the Chief passed him the frayed rope, and he saw where Jook had gnawed it to free himself. The Chief pointed to a hole and claw marks. "He dug himself out."

Zoya sniffed the tugline. Her snout pointed, her shoulders strained. What could she smell, what did she know? Garris unclipped her leash, and she bolted forward, mounting the tumbled slope without hesitation.

She darted to one side, then switched to the other. Two hundred yards from the sled, there was a hollow. Zoya dove into it.

When the group reached the spot, they saw her at the bottom, digging loose snow away with her paws. Within moments, Jook's fur appeared beneath the white crush. Garris and two others descended with shovels and uncovered the dog. Ice had balled on his legs and side. His forepaws were bloody.

Garris cleared a space around Jook's head. A frozen hand appeared, fingers curled around the dog's muzzle.

"Andy's below," he said.

They shifted Jook's body aside and continued digging. Rezkov was buried like Mattie had been—the snow was like poured concrete. His shoulder appeared, then his cheek, pale and frozen. He'd been entombed by the slide at an angle, face inclined, one arm raised shoulder high, like a weary traveller who'd fallen asleep on his side.

His brow was waxen and hard to the touch. His eyes were clear and blue, and there was a glint of afternoon sun in them. He'd been able to clear a small space by his mouth, and Garris could see the telltale shell of ice marking its boundaries. He'd lived awhile—long enough to hear Jook digging, to hear his whimper and huffing breath; long enough to feel Jook's warm nose with his hand and grasp it.

Rezkov had been thrown from his sled and buried here. When the sled came to rest farther down, Jook chewed himself free. He found where Rezkov was buried and was trying to dig him out. And he'd reached him. Why had he stopped digging?

His forepaws were bloody. The claws were torn out and the toes were broken. But there were no other signs of injury. And his fur was equal to the cold. The dog's death was a mystery until they lifted him out and saw the large bowl of frozen blood beneath his muzzle. Jook had dug till his heart burst.

Garris removed the gobbets of snow from Jook's brows. The lids were closed. Had Andy been alive? he wondered. Had he felt Jook's last breath and known that the dog had no more to give? There was no sign of fear or regret in the musher's face.

Not a trace of it. Garris thought of Koopman's kingdom to come. Jook wouldn't have to wait. He was one of the blessed, the angel of a god unknown to man.

As they were wrapping the two bodies in canvas, a pair of rescuers approached from downslope.

"We found the trapper," one said to the Chief.

The other shook his head. "Of all those who died here—" He looked at his partner.

"This one's the worst," the other said.

"Where's your third?" the Chief asked.

"She's with the body," the man replied, "trying to keep the birds off."

The sun was setting. The slope was dim now, the air growing cold. A crescent moon hung in the eastern sky.

As the group approached, they heard razzles and croaks. Ravens swooped low and hopped on the snow. Others were perched on boulders nearby. A woman was turning, arms raised, trying to chase them away.

Garris saw Tom Astley's face staring out of the snow. It was rigid, mouth open as if frozen mid sentence. He seemed to be wearing a monocle, but as Garris drew closer, the unlikely lens grew deeper. It was a hole. The ravens had consumed Astley's eye and continued into the brain behind. The remaining eye was wide with petrified horror. His cheeks and most of his nose had been pecked away. So had part of his upper lip. The chin remained, along with jawbone and teeth. His canines were visible now, filed to points.

The ravens squawked as they swooped, challenging the

238

rescuers. They were enjoying their meal, and there was still plenty left.

The Chief knelt and inspected the remains. "His back is broken," he pointed, "and so is his leg."

The slide had folded Astley at the waist and sunk his middle so deep in concrete that he couldn't move. But he hadn't died quickly. The snow rumpled around his shoulders confirmed his struggle, and the clear ice that cradled his head was proof he'd been conscious for quite a while.

"What time is it?" Garris wondered.

A rescuer checked his watch. "Nine."

"He's as warm as I am." The Chief had slid his hand through the gap in Astley's shirt. "He just passed."

Unlike the others, Astley wasn't entombed. He'd tried to free himself, Garris thought. But his body was tangled in noose wire and trap chains. The splintered end of a stanchion had pierced his side, and three dried heads—two minks and a crane—clung to his uplifted elbow, hanging on strings.

He'd been able to breathe. And with the eye that remained, he'd been able to see. He'd come to rest with one leg protruding. The slide ripped the boot off his foot. Maybe the birds tore his sock away. The toes were gone. There was nothing left but a rake of bone. While his bosom friends enjoyed their feast, Astley had watched from the head of the table.

The rescuers used their picks and shovels to free what was left. Black pin feathers were mixed with the flesh. Astley's pants were ripped, but his thighs were intact. Garris noticed the turkey stitches on one, where he'd sewn himself up.

The Chief spread the trapper's parka on the snow, and they set his parts on it. "Use those wires to bind him."

"What are these?" A rescuer touched one of the parka's buttons.

"From a moose's spine," another replied.

The ravens still hopped on the snow, razzling, and the ones perched on boulders were razzling too. Garris wondered what they were saying. And he wondered what they had said to Astley when they entered his brain and dined on its contents as far as their beaks could reach. The trapper had spent his life with them—he probably knew.

SEVEN DAYS EARLIER. APRIL 17, 1922.

Garris dreamed of the blizzard all that night, while Yvetta cared for John and Mattie tended his wounded leg. The storm was still raging the next morning, and when Garris left the cabin, every dog was a snow-covered circle with its nose under its tail.

He leaned into the wind and struggled down the path, trying to buttress himself. I'm her father, he thought. But his authority had abandoned him. When he reached Mattie's door, he stood for a moment, feeling feeble and inept. He hoped she'd forgive him.

Garris knocked. The door opened, and without a word Mattie let him in.

Koopman was feeding wood to the stove. Beside it, Yvetta's clothes hung from a line. On the table the nurse's satchel stood open, along with a kettle and basin. Yvetta sat on a stool, wearing Mattie's shirt and pants, holding John's hand. He was asleep, with his legs beneath the blankets.

"The bones are whole," Mattie told him.

"That's a relief."

Yvetta turned away.

"He passed out from the pain," Mattie said, "while I was sewing him up. Then he woke and they talked for a while." She eyed Yvetta, whose back was to them. "John is strong, but it's best if he stays in bed for a few days, so the wounds don't reopen. He's welcome here—"

"The People need him," Yvetta said.

Koopman rose. Mattie glanced at him.

"He's a remarkable young man," she said, "with great promise. But he's caught between two worlds." She peered at Yvetta. "We're fond of him. We still hope he'll be a voice for Jesus."

"Last night, I asked him about our lessons," Lars confessed. "I was angry. Upset. I shouldn't have done that."

Mattie shook her head. "No, you shouldn't have."

Garris was watching his daughter. She was furious with Lars and furious with him. "Can I speak to you privately?" he said.

She seemed reluctant, but she let go of John's hand and rose from the stool.

Mattie handed her a parka. There was a shed out back. When they reached it, Garris faced her.

"I know how angry you are," he started. "I should have trusted you."

He wanted to put his arm around her or take her hand in his.

"I should have trusted you," he said again. "Your mother and I—" He saw something new in her face. More than contempt. Hatred.

"Everything was ready," she said. "John licked the blade with his tongue. Astley would be dead now, and John would be fine. The nightmare would be over."

"Yvetta, please—"

"No," she shook her head.

"This isn't your—"

"No!"

Garris stiffened. His eyes were on the scar that stippled her chin. "I was frightened. You're seventeen. Astley's a madman."

"John has powers too," she shot back.

"I misjudged him," he nodded.

"We failed because of you."

"I know." Garris sighed, "What's done is done. Astley's no fool. You're not going to trick him again. John needs to heal. We'll go to Nome—"

"The People need John, and John needs me."

"This isn't your battle." And it wasn't his either, Garris thought. He'd been a fool to listen to Rezkov.

"You don't understand," Yvetta said.

Garris was shaking. All the fears that had plagued him since Mirabel's death seemed to surface at once. "Please— Humor your father. Can you do that?"

Yvetta stared at him, then she seemed to soften. She extended her arms, and he accepted the embrace, hiding his face in her shoulder, mortified by his weakness.

She stroked the back of his head.

"Look at me," she said.

He drew a breath and lifted his chin. She was no longer angry with him. She seemed sorrowful. Pitying. Instead of seeing a man who had command of his life, she saw someone who couldn't handle its threats.

"That first time I was with John alone—" Her voice dropped to a whisper. "The place by the stream, where the wheatears came—"

Garris nodded.

"We were married that day."

A woman was speaking.

"I know how much he means to you," Garris said.

"We fell asleep with our noses touching." She raised her fingers to her nostrils. "Our Real Selves rose together, from our breath. They flew while we slept. Our bodies were nothing but shadows below."

He didn't speak.

"I love John," she said.

The silence drew out. The wind was blasting the cabin's hoarfrost, and bits of ice struck the shed with a *ping-ping-ping* like a hammer striking nails.

"I'm not leaving him," Yvetta said. "Not now, not ever."

The following day, in the midafternoon, after Toluk had driven the communal team back to the camp, Yvetta returned to the cabin to gather her things. She took her clothing, a few books, the blue ribbon she'd worn in her hair for so many years, the framed picture of Mirabel, and the snowshoes he'd made for her. She stripped the blankets off her cot, and Garris watched while she bundled the possessions together.

"Must you?" he had asked.

"I don't want us to argue," she said.

She put on her parka and carried the bundle to the door. Then she set it down and returned to the stove. Garris watched her kneel before it. She raised the latch, opened the door and placed wood on the grate. She used a stick to fire the wood, then she closed the iron door and rose.

The Yvetta before him was split, an image seen through bevel-edged glass. There was the child who couldn't survive without him, the creature he'd devoted his life to; and there was the woman who could fend for herself, who didn't need him at all.

Had the child been a falsehood? A puppet of cloth and sawdust?

Garris swallowed his pain. Somewhere inside the woman, hidden from sight, was the root of Yvetta. Eager to help, anxious to please—a girl who could laugh and listen and sing, who loved fanciful thoughts and beautiful things—

John was waiting by the cabin door, amid whirling snow.

Garris followed Yvetta out. John offered to take the bundle, but she refused. He had a branch of driftwood in his hand. She looked back with a trace of a smile—just a trace—and the two of them started down the trail together toward the Eskimo camp. John walked with a limp, using the branch as a makeshift cane.

Garris stood watching till they disappeared around the bend.

He spent the rest of the day at his workbench. He sharpened his plane blades and honed his drills. His vises needed greasing, and his saws needed filing. There was no work in Rightful, but a carpenter didn't neglect his tools. As the light grew dim, he found himself turning a bleached block of wood in his hands. Without thinking, he secured it in a vise and began to chisel.

Just before nightfall, the bad weather let up. He was sanding his creation when there was a knock on the door. It was Blinne. She had heard about the night in the storm and

Yvetta's departure. They sat on the cot and talked.

"Let's be glad they came through it," Blinne said. "You're lucky, you know. All those years together. I envy you, Garris."

He nodded.

"You shouldn't have said what you did to Pike." Her expression was sober. "It hurt him."

"I'm sorry."

Blinne sighed. "He knows—you spoke the truth. And I know it too."

"I'll talk to him," Garris said. But she seemed not to hear. "Astley, the Meeting House, the fading glory of Rightful— It's a lot of grief to protect him from. I'm just a shanty girl with a short fuse." Her eyes wandered the shadowed bench and his ranks of tools. "It may not be love, but I know he needs me. And I need him. We're at the end of the world, just trying to hang on."

Her sad eyes settled on him. "His belief in Rightful's future is a lie. Maybe my belief that he loves me is too. Sometimes I think lies are all that we have. Without them, what would become of us?"

$$\wedge\!\wedge\!\wedge$$

He rose the next morning thinking of Kiachuk, wondering if he was in her thoughts. He longed for her warmth and her wisdom. She had given him strength and hope, and now he had neither. He'd cursed her, he'd deafened himself to her pleas. He'd beaten her father and wounded her brother. Was there any path to forgiveness?

Garris slid the carving into his parka pocket and started along the trail. As he rounded the bend, a woman's sobs reached him. Mattie appeared, and Lars with his arm around her. The pastor saw him, shared a despairing look and slowed.

"What is it?" Garris said.

"We've met our Judas," Lars replied. "You were right."

"They took the children from me," Mattie whimpered.

"You know what the mission means to us," Lars said.

"'Don't come back.'" Mattie cringed at the words.

"He threw us out of the camp," Lars said.

"I didn't believe," Mattie shook her head, "he had that kind of power."

Garris was silent. This, too, was his doing.

"John's faith—" Mattie's eyes were fearful. "It has nothing to do with the message of Christ."

"It's worse than it was," Lars said, "when we got here."

"Your daughter is with them," Mattie said.

Garris nodded.

"Be careful," she warned. "They're taking Ned's beating very hard."

Garris continued along the trail. When he entered the camp, it seemed nothing had changed. Children were playing in the yard. Women were down by the river, doing their wash. But the One-Eyed Man was standing with a knife in his hand, speaking Inupiaq to three others. As Garris passed, their heads turned. One of them scowled, as if offended by his presence. A mother emerged from her hut and shouted at the children. A young boy hurried to her, and she pulled him inside.

Garris came to a halt by Ned's hut.

Was Kiachuk feeding her father? Treating his wounds? Garris had thought he would announce himself. But the One-Eyed Man was watching, and so were the others.

Garris drew in his gaze, seeing the spot where Ned had curled beneath his blows. He remembered Kiachuk's scream and how he'd hurled her aside. And it seemed an impossible thing—that she would accept his remorse.

He reached into his pocket, grasped his carving and stooped, setting it down by the hut entrance. He'd fashioned a head the size of his fist, with an unlikely face; of uncertain gender and age, with the purity of a child and the confidence of a sage. The idea sprang from the double image of Yvetta, and the hope there was a little girl inside her that would never leave. It was a hope, as well, for himself—for a probity beneath his anger. And as he'd carved, the face became a hope for Kiachuk too—that the root of childhood was part of her nature, precious and secure, proof that she had never been barren and would never be.

As he straightened, he saw Sara and Somebody on the far side of the yard. Kiachuk would come to the wedding, he thought. He'd have a chance to reconcile with her there.

The couple were speaking to Yvetta, motioning and laughing. They turned and stepped toward him. As he approached,

Sara smiled. She had a basket on her arm, loaded with small envelopes.

"Good morning," she greeted him, as if all was well.

Somebody thumbed through the basket and retrieved an envelope with his name scribed on it. "We were going to stop by your cabin," he said. "This is for you."

Garris took the envelope. The wedding was two days hence.

"Right on time." Somebody admired the basket's contents.

"Aren't they nice?" Sara rubbed her thumb across the embossing. "We're so glad we did this. Everyone here is coming. Yvetta promised."

Over her shoulder, Garris could see his daughter standing by John's hut, staring at him with an invitation in her hand.

"What about Ned and Kiachuk?" he asked.

"They haven't said yes," Somebody winked, "but they'll be there. You'll see."

"We had an idea," Sara said. "Would you carry some of them to the wedding in your sled?"

"Have you talked to John?" Garris asked.

"He'll love the idea," Sara replied.

"If he does, I'm happy to do it."

Somebody's brow rumpled. "Is the march—"

"Don't worry," Garris assured him. "I can play it in my sleep." He nodded to the couple and continued forward.

Yvetta watched him come.

Garris remembered how eager she'd been to help Mattie

and Lars. Now she and John were casting them out to preach a new faith to the People. As he approached, she turned and crawled inside. A moment later, John emerged.

"I want to see my daughter," Garris said.

John shook his head. He rose, supporting himself with the driftwood cane. His pant leg was rolled, and the bandaged calf was visible.

"A man's actions," Garris said, "can have results he doesn't intend."

"You betrayed us," John replied. "My sister betrayed us. My father betrayed us. I'm not forgiving in the Christian way. My Real Self refuses to do that."

"Your sister wanted to protect you."

"The People are weak," John said. "Some were born weak. Some were fed weakness and grew to accept it. The People need strength, not weakness."

"She's your blood, John. And Yvetta's mine."

John gazed at Ned's hut. "He's chosen her to share his shame. They can stay shut in there forever. It doesn't matter to me." He looked at Garris. "That's Ned's way, the way of weakness. He thinks his daughter's unworthy. And he wants to hurt you.

"So do many here. They hate what you did to him, and they hate what you did to me. But the anger is worthless. It's of no use to us. We need pride and faith. You can't give us that, and you can't take it away. It will come with the new idea of who we are."

"Protect my daughter," Garris said.

"You're my last stop." Rezkov lashed the tarp over his drift sled. "Everyone will be warm and cozy this spring, including the newlyweds." He pulled an envelope from his parka pocket. "Is the entry march smooth? Somebody thought I should ask."

Garris laughed.

"You know what he told me?" Rezkov raised his brows. "'Me and John—we're the important figures now. John's in charge of the camp, and with Jonas passing the store to me, I'm the one in Rightful everyone will look to.'"

"The boy's a buffoon," Garris said. "Come inside. I've missed you."

He brewed some Eskimo tea, and they sat at the little table.

"You're coming to the wedding?" Garris asked.

"Oh sure. Was Astley invited?"

Garris was silent.

"Too bad what happened at the Flying Man's shelter," Rezkov said.

"Everyone knows," Garris guessed.

Rezkov nodded.

"The storm was brutal on the way back. Zoya saved us."

"That's why you have her."

"That blizzard—" He peered at Rezkov. "I've never experienced anything like it. With all that's happened— It's like I'm still in it. Lost, without control."

"That's not good."

Garris sighed. "Pike's scales are tippy. Jonas is struggling with Ruth and Sara. Ned hasn't left his hut. As for Koopman—"

"He's in a bad way," Rezkov agreed. "He's sitting in his shack right now, writing letters—to the Friends, his superior, his aunt."

"Seeking advice," Garris said.

Rezkov regarded him. "He's afraid to tell anyone what's happened. They don't know the Meeting House has burnt down."

Garris was silent. It was worse than he thought.

"Before I left," Rezkov said, "he shared his ideas for a new lesson."

"The camp won't want it."

"He can stand on a sandbar and lecture the birds. Mattie thinks they'll have to abandon the mission. She's probably right."

"The wedding will give him something to do," Garris said.

"What about you?"

Garris gazed at his workbench. "Even if Yvetta was willing to go, we'd be stuck here till breakup. And the way it's looking, she's not going to leave."

Rezkov squinted at him. "You were right, my friend. You've been right, through it all. John was brave to go after Astley, but he didn't have to drag Yvetta along. Ned should have stopped him. Ned deserved what he got. Astley's the poison here. That's what's wrong. Something has to be done about him."

252

Garris smiled at his confidence. "We'll see him again, I'm sure."

"And I'll be with you," Rezkov promised.

Again Garris smiled. But with all Andy's heat and gravity, the prospect of an end to the trouble inside him didn't seem real. He wasn't sure how to express that or if Rezkov would understand. But he freed his heart and began to speak.

"I'm not a gloomy man," Garris said. "I'm a simple one. I have my tools, I love using them. Like you, I love wood. I love being close to it, seeing it take a new shape in my hands. There have been people I've cared about. A few I really loved. I could say, 'I need you' to them and mean it. And I've felt something like that in return. But . . . for some reason— I've learned to dread life, and the dread is increasing.

"I don't know why. It's like being in that blizzard. You can't see or hear, you have no control. And there's no Zoya running ahead, finding the way.

"I'm not a coward. But what happens in this life seems cruel. We're all dreaming things will be 'right,' but life isn't listening. The dread I'm feeling is bigger than Astley.

"Something bad is going to happen, Andy. I can feel it, the way I can feel when a timber I'm working on has a hidden check and is going to split down the middle."

$$\Lambda^{\prime}\Lambda^{\prime}\Lambda$$

Jonas looked commanding in his dark suit and tie, but

Garris could see the relief in his eyes. The storekeeper cued him with a raised forefinger, beating a count of four. And Garris began to play.

He was seated on an upended log at the edge of the assembly. He rocked as his right hand picked and the fingers of his left trooped on the fretboard. The march had a buck and brightness, and its jaunty skip begged a laugh for its impudence.

There weren't benches enough, so they'd carried hay bales and empty buckets into the store for seating. They'd straightened the bolts of cotton and bags of rice that lined the corridor, and the bride and groom appeared now, stepping slowly down it. The pastor stood at the center of the room, before the big iron stove. The buffet behind him had the cake on it, along with the Edison phonograph Jonas had found in Nome.

Sara and Somebody were beaming. He was dressed in the tux Jonas had rented and carried himself with the new pomp they were all trying to get used to. Sara was wearing her mother's gown. She was shorter than Ruth and didn't have her bust, but despite the poor fit, Garris was surprised at how similar they looked. Sara's hair was piled high like her mother's, and there was a stateliness in her carriage that vied with Ruth's. The graying woman stood stone-faced, mastering her emotions, eyes swollen from a last-minute dispute about how things would be ordered after the waltz.

Yvetta and John were seated in front. The Eskimos' attention seemed equally divided between the approaching wedding couple and the young pair they now trusted to chart their future. As Sara came to a halt, she signaled Yvetta with a grin and a nod. Yvetta began to clap, and the rest of the gathering joined in. Sara curtsied and Somebody bowed. The pastor lowered his hand to quiet the guests, doing his best to maintain an air of solemnity.

Garris smiled and rocked in time to the tune, but inside he was feeling sad and alone. As the guests were seated, he had watched the door, hoping that Ned and Kiachuk would show. It was clear now, they weren't coming.

Yvetta seemed in high spirits. Her hair was parted in the middle, with a braid on each side, like an Eskimo woman. The children from the camp were restless, and the mothers were trying to settle them. By the wall, Mattie stood between Pike and Blinne. The two looked concerned about her. Mattie's head twitched, and her lips were trembling.

The bride and groom came to a halt before Lars. He smiled and patted the Bible in his hands. Garris struck the last note of the march, and as it faded, the pastor cleared his throat. He glanced at John and began to bless the occasion with his thoughts on matrimony. This lesson was to be given without a translation.

Yvetta rose quietly, circling behind the gathering. There was a bounce in her step, as if some girlish impulse had awoken momentarily. She drew up beside Garris, eyed the guitar and laughed. Then she bent and kissed his cheek.

It was like the moment, after careful chiseling, when two rabbeted boards were flawlessly joined. That was all. Before he could speak, she turned and hurried back to her seat.

"Garris," a voice hissed.

Rezkov stood by the door, staring at him, squint-eyed. He sniffed—loudly enough to turn heads—and motioned.

Garris rose with his guitar in his hand. Rezkov grabbed their parkas and slid through the door. As soon as Garris crossed the threshold, he smelled the smoke.

The night was dark, but the sky was clear. A crescent moon shone through a curtain of lime aurora, and reflections rippled over the snow. Their sleds and dogs were parked outside, along with the Eskimos' team. Garris tossed the guitar in his basket and pulled on his parka.

"It's the shed," Rezkov said.

Garris could see the flames. "Let's clear the store."

"Let them be." Rezkov grabbed a shovel from his sled. "We can put it out."

Garris retrieved his, and the two doused the flames.

As he set the shovel back in his basket, Garris turned slowly, scanning the valley and the surrounding snows. A man's silhouette stood motionless at the foot of Butcher Peak, a hundred yards up the slope. Tom Astley was watching them.

"Andy—"

"I see him," Rezkov said, pulling his anchor and stepping onto his footboards. "Let's see if he's game."

Jook rose to his feet, and so did the team.

Rezkov shouted, and his sled took off.

Astley reacted, doing the same.

Garris called to Zoya and yanked his snow hook, following

Rezkov. The gun's in my kitbag, he thought, with a bullet in each chamber.

The snow was hard and fast, and the incline was low. Zoya tore forward.

Astley's fox parka flew back. His team was running flat-out, dusted with snow, the aurora glittering on their loping bodies. Rezkov's dogs were charging after. Andy danced on the runners. Jook was going full steam.

Garris' sled scraped a ledge. He struggled for balance as the nose struck ice. The runners whipped, tore through a shelf and careened off a boulder. Rezkov was skittering over wind-scoured shelves, bucking and banging against protruding rocks.

Astley took a dip at full speed and vanished from view, and then Andy, his team first, down and back up, sled swinging half around. Garris braced himself, a jolting descent, down and back up, and the view returned.

The trapper's sled reappeared, topping a rise. Astley had one foot on a board and was pedaling the other. Rezkov followed, and Zoya right behind. The running was soft and smooth now, and the wind was silent. There was nothing to hear but the hiss of sled runners, the united panting and the padding of paws.

Then abruptly, the way steepened. What was Astley doing? Did he think he could drive his dogs up Butcher Peak?

The trapper stepped off his runners and raced alongside. Rezkov did the same. Garris followed suit. The hunched shape of the butcher rose before them, head bowed, the blade of his rocky cleaver flashing. Astley had reached the butcher's lap, but he wasn't stopping. He and his team headed straight for the blade.

A trick, a ruse, Garris thought. It was some kind of trap. But Rezkov didn't slow, and neither did he. Astley leaped onto his boards, and his team swung left. He was driving his dogs across the Peak's middle.

Rezkov was following, springing back on his boards as Jook made the turn. Garris leaped too, finding his footing, and the next moment Zoya took the pivot at high speed. It was all he could do to hold on.

His team was all in, every tongue hanging, every throat panting. Their combined breath left a stream of fog, and the aurora made its flowing magical, lighting their power and speed. Why was Astley crossing the Peak? Where was he leading them?

Beneath Garris' runners, the crystals hissed like fat in a skillet. The nose struck a windrow of snow, skewing the sled, fooling his balance.

Astley was past the cleaver. Rezkov followed.

Garris was beneath it.

The moon flickered on the blade's sharp edge, as if the hand that held it was quivering, as if the cleaver was about to fall. And then Garris heard a hollow thump and a long exhale, a releasing that shook the whole mountain.

He saw Astley and Rezkov crossing the incline beyond,

and then something tugged at his runners. A sucking sound, and the surface around him began to move.

Garris jerked to right his sled, but he lost his grip and the basket spilled. As he went down, he saw the face of Butcher Peak dividing around the cleaver. On either side cracks rayed across the slopes, snows shattering to fragments, crumbling and collapsing and tumbling down. It was as if all the Peak's snow was a rug, sliding toward the valley below.

He looked again for Rezkov and Astley. Through the whirling ice, an impossible sight: a large cake with two mushers on it—men and dogs and sleds—all balanced on the teetering mass. Then the giant slab tipped to the side, heading down the mountain's west flank.

An ominous rumble. Above him a giant white wave was cresting, cakes tumbling inside it. Goodbye, Garris thought. But the wave struck the cleaver and split, twin rivers flowing to either side, raging and white. Blocks tumbled past, crashing against each other. Flying ice, swarming like insects, biting. All around him, billows were rising—nested arches, upended bowls, vaults over vaults, a milky blooming. Every boom triggered another—a deafening blast, more consuming and senseless than any man-made destruction loosed in the Great War.

The store lay below, and the furious snows were sliding toward it.

A cloud of ice dust billowed around him. He was drowning in powder, seeing only white, moonlit and ghostly: swirling tissues, glittering, spectral; bunching and coiling like the entrails of Astley's prey. Garris was inside the cruelty now, feeling its cold, hearing its promise. The soul of the north, father of blizzards, cared nothing for life, or right or wrong, or anything else.

He was blind to the world, but he could still hear. The slide's roar reached him, along with the clatter and rumble and shriek of wood as it struck the store.

10

*D*arkness had settled on the Rightful Valley when the searchers made their way down the Peak's west leg. The Chief was in front. Four men were on ropes, pulling a sled bound with Rezkov and the remains of Tom Astley. Garris followed slowly, by himself, thinking about Andy's last moments with Jook, and the ravens' long and reluctant leave-taking.

The avalanche fan appeared, heaped and furrowed in the moonlight. It had yielded up its lives, its mercies and tragedies. All but two. Rescuers were seated or curled on the ground, asleep or eating, trying to work out the aches and stiffness in body and limb.

As Garris descended, Koopman trudged to meet him.

"You found Andy."

Garris nodded.

"There might be people who would want his body," Lars said. "She was from Indiana. Did you know that?"

Garris peered at him. "Mattie."

"Her father was a wheelwright." Lars frowned. "I thought I could make some sense of it." He seemed as distracted as ever, but his manner was oddly calm, as if his distress had somehow been resolved.

"A couple from Pleasant are headed to Nome," Lars said. "I'm going with them. I hate to ask this—"

"What?"

"When breakup comes—" Koopman sighed. "I don't have enough for passage south. Can you help me?"

Garris searched the pastor's face. Then he motioned for Lars to follow him past the fan's border. When they reached Garris' sled, he knelt and stroked each of the dogs. He gave Zoya a hug, and she licked his face.

"Take them," he said. "They'll get a good price in Nome. Especially her. She's the brains of this outfit." He scrubbed Zoya's ruff. "I'll keep the sled."

"Are you sure?"

Garris rose. The dogs had made him feel like he had control of his future. "I'm no musher," he said. "Sell them to someone like Andy."

"I'm sorry." Lars seemed on the verge of tears. "You must think I'm daft." He gazed at the corpses lying in the morgue.

Garris shook his head, uncertain what he meant.

"Waiting for the last trumpet," Lars said.

The moon lit the morgue and the tilled fan like a mystic lamp—a lantern burning in a hall of justice. The cold court of the slide, Garris thought. Absent law, and unjuried by others. This court was a private place, where intimate voices spoke and gave witness, if they were able. Where the heart delivered its own verdict.

"There was a kind of judgment here," he said.

"Not by God. There is nothing of God in this."

"Maybe not," Garris said.

A breeze blew past them.

"You're a good shepherd," Garris told him.

"Without my faith or a flock."

"If your god didn't reach them, your friendship did."

Most of the white victims, as Koopman suggested, had relations in the States. But sending the bodies back presented so many challenges, the Chief set the idea aside. The ground was frozen, so they couldn't be buried; and freeing enough rock to cover them all would have been a project. So it was decided that the white dead would be put to rest the Eskimo way.

Timbers were picked from the ruins, and under Garris' direction, a simple scaffolding was erected below the Peak's west leg. A search began for fabric and hide to bind the dead. They found garments among the cabin remains, and the Eskimo rescuers from neighboring villages headed for the empty camp to collect more, along with objects the dead natives would need in the afterlife. When they returned, Ned and Kiachuk were with them.

Garris was hammering nails into a truss. The Chief raised his head. "They've come," he said.

Garris turned to see Kiachuk on the river trail with the One-Eyed Man beside her and Ned behind, rounding the bend. The Chief went to greet them and so did others. Garris stood with his hammer in his hand, wanting to follow.

She had thought of him, no doubt. But he feared those thoughts—their harshness, their finality. Why hadn't she come? Why now, why so late? Her dark hair was unbraided, and a breeze lifted a lock from her brow. She didn't see him. Garris set his hammer down, uneager to draw attention, watching as the Chief and the others led them to the morgue.

A rescuer moved snow with a shovel while the Chief lifted tarps and peeled away canvas. Ned and Kiachuk stepped among the corpses, speaking solemnly. Saying goodbye to cousins and neighbors perhaps, or uttering words prescribed by tradition. The few phrases that reached him were in the native tongue.

They paused beside a body and knelt. Kiachuk bowed her head. Ned broke down and hid his face. Kiachuk raised a small bundle and straightened the blanket in which it was wrapped. Ned's retching sobs carried across the fan. With all the grim history the old man bore, there were more tears to shed, more pain to feel. A few of the rescuers watched. Most turned away.

It was all so senseless. Ned missed the wedding because of the beating, because of his shame. And the others—who had come in goodwill—had paid with their lives.

Kiachuk helped the old man up. He seemed to collect himself. Then he scanned the slopes and spotted him.

Ned stared for a long moment, then started toward him, crossing the diggings. Kiachuk followed, her gaze averted.

Had the tragedy changed the Eskimo elder? The bitterness between them seemed meaningless now.

Ned halted a few feet away and scanned the fan, his jaw chewing. Then he peered at Garris. "What they doing?" he said.

Garris looked at Kiachuk. Her world was in ruins. The divide between them— Could it ever be crossed?

The creases in the old man's face deepened, and his tears came again. "What they doing?" he said.

"They're gone," Garris replied.

Kiachuk smiled—a smile so dark and sad that it stopped his breath.

"John has hidden himself," she said, "to keep me guessing."

$$\wedge\!\!\wedge\!\!\wedge$$

In the late afternoon, the binding of corpses was completed. At dusk, Garris asked Kiachuk to walk with him along the hidden course of the river.

She didn't answer. She just faced the frozen bank and sighed.

Garris led the way. Minutes passed. Finally he spoke.

"What will you do?" he asked.

She shook her head.

In the quiet, Garris could hear meltwater trickling beneath the snow.

"I'm staying," he said.

"Here, in the valley?"

He could feel her puzzlement.

"The snow will melt," he said. "Summer will free her. And John too." He stopped.

Kiachuk halted and turned.

"I'm not ready to lose her," he confessed. "Will you stay here with me?"

Her face was expressionless. There was only silence and uncertainty.

/\\/\/\

The ceremony for the dead occurred the following morning.

The Chief appeared during breakfast, without his balaclava. He wasn't recognized and had to introduce himself around. Garris was speaking to him when Lars approached, carrying the vestiges of his Bible. He handed the broken volume to the Chief. "The couple I'm traveling with are leaving."

The Chief peered at him. "I thought you might say a few words over the dead."

"What would I say?" Lars replied.

266

His gaze wandered. It seemed he was going to walk away, but at the last moment he turned with a mewl and embraced Garris.

After breakfast, the bound bodies were carried to the foot of the scaffolding. The Eskimos refused to have Astley's parts near their people, so the bundle was set aside. The Chief removed a few loose pages from Koopman's Bible and placed them in the bindings of each of the white villagers. When he'd finished, Garris took what was left of the volume and bound it to Mattie with a length of twine.

The bodies were stacked three-deep on the scaffold. A tarp was placed over them and secured with ropes. The Chief invited the Eskimos to place objects belonging to the deceased around the scaffolding or affix them to the posts. Men were given spears and paddles, vests and mukluks, snow goggles and fish nets; women were provided with needles and thread, bracelets and belts, *ulus* and baskets. Portions of food were set on the ground, and water was poured on the snow nearby.

The Chief asked for a minute of silence, and those present stood with heads bowed or eyeing the dead, while the wind slapped their pants and ruffled their furs. When Garris glanced over his shoulder, he saw a dog team rounding the bend in the river. Zoya and her mates were hitched in behind. Koopman was walking beside them. By the time the silence had ended, they were out of sight.

Ned and Kiachuk joined the Eskimos from neighboring camps and villages, and they cried and embraced. Then the rescuers said their goodbyes. Toluk, who'd mushed to Pleasant for help, had a cousin there who had room for him. The granny and the little girl were offered shelter with a family in Teller. The Chief said he'd escort the One-Eyed Man to Nome, where he could sleep in the jail till they had space for him in the mental home in Fairbanks. Among the rescuers was a Catholic priest who lived at the mission in Pilgrim Springs. He thought they might take Ned in. He offered Ned a seat in his sled.

Garris heard the offer and Kiachuk's translation. Would she leave with her father? Had she made other plans? When Ned said yes, they set out for his hut to gather his things. Garris went with them.

Heirlooms, clothing, spears and hooks to fish and hunt— Would the old man ever use them again? Kiachuk didn't touch her own things. "You're staying," Garris said. His words were gentle, tentative. She didn't reply at first. Then her dark eyes met his and she nodded.

When the priest's sled was loaded, Ned climbed in and seated himself with the bundled remains of Tom Astley between his legs. He gave Kiachuk a pinch, and the sled departed.

They stood in silence, watching. Then Kiachuk sighed.

"I heard the rumbling," she said. "Ned was asleep." She turned and gazed at the empty huts. "In the morning, the camp was still empty. I knew something terrible had happened."

She faced him with a pleading look. "I should have come, but I was afraid."

On the way back to the village, they stopped at Garris' cabin. A wall had shifted and the door was jammed, but he broke a window, climbed in and found his tent and some blankets.

They chose a spot on the Peak's east leg with a view of the fan, set up the tent, and returned to his cabin with the dogless sled. They loaded it with wood, pails for melting water, and food enough to last through the week. With a length of rope, Garris hauled the load to the campsite. By then, the day was drawing to a close.

They gathered rocks for a firepit and built a low wall for shelter from the wind. Then Kiachuk started a fire and made their first meal. As the sun went down, they sat on folded blankets, facing the slide and the Rightful Valley.

"I was hoping you'd come to the wedding," Garris said.

"Ned was drowning in shame."

"I thought I'd lost you."

"When he asked me to stay," she said, "I agreed. I couldn't face you." She looked away. "I couldn't stop crying."

He reached for her hand.

"The child's head," she murmured.

"I meant to give it to you, but— I lost my nerve."

She closed her eyes. "You'll think me odd."

Garris waited. She drew a breath.

"I imagined it was ours," she said. "A child born not from love, but from anger and pain."

"A child with the wisdom I lack."

Silence crept into the space between them.

"I wanted to ask your forgiveness," he said. "I was out of my head."

"Raging at life."

He nodded. "And afraid for Yvetta."

Her eyes met his.

"They were sitting next to each other," Garris said.

Kiachuk didn't reply.

"They were buried together," he told her, as if he knew. "They were holding each other. Speaking words of faith and love."

"I hope that's so."

"His convictions bound them." Garris felt a regard for the young man he'd never felt in life. "I knew so little about him. When Yvetta moved into his hut, what did you think?"

"I remembered how proud he was the day he caught his first fish."

"They wanted a new dignity for the People."

"John persuaded many, in the last days—that the Real Selves of the dead were about to appear." Kiachuk seemed burdened by her thoughts. "They would bring a *kazgi* with them. And our Real Selves would join those from the past and future."

Garris squeezed her hand, feeling its warmth.

"A dream for lovers," he said. "She was so devoted to John's ideas—" He imagined the couple embracing, whispering to each other beneath the snow. "Do you think they let go of them at the end?"

In the days that followed, they collected things from his cabin and the ruined dwellings—his tools, some pots, clothing and the cello case with the guitar inside, wrapped in a pair of pants. Pike's storage locker was full of food. The firewood Rezkov had delivered was enough to last them for months.

A spring storm struck. It added snow to the fan and the valley. When it cleared, they emerged from the tent into an eerie silence. Garris gazed at the scaffold, imagining that the bodies were the last people on earth. The world had gone back to the way it had been: intervals of quiet, violence in the sky or a chance slide, and then quiet again.

They visited the Eskimo camp just once. The huts were no different without the People. Kiachuk collected her clothing, her coat, utensils and a crate of fish she'd dried. They entered John and Yvetta's hut. Kiachuk noticed the sky blue ribbon on a shelf and put it in her pocket. She found the elders' harpoon and the Guide, and she wrapped the Guide in a seal fur and put it under her arm. Yvetta's snowshoes were propped against the wall. Garris took them.

In the tent that night, Kiachuk removed his clothes. Then she removed her own, and they slid beneath parkas and blankets. She drew close and they kissed. He felt her nakedness and her warmth, but tragedy had sapped his desire. It touched and withdrew, circled and hid. Finally it asserted itself and stood in the open, like a table with four legs.

Afterward they lay quietly, thinking their separate thoughts. If Yvetta's ears were packed with snow, and her mouth, he could ask Kiachuk to clear them. He wanted to believe his daughter had been able to hear and speak.

Garris felt her hand on his shoulder.

"The summer will come," she said, "and the snow will melt."

In the third week of May, the slide began to thin. They crossed and recrossed it together, checking where the snow had slumped, hopeful but fearful about what they might find. "If you see something grim," Kiachuk said, "look away. I can manage Yvetta. If it's John, I'll do the same." When they'd covered the fan, they climbed the boulder bed and scouted its holes and fissures.

Every day the fan shrank and there was more earth to see. Patches of tundra appeared, winter brown. Meltwater trickled across them, rills winding and weaving, disappearing beneath snows nearby. On the riverbank, the tips of the willows turned green. "They're missing us," Kiachuk sighed. "They remember how we tickled their buds and plucked their shoots."

The two of them were clambering over the boulder bed when Garris froze.

"It's her," he said.

Kiachuk led him aside and returned to make a closer inspection. It was a limb of gray moss that the slide's churning edge had raised from the rock.

The summer rains came, and the air was damp velvet folding onto the ground. As July advanced, the fan divided into white islands, and the islands shrank. Between, the earth turned jade and chartreuse as the heathers and moss were renewed. But there was still no sign of Yvetta and John. A stream emerged from the largest remnant of snow. It spilled over a ledge, dashed into bubbles and wound down the slope toward the river. From the seam, emerald sprigs rose. Kiachuk knelt, fingering the growth. Garris stood beside her, looking around.

"Where have they gone?" he said. The river was purring, and his words sank beneath. Would even this simple wish be denied?

Kiachuk stood. She held him and they mingled their tears.

"Some *angakoqs* flew away," she said, "and they never came back."

That night, after she removed his boots, she turned to face him.

"Maybe they're here," she said, "and we're just not seeing them."

Garris shook his head. What was she saying?

The rain lasted three days. They remained in the tent. The vigil was approaching its end. The only place left was the boulder bed; the fissures were deep, and many were choked with ice. But if the slide put John and Yvetta there, they would never be found, as the holes would be packed through September when the first snows of winter fell.

After the rain stopped, Kiachuk led him back to the stream and the green seam. The water wound its way through the rocks, dishing from edge to edge. It chirped and gurgled and split into cords, and the sun flashed on the silver lattice.

She put her hands on her hips and turned, with an air of deciding.

"This is their place," she said.

Their place. What did that mean? Had they vanished beneath the tundra? Was the realm of summer their new home?

Yvetta— His heart cried out. *Where are you now? Your freshness, your faith, your unyielding dream—* He remembered the day she had called the best in her life.

Kiachuk was still standing there, looking around.

Beside the stream, a few yards from where she stood, Garris noticed a bowl. Willows had risen around it, like the bowl Yvetta described. It was rimmed with rocks and there was a green mat at its bottom.

He crossed the heather, and when he reached the bowl, he slid into it. Then Kiachuk was sliding beside him, shouldering with him against the soft growth.

Azalea, he thought, touching a cushion between them.

The cushion was covered with buds red as blood. Garris grazed his palm over the buds and the tiny pink flowers.

They had revealed their Real Selves to Yvetta.

The bees had Real Selves too, and the hoppers and willows, with their catkins hissing like candles. The rocks on the rim, and the windflowers too. For a moment, everything in the bowl had a hidden identity—a secret self. Prized and held dear, honored, exalted. Or cast off and abandoned.

"What is it like," he said, "to be your Real Self?"

The question hung in the air between them.

"I breathe," Kiachuk answered, "and air fills my chest."

A passing breeze rang through the rocks.

"I put my hand to my heart," she said, "and I feel it beating."

She spoke softly, simply.

"I open my eyes," she said, "and you are here."

Garris remembered Sara's glittering gown, and the strobe of sun that pierced Blinne's mask.

That night, while Kiachuk cooked, he thought about the dead of Rightful, their struggles to hide or free their Real Selves, and the verdict the struggle had delivered to each. He imagined Yvetta and John in a cocoon of ice, love like a fire Rezkov had lit, burning between them. As his thoughts ripened, Garris opened the cello case and removed his guitar.

His fingers wandered, and so did his hum. The mood was dark, too dark for a child's ears. But there was something he had to express. Not for Yvetta. For himself and the woman with him.

He'd lost his daughter, but he still had something of her. Her blazing essence, her unwavering spirit. And that was a kind of joy—painful, mournful—unlike any he'd known. Kiachuk was silent, but as he stumbled from note to note, he felt her near.

The next morning, the wheatears arrived.

He and Kiachuk were in the bowl. The birds circled and perched on the rocks, peering at them through their black eye masks and flicking their tails. One faced him and called. A trill and a buzz, a trill and a buzz. Garris heard it clearly. "Yvetta," the wheatear cried, "Yvetta." And the others joined in, "Yvetta, Yvetta."

When the song was finished, Garris played and Kiachuk sang the words he'd written, shading their meaning with raw acceptance. When the last verse ended, they closed their eyes and imagined: at the moment they'd passed, Yvetta and John were their Real Selves, and that was a triumph and reward of its own.

In the days that followed, Garris did the same for others the slide had taken, trying to capture in song what he'd seen and heard. He puzzled and wrote, and Kiachuk puzzled with him. And the more he thought about the glimpses he'd gotten of people he knew, the more he wondered at what emerged when their time had run out.

In the middle of this, the anger so often brewing inside him seemed to fade. Those who had found their Real Selves— They left knowing the mercy of life. The others died shrouded and masked, lost to themselves, condemned to the cruelties and mischances of an uncaring fate.

On a windless day, beneath a clear sky, they played the last song for the dead. Kiachuck faced the scaffolding and sang to the bodies suspended there as if they could hear her. When the last note ebbed, Garris set his guitar aside. It was noon and the air was hot, so they descended to the river, hand in hand. At a spot where it was deep enough, they removed their clothes, waded in and stretched out faceup. Garris felt the current riffle over him, stroking his sides, licking his feet. Two ducks floated on the surface nearby, letting the current carry them south.

Once the sun had dried them, they dressed and Garris led the way down the trail to the bend in the river. Fifty feet from the Meeting House, they stopped and stood, gazing in silence at its charred remains.

The warmth continued into the evening. They lay on the tundra together beneath the arctic sun.

Sometime past midnight, Garris fell asleep.

He dreamed he was up to his knees in snow, using his shovel, trying to reach someone who was buried. The spiral aurora—that giant blue screw-thread—was turning above him.

Suddenly, from the ice beside him, not a dozen feet away, Yvetta emerged. She was pale and luminous, and he knew without thinking—this was her Real Self, and it was free of the slide now, finally free. He had a Real Self too, and magically, while his earthly self shoveled below, his Real Self rose to follow Yvetta's.

The sound of the wedding march reached him.

Something momentous was happening. The dwellings on earth had all been destroyed. Not just the Mercantile and the cabins and Meeting House. Every shelter on earth. The wedding march was a processional for Real Selves, and they were rising together—all of them, not just from the Rightful

Valley. They were ghostly and glowing, and they were headed for the only home left—a home of coiling light. It was a ribbon, Garris saw, the color of the one Yvetta wore.

Her body was fibrous now, like flowing hair. He lightened himself, letting the night comb his body. Ahead, the celestial *kazgi* grew larger and brighter, its great curtain rippling, blue pillars flashing.

On all sides, the Real Selves were arriving. Fibrous, irising in the light, Garris saw them passing through the *kazgi's* translucent walls. Yvetta approached the glowing ramparts, the auroral lines flexing around her. Fishbone ripples, fern fronds and barbules, then a burst of stars—she was slipping through. And Garris was right behind her.

Animals, plants, water and wind— Races inhuman, unthinkable natures, free now to mingle. Garris felt the uncountable Selves in the *kazgi* teeming around him.

Blue light infused the curving corridor, and the arriving people lapped over each other. The *kazgi's* light shone through them all. They were whispering, mixing and melding, laughing and weeping; and their bodies flickered, joining and parting as the hanging walls rippled and glittered around them.

No carpenter's work, no timbers or siding— The home for Real Selves was made of aurora, and eternity glowed through its spiral halls. It was a heaven with no regard for law, for the wrongs Rezkov tried to make right, for those who cherished the Word or tipped Pike's scales. It was a Meeting House, a place of weaving together, of knowing each other and being known. For all those true to their hearts and eager to join

John's kingdom come, this was the journey's end.

John was here, Garris saw. He threaded the throng, approaching Yvetta.

As the lovers embraced, they were like reflections in water—blurry, rippling, fluid and pale. The Real Selves were turning to watch, sober now, sober and staring. They were staring not at Yvetta and John, but at Garris and the strange woman—a white Eskimo—standing beside him, holding his hand.

John and Yvetta kissed, and the Real Selves began to sing.

Garris turned, listening and trembling. Was the chorus for him? The heavenly throng was singing, and the melody was one he knew. In this place of rapture and mingling, the hymn seemed to enter from every quarter, echoing, suffusing his thoughts, his feelings and the germ of his faith.

When it ended, John led Yvetta away.

Garris was sad, but he let her go. Someone with wisdom held his hand, and he had a little inside him. He watched till his daughter was lost in the crowd.

$\Lambda\!\wedge\!\Lambda\!\wedge\!\Lambda$

Early the next morning, before Kiachuk woke, Garris put words to the hymn he'd heard in his dream. The Real Selves had been singing "Why Do We Mourn?" The melody spoke to their hearts, as it had spoken to his. He turned the hymn into a pledge, for himself and everyone in the world—a world he'd given up hope for and abandoned.

As he trialed it on his guitar, Kiachuk raised her head. He showed her the words. Then they sat together and brought it to life.

When the last verse ended, Garris faced her.

"This is our song," he said. "A song of union, a promise to each other."

Kiachuk raised her hands and took a dark braid in each, accepting the vow.

"It's time to leave," Garris said.

They ate a small meal and loaded the sled in silence. His tools and the cookery went first, then the blankets, furs and clothing, and what remained of their food. They lashed the cello case on top, with the guitar inside.

Garris secured the tent canvas over their belongings, binding it to the sled rails with rope. Then they descended the butcher's east leg, headed for the scaffolding where the dead had been placed.

Kiachuk set the Flying Man's Guide on the planking and hung the elders' harpoon on one of the posts. Garris used a rock to nail the blue ribbon beside it. On the ground nearby, he set the snowshoes he'd made for his daughter.

"There's no forgetting," he said.

"No forgetting," she agreed.

"Every time I see a little girl, I'll remember."

Kiachuk regarded him sadly. "The world is full of children."

Garris grabbed the tugline and began hauling the sled down the slope.

They took the trail that ran south along the river, the same trail Garris had trod in April of the previous year. As they reached the mouth of the valley, they paused to look back.

The place was as it always had been. The sun's rays fought to reach the earth through the shifting clouds. Fierce winds waited for an unguarded moment. And to the north, around the bend, the Teeth were visible above the steep slopes. Kiachuk looked at Garris. He nodded and turned, rope in his hands, departing as he'd come, with someone he loved and a few possessions dragging behind.

Rich Shapero's novels dare readers with giant metaphors, magnificent obsessions and potent ideas. His casts of idealistic lovers, laboring miners, and rebellious artists all rate ideas as paramount, more important than life itself. They traverse wild landscapes and visionary realms, imagining gods who in turn imagine them. Like the seekers themselves, readers grapple with revealing truths about human potential. *The Slide That Buried Rightful* and his previous titles—*Dissolve, Island Fruit Remedy, Balcony of Fog, Rin, Tongue and Dorner, Arms from the Sea, The Hope We Seek, Too Far* and *Wild Animus*— are available in hardcover and as ebooks. They also combine music, visual art, animation and video in the TooFar Media app. Shapero spins provocative stories for the eyes, ears, and imagination.